Eccentric Circles

Volume 1

Eccentric Circles

Volume 1

Short Stories by Encircle Authors

Edited by Cynthia Brackett-Vincent

Encircle Publications
Farmington, Maine, U.S.A.

ECCENTRIC CIRCLES © 2022 Encircle Publications

Paperback ISBN 13: 978-1-64599-346-9
Hardcover ISBN 13: 978-1-64599-347-6
E-book ISBN 13: 978-1-64599-348-3

ALL RIGHTS RESERVED. In accordance with the U.S. Copyright Act of 1976, no part of this publication may be reproduced, distributed, or transmitted in any form or by any means, or stored in a database or retrieval system, without prior written permission of the publisher, Encircle Publications, Farmington, ME.

This book is a work of fiction. All names, characters, places and events are products of the author's imagination or are used fictitiously, and any resemblance to actual persons, living or dead, or to actual places or businesses, is entirely coincidental.

Editor: Cynthia Brackett-Vincent
Cover design by Christopher Wait

Published by:

Encircle Publications
PO Box 187
Farmington, ME 04938

info@encirclepub.com
http://encirclepub.com

contents

American Justice by Sharon L. Dean 1
The Bank Robber by Vaughn C. Hardacker 14
Baptism by Kevin St. Jarre 24
The Burns Family by A. J. Thibault 28
The Case of the Missing Gnome by Dane Cobain 37
The Cat's Clue by Lois Schmitt 43
Choices by S. Lee Manning 59
Cindy's Storm by Catherine Dilts 71
The Day of Reckoning by Karen Hanson Stuyck 88
Go Fish by Lara Tupper 100
Jennifer Jacobson, Private Eyeball by Mike Befeler 115
Lady of Bureba by J. K. Knauss 132
Lily Robinson and an Ab-breve-iated Mission by BJ Magnani 143
Mainely Trapped by Matt Cost 149
Moonlight by Scott Lipanovich 165
Mother's Day by Saralyn Richard 172
Nuns Fret Not by Jay Ruud 181
Old Friends and Zip Drives by CB Shanahan 192
Patsy of Harlan County by Sue Baumgardner 204
Sisters of Grace and Mud by Alison L. McLennan 219
The Terrace, Saint-Tropez by Bruna Gomes 228
Ulnar Splint by Anne Britting Oleson 241
Waitin' for the 12:15 by Joe Kilgore 248
What's Your Name? by Richard J. Cass 258
About the Authors 265

Sharon L. Dean

American Justice

First degree assault. Do you know any of the people named who will testify? Know the lawyers? Have family members in law enforcement? Been the victim of a crime? I strain to hear the excuses of those who approach the bench. They speak too quietly to the judge and the lawyers. I create a story about the blond with the nose ring and the black T-shirt over jeans so tight she must have sat in a tub of hot water to shrink them to every curve in her very curvy body. She's in drug rehab. She's a prostitute who's been assaulted by half a dozen of her clients. I'm not being fair. She's probably married to a cop. Whatever her excuse, she's dismissed. So is the girl whose red braids make her look like Pippi Longstocking and the Black woman in the power suit even though they're both among the few who have followed the instructions to dress appropriately. Between the people dismissed and the jurors seated, I've counted eight pairs of jeans, varying from designer to Walmart specials; four T-shirts, clean though not ironed; three female tops that show too much cleavage; two pairs of dirty sneakers despite the cold weather; and a pair of heels so high the woman wearing them will soon be a lucrative client for a podiatrist.

I hear my name. "Deborah Strong." I search quickly for an excuse, but I have none. I take my seat as a potential juror and pull my sweater tight around me. The courtroom is as cold as its drab walls. Nothing to distract us from the case we'll hear. The twelfth name they call is Susan Warner. I know her. She must have come in after me. I would have recognized the silver hair she used to highlight with a streak of lavender or maroon or copper to annoy the administration at Souhegan College. No streaks now that she's retired.

Two more jurors are called as alternates. A woman with a tattoo along the side of her neck who looks like she could be a member of Hell's Angels and a woman who wears a blouse too sheer and too low for the courtroom are named as alternates.

I look at the jury. A man in a suit, one in khaki pants and a sweater, one in jeans and a sport shirt. An Indian man and a flamboyant young man who doesn't look old enough for a driver's license. I wonder if they've been chosen for a show of diversity. A woman in a flannel shirt, a woman who is visibly pregnant, and one in a V-neck sweater showing just a hint of cleavage on a body that could model for a runners' magazine. They look about thirty. Two of the other women look, like me, to be approaching fifty. One of them could exchange wardrobes with me, conservative but sporty. The other wears enough jewelry to start a silver-smithing shop. Five men, seven women, not a good ratio for the accused whose name we've learned is Leonard Plant.

The judge dismisses us and tells us to report in the morning for the beginning of the trial.

Tuesday morning I park my car in the city garage and step out into the bone-cold air of a New Hampshire January. I'm wearing heavy-weight corduroys and an extra layer under my sweater. Ahead of me, I see Susan. She's close to seventy, short, thin, and still fit and feisty.

I catch her and say, "Susan. I tried to find you yesterday when we were dismissed."

"I had to leave to pick my husband up at the airport."

We reach the courthouse and find our way into the assembly room where jurors slowly arrive for the different cases they'll serve on. A few whisper to a neighbor, but most sit quietly reading a book or a magazine. One man works a Sudoku. Beside me, Susan crochets a baby sweater in a color as neutral as the courtroom walls except for the threads of pink that announce the baby as a girl.

"Expecting a granddaughter?" I whisper.

"Due next month. I'd rather be knitting, but knitting needles are banned."

"Hard to imagine anyone using them as a weapon in here."

The bailiff comes in and directs us into the courtroom. The judge puts on glasses that hang from a chain around her neck as she reads the standard trial procedure. When she's finished, she takes off her glasses and scowls at us. "If you speak about this case or research it in the newspapers or whatever social media you use, you will be charged with a crime and I'll see to it that you spend time in jail." She sounds more like a prison warden than a judge.

I study the prosecuting attorney. She introduces herself as Attorney Judith Webb. She's young, petite, dressed in a gray lawyer suit and wearing comfortable pumps. Her voice is surprisingly deep, impassioned as she relates the events from the victim's perspective.

"In the course of this trial, I ask you to imagine yourself as Mackenzie Shaw. At the time of the assault, she was just nineteen years old, studying massage therapy at Hillsboro Community College, living at home, free to come and go now that she's legally an adult in everything except her right to drink a beer. But drink a beer she did, like most American nineteen-year-olds. In fact, she drank three beers. Too many, she admits, but not so many that she doesn't know what happened. Picture her on a Friday night. She's put on a pair of shorts, a light-weight T-shirt. Comfortable but not provocative. It's August 26th and the weather is warm."

Webb holds up a pair of shorts and a T-shirt. The shorts are the kind I wear, the kind you buy at an outdoor store to take on a camping trip. The T-shirt has some kind of design I can't read beneath the dirt that covers it.

"Imagine that night," Webb says. "Mackenzie Shaw meets the defendant, Leonard Plant, a blind date arranged by another student in her massage class. Mackenzie has no reason to fear for her safety when they walk from her home on Brookings Street to a party four blocks away on Powell. They talk about things young adults talk about. Their favorite music, the latest movies, what social media they use. They reach 259 Powell Street and go inside."

Webb points to a chart with a map of the city's streets. A middle-class section of town, tree-lined, safe to walk at night. She continues in her deep voice. "Mackenzie thinks she'll meet some of her classmates from massage school at the party. Instead, she finds four people she doesn't know. It's a warm evening and they sit outside drinking beer and talking. Imagine Mackenzie's discomfort when they start to swallow pills with the beer. Picture Mackenzie leaving the party alone. Beer is one thing, drugs are another. It's not late. She knows the streets. She's half-way home when she feels Leonard Plant pushing her from behind onto the cement sidewalk. He threatens to kill her if she tells anyone about the pills. He kicks her in the back, pinning her arm behind her. He rolls her over, sits on top of her, and says he'd rape her if he found her attractive. He gives her a last kick on the side of the head then goes back to the party. Look at these clothes again."

Webb parades Mackenzie's soiled and bloody clothes in front of us. She puts them into an evidence box and concludes. "During the course of this trial, we will demonstrate how the defendant, Leonard Plant, found a blind date to take to a drug fest. When Mackenzie Shaw doesn't accept the drugs, he threatens her, beats her, and leaves her, half dead, to find her way home."

I look at Leonard Plant. He's good-looking, someone a nineteen-year-old girl would be happy to find is her blind date. They're the worst. The guys who use their good looks to manipulate young women into sex, then leave them for their next conquest.

The defense attorney stands, pats Leonard Plant on the shoulder, and introduces himself to us. Attorney James Dickens or is it Dickson? Whatever his name, he's tall, self-confident, middle age. The slight stoop to his shoulders tells me that he spends too much time hunched over a desk.

Dickens or Dickson is convincing. "Mr. Plant," he says in a voice coated with authority, "is a pharmacy technician who's earned the respect of his colleagues at the Hillsboro County Hospital pharmacy. He knows too much about the danger of recreational use of prescription drugs to use them. He, too, drank at the party. It was a Friday. He'd had a long week. He had a couple of beers, nothing illegal about that for someone over twenty-one. He admits that he saw people swallow pills, but he refused them. He went into the bathroom and when he came out Mackenzie had started to walk home alone. They hadn't clicked very well during the evening, so he didn't follow her. He wasn't worried because the street was lighted and safe and the weather still warm."

Dickens or Dickson points to the evidence box. "Clearly something happened to Mackenzie Shaw on her way home. A passerby saw her lying in the street and called an ambulance. You'll hear the doctor who attended Ms. Shaw say that she was drunk. She likely was attacked, but her injuries could have come from falling down. She declined a rape test because she hadn't been raped. Listen closely for the next few days and I'm sure that you will judge my client innocent of everything except being talked into a blind date with a girl he didn't know was still a teenager."

All morning, I listen to the lawyers examine and cross-examine the four people who were at the party. Two male and two female. One of the males has put on a polo shirt for the trial despite the cold weather. The other wears a black T-shirt with a photo of some band I've never heard of. Both of the women wear jeans and sweaters that are too loose for the cold courtroom. One of them twirls her long hair through the twenty minutes of her testimony. She confesses that she was too stoned to notice if Leonard Plant followed Mackenzie Shaw when she left the party. The male wearing the polo shirt doesn't even remember meeting Mackenzie.

When the bailiff comes in at noon, my stomach is growling, my back is aching, and I'm despairing about the future of our country left in the hands of these young people. He leads us into the deliberation room and asks if we want sandwiches brought in or want to leave the courthouse. Susan and I decide on a local sandwich shop.

We arrive and place our orders. Three other jurors come in behind us. The juror who wears a suit orders, then sits in a booth alone. He takes out a cell phone. He must think his business life is important. The Indian man reads a book that looks like it's about Colonial America, and the woman wearing a silver mine talks loudly about her fascination with jury duty as she orders soup.

Susan nods toward silver mine. "She's going to be difficult."

"I know." Susan had been involved in three murder investigations, been nearly murdered herself, so I ask, "Is this hard for you? You must have had to testify."

"It's easier not being involved."

"I did what you asked."

"What I asked?"

"About that letter Abigail Brewster wrote." Susan had written books about Brewster and the letter I found told me what had happened to her in the 1870s. We never spoke directly about it. We'd let the dead rest in peace.

We bus our table and leave at the same time as Business Suit, Indian Man, and Silver Mine, who's the only one who doesn't put a tip in a cup on the counter. She must save all her money for the mother lode she wears on her body.

The cold has moderated when I walk to the courthouse Wednesday morning. I catch up with Susan as I did on Tuesday. We should carpool.

"Good morning," I say.

"Not sure how good it'll be. We get to hear Mackenzie and Leonard today. I've been watching him during all the testimony. As terrifying as Ted Bundy. All charm on the outside, all evil inside."

I understand Susan more than she can imagine. I point to Silver Mine who's walking in high-heeled boots in front of us. Sylvie, she announced to the entire jury yesterday. I wanted to ask her if she changed her name to match her jewelry.

We reach the courthouse and are sent to the assembly room. A few people talk. The man in the suit is reading *The Economist*. Susan works on the sweater she's making for her soon-to-be-born granddaughter, and the pregnant woman pages through a copy of *Your Baby's First Year*.

We've been waiting a long time. I look at the clock, fearing that the case of Shaw vs. Plant won't come to as neat a conclusion as the plot of an Agatha Christie novel. 10:04. When the bailiff opens the door and calls us to the courtroom, I know the parties haven't settled. I sit at the beginning of the back row in the jury box and try to ignore the perfume that Sylvie douses herself with every morning.

The prosecutor calls Mackenzie Shaw to the stand. Mackenzie wears a gray wool sweater and black dress pants. She's visibly nervous but when she speaks, she's clear and articulate.

Webb is dressed in a dark blue lawyer suit that's a twin to the ones she wore on Monday and Tuesday. "On Friday, August 26th of this year, did you go to a party with the defendant, Leonard Plant?" she asks Mackenzie.

"I did," says Mackenzie. "He was a blind date."

"Describe in your own words what happened at the party."

Mackenzie uses a handkerchief she's holding in her lap and wipes her eyes before she begins. "At first I thought we were going to hit it off. When we got to the party, everyone was friendly. Leonard offered me a beer. I'm not used to drinking, but I said yes."

"Did you have just one beer?" asks Webb. She's laying out Mackenzie's culpability so the defense attorney won't corner her client during cross-examination.

"I had two. Before I finished the third one, they took out drugs so I decided to leave."

"They took out drugs? Can you say who provided them?"

"Leonard Plant. He stole them from a hospital pharmacy."

Dickson jumps up. After three days, I remember his name. "Objection. Where the drugs came from is not an issue."

"Sustained," says the judge.

Webb rephrases her question. "Did Mr. Plant offer drugs to you?"

"Yes, but I said no, and left."

"Tell us what happened then."

Mackenzie wipes her eyes and blows her nose before she continues. "I heard someone walking behind me. When I turned around, I saw Leonard. He said that if I told anyone about the drugs, he'd kill me. I started to run. He grabbed me and pushed me down and started to kick me. The next thing I knew, I was waking up in a hospital bed."

"Could you have been mistaken that it was Mr. Plant who attacked you?"

"No. It was him for sure."

"Mackenzie, I'm going to play the voice message the jury listened to yesterday. I want to know if you recognize the voice." Webb turns on a recorder and we hear a male voice say, "Why'd you have to storm off like that? If you stayed, I wouldn't have hurt you."

When the recording stops, Webb says, "Can you identify that voice, Mackenzie?"

"Yes. It's Leonard Plant's."

"How can you be sure?"

"He screamed in that high-pitched voice while he was kicking me."

"Thank you, Mackenzie." Webb is manipulating our sympathy by using Mackenzie's first name.

Leonard Plant says something to his attorney, who nods and stands up to cross-examine Mackenzie Shaw. Dickson's wearing the male version of the prosecutor's lawyer suit. I don't like his tie. It's too bright a blue and the design looks like some kind of bug. I've already decided he's a parasite. He presses Mackenzie on her drinking. How much beer is usual for her? Could she have stumbled? Isn't it possible she misidentified Leonard Plant? Why didn't she call the police when she saw the drugs? Mackenzie is flustered. She twists the handkerchief in her hands and keeps glancing at her lawyer.

"Thank you, Ms. Shaw." Dickson uses Mackenzie's last name as he dismisses her.

Webb calls Leonard Plant to the stand. He wears a sport coat and dress shirt in a blue that matches his eyes. He's playing up his good looks. I recognize the high pitch of his voice from the recording as he describes his version of events. Yes, he knows the effects of various drugs, including the ones at the party. He says he did not take any drugs. He was relieved when Mackenzie decided to leave the party. He didn't follow her.

Webb sits down without pursuing the voice message. She'll let Dickson figure out how to get his client to explain it.

After preliminary questions that go over facts we've already heard, Dickson addresses the voice mail. "Did you make the call Attorney Webb just played for us?"

"Yes." Plant makes no effort to deny the evidence.

"Can you explain that message?" says Dickson.

Plant looks at the jury. He's charismatic, someone easy to believe. "I thought

Mackenzie left because she was afraid I'd want to have sex with her. I didn't like her, but I didn't want her to think badly of me. I never saw her again."

Nothing hangs on the pale walls of the deliberation room. Even the curtains that frame a long window are the same beige as the walls. The carpet is darker than the walls, textured. I can see splotches of dirt that we've brought in on our shoes.

The chairs are comfortable, cushioned, unlike the ones in the jury box. I choose one that faces the window. Outside I see the brick of one of the city's old mills. A lone tree, bare of leaves, stands on the courthouse side of the road. It's as stark as the inside of the deliberation room.

The table is long and oval, with a pad of paper and pencil neatly placed in front of each chair. It would fit at whatever business I imagine Business Suit works in, except for the paper, which is small and white and inexpensive because of our cash-strapped legal system. I look at the jury that has the fate of Leonard Plant in its hands.

If someone doesn't speak quickly, I'm afraid that Sylvie will volunteer to be Chair. Anyone who looks like a silver smithing shop shouldn't be allowed on juries. I suggest the juror who shares my taste in clothing. Leslie. I've learned her name and that she's a high school principal. She should know how to handle disputes. Sylvie objects, saying there should be nominations. She waits for a reaction, then nominates herself and asks for a paper ballot. Kate, the pregnant woman, stops her and says a simple show of hands with be enough and will speed the process. Sylvie votes for herself and everyone else raises a hand for Leslie.

Leslie asks that we go around the table, give our names and an initial verdict of guilty or not guilty. The youngest woman, Elise, the one I thought could model for a runners' magazine, says not guilty. Flamboyant Ted surprises me with a not guilty vote. I imagine him as vulnerable to the homophobic attacks of people like Leonard Plant. After I vote guilty, Sylvie lectures us on the concept of doubt. Leslie interrupts and asks, "Guilty or not guilty?"

Sylvie stands up and puts her hands on the table and announces, "Not guilty." When she sits down, the charms on one of her bracelets scrape on the table.

"I think guilty," says Leslie. "That's nine to three. Who wants to argue their case?"

Raj is the first to defend his guilty vote. He speaks with the logic of a software engineer in the accented legacy of British East India. "Mackenzie wasn't using drugs that Leonard Plant stole. She wouldn't have mistaken her assailant."

Sylvie leans across the table at Raj. "That was struck from the record."

Leslie moderates. "We can't talk about stealing drugs, but we can talk about using them."

Sylvie challenges him again. "What makes you so knowledgeable about American law?"

Raj copies her body language. "I've studied the Constitution."

Raj must be a new citizen. I suspect he knows more about American law than any of us. When I look around the table, I realize that we're lucky. Only Sylvie is a problem. We could have had anyone with a driver's license on our jury. None of us seems to be racist or homophobic or just plain stupid. Our justice system doesn't consider IQ.

Sylvie lectures us on alternate theories. Mackenzie could have fallen. She was drunk and it was dark. She could have mistaken a stranger for Leonard Plant. "There are alternate theories. It's not a hundred percent."

Leslie loses patience. "Nothing is a hundred percent. Get on with it. Nine of us think he's guilty. We should continue to say why. Maybe that will convince you holdouts."

I make my case. "It's clear that Mackenzie was injured on both the front and back of her body. She also had a concussion. It's difficult to imagine her falling this way even if she was drunk. If she fell on the front of her body first, she would have broken the fall with her arms and avoided rolling over."

Sylvie objects. "How would you know? It's possible to fall all kinds of ways."

"Possible but not probable. There's a bigger chain of evidence. The phone call. Why would Leonard Plant say 'I wouldn't have hurt you'? That tells me that he did hurt Mackenzie."

Again Sylvie objects. "I can imagine all kinds of alternate theories. He thought Mackenzie left because she was afraid of him."

Before anyone adds another reason for a guilty verdict, Elise changes her vote. "Deborah is right. If you fall when running or even walking, if it's face first, you break the fall with your arms."

Sylvie continues to object. "The street was a safe one. There was no reason not to let Mackenzie walk home alone."

Ted looks at Sylvie and changes his vote. I wonder if he believes guilty or if he doesn't want to be on the same side as Sylvie.

The bailiff knocks on the door. We can't go out for lunch during deliberation, he tells us. Will we be needing lunch brought in or have we almost reached a verdict?

"Lunch," Sylvie says, looking around the table. "You haven't convinced me. I still have doubts."

Lunch arrives. We stand, stretch, talk in general about our personal lives. Sylvie stands close to the door. She's cornered Susan, who's too polite to stop her talking. I hear Sylvie say, "That Deborah's a problem. She's critical of everything."

Susan defends me. "She's a friend. She makes good points."

"Never trust a woman who's so assertive," says Sylvie.

Raj knows I'm listening. "It's okay," he says to me. "You're just observant." He looks at the jury members. "I'm listening to how you all negotiate to get a guilty verdict. In India, we still have honor killings of women who commit adultery and we tolerate rape. I became an American citizen to get way from all that. I'd rather my daughters grow up to be like you than learn how to make a good curry."

Leslie calls us back to the jury table. Sylvie is becoming more illogical. "It's not a hundred percent. There's doubt. That poor boy is going to have his life ruined."

"What about Mackenzie's life?" asks Susan. "If we don't hold people like Leonard Plant accountable, life will be no safer for my granddaughter's generation."

"You don't have a granddaughter," says Sylvie. "Just that stupid sweater you're knitting."

"Crocheting," says Susan, who's lost her ability to be nice.

Ted gives up. "Let's call it a hung jury. We're getting nowhere on this. Who's ready to call the bailiff?"

I suspect everyone shares my thoughts. Sylvie's on a campaign to earn bragging rights for having hung a jury.

"Last chance, Sylvie," says Susan. "We all think there's more than enough evidence to convict Leonard Plant."

"Call the bailiff," says Sylvie. "There's always doubt."

Leslie sends a note to the judge that we are hung on the charge of assault. We stand up to stretch while we wait. I look out the window at the leafless tree and the hard bricks of the old mill. Only Sylvie doesn't stand up to stretch. She looks as cemented as the bricks in the wall I've been looking at.

The bailiff comes in and hands a note to Leslie. She reads it and says, "We need to sit down. The judge says keep trying."

We go around the table and explain again why we say guilty. Sylvie keeps presenting increasingly absurd alternate theories. At 4:30 the bailiff knocks and announces that the judge is ready to accept a hung jury if we are no closer to a verdict. Leslie fills in the official documents. A few minutes later we are called back into the courtroom and state our failure to agree on a verdict. The judge declares the jury unable to reach a decision and tells Leonard Plant that he is free to go.

I watch him shake his lawyer's hand. He looks at Mackenzie, who does not raise her eyes. She is shaking. The prosecutor tries to comfort her. She puts her arm around Mackenzie and walks her out of the courtroom.

I leave the courthouse with Susan. I'm too angry to trust myself to speak to her. Sylvie is walking in front of us talking loudly on a cell phone. "I did what we planned. I hung the jury." She is swaggering. I hope I'll never again hear the words "alternate theory." I think of Raj and India and wonder if he still believes in the American justice system.

A windstorm has left the streets littered with trash blown from cans that were put out for pick-up this morning. The air smells of gasoline fumes from a traffic jam where wires have fallen onto a light and impatient drivers lean futilely on horns. I get into Susan's car. I'm glad she drove us today. I'm angry enough that I don't trust myself behind a steering wheel.

The traffic jam forces her to turn onto Powell Street. A man and a woman are stopped in front of the house where the party happened. They have their arms around each other and look like they're waiting for someone. I see that it's Dickson, or is it Dickens? I've forgotten again. And Sylvie. They wave at Leonard Plant who is coming down the steps.

Susan sees what I see. "They planned it all. I hope they didn't see us. People have killed for less." She guns the car.

I turn my head and watch them from the side window. Sylvie sees us and raises her middle finger. Her silver earrings sparkle in the sun.

Vaughn C. Hardacker

The Bank Robber

Elisha Worthington, the bartender/owner of The Old Watering Hole, the only bar in Jemptland, Maine, was wiping the bar when the light coming through the entrance was blocked by someone standing in the threshold. He looked and saw a tall man holding a briefcase. He was about six feet one, wore a red and black plaid hunting jacket, and a pair of Red Wing work boots. He stepped inside and approached the bar. As he closed the distance, Worthington noted that he had not shaved for several days or more and looked like a cross between Don Johnson and Clint Eastwood… either way he immediately got the impression that this man was a member of that lucky group that make women go weak at the knees.

He slid onto the bar stool and nodded to Worthington. His eyes were slate-gray and crow's feet spread out from the corner of his eyes, making the saloon owner believe that those eyes had spent a lot of time staring into the harsh sun.

"What can I getcha?" Worthington asked.

"Do you have iced tea?"

"Yeah?"

"Unsweetened?"

"Yeah, you want one?"

"Sure, put a lemon wedge in it, please."

Worthington was surprised when he spoke. He may have looked like a logger, but spoke like a Rhodes Scholar. He poured him a large glass of ice tea, squeezed the juice out of a lemon before dropping it into the glass, and then skewered another slice on the glass's rim.

The stranger took a large swallow, sighed and set the glass on the bar. "It's hot today."

"Yup, has been all summer."

"This is a nice little town… small but nice."

"Jemptland isn't exactly a metropolis. It's seven blocks long and five blocks wide. The population, counting dogs, cats, and other domestic pets, is less than four hundred. That number swells some when the potato harvest is in session and the number of migrant workers is at max. What brings you to our fair town?"

"I'm looking for someone."

Worthington's curiosity was piqued. As the only bar for twenty miles in any direction, he was used to being a clearing house for information. "You a cop or something?" he asked.

"Or something. I'm a lawyer and licensed investigator from Portland."

II

Worthington stood, unable to move away from him. The tall, dark stranger held his hand out. "Dylan Thomas."

"Like the poet?"

"Yes." The stranger looked exasperated. "You have no idea how many times a day I have to answer that question."

"How can I help you, Mr. Thomas?"

"Please, call me Dylan."

Thomas placed his briefcase on the bar. "I've learned that in a small town there are two places where you can find people—barber shops and bars. I don't see a barber shop in town, so I came here."

"Okay… how can I help you, Dylan?"

"Do you know a writer named Robert Lyle?"

"I've don't think I've heard of him. So, I don't think that he ever wrote anything of significance."

Thomas smiled. "Unfortunately, that holds true for most writers. Nevertheless, it's my belief that Lyle was unique…"

"How might that be?" I asked.

"He wrote as if he'd actually done some of the things in his novel."

Worthington hoped that the look on his face wouldn't give away the fact that he did know Robert Lyle.

III

Nine Years Ago.

Robert Lyle opened his mailbox and saw the self-addressed, stamped envelope that he routinely included in his query letters to publishers and literary agents. He was shopping his first novel and thus far had accrued nothing but rejection letters. His stomach was in a knot as he ripped the envelope open and saw the small card inside. "Shit, rejection number 205." He crumpled the card and envelope in his fist and stared at the other correspondence: utility bills, phone bill, and three bills from *maxed-out* credit cards, two of which were at least one month past due. Financially, he was in dire straits—so broke that if air cost a nickel, he'd suffocate. Not that he didn't have skills. He was often described as the proverbial jack-of-all-trades. The problem was that he was out of work in each of them. He took a furtive look through the glass insert in the door of his apartment building…he was two months behind on his rent, too.

He opened the door, trying to be as quiet as possible. Mrs. Scribner, his landlady, had the apartment just inside the entrance on the right. Lyle was on tip-toes and almost to the stairs when her door opened. "Are you avoiding me, Robert?"

Caught! He turned and smiled his most alluring smile. "Of course not, Mrs. Scribner."

Sarah Scribner was not the typical give me your rent or get out sort of landlord. If anything she was more of the favorite distant aunt type. She went further than most proprietors would. The fact that the locks on his small efficiency apartment had not been changed was proof of that. She looked at the balled-up paper in his clenched fist and sadly shook her head. "Another rejection?"

"Yeah."

"Robert, I know you want to be a successful writer in the worst way, but you still have to meet your responsibilities. Have you thought about how you might get some money?"

"I've tried getting a job as a writer, but it's tight right now."

"Then I suggest you consider other types of work. I don't want to be pessimistic, Robert, but maybe you're trying to be something that you're not meant to be. The Lord has a purpose for all of us…maybe yours is to do something besides writing novels."

"But, I'm a good writer, Mrs. Scribner. All my friends have read my work and agree that it's better than a lot of the stuff being published today."

"That's what you would expect your friends to say. Have you considered getting feedback from other sources?"

Lyle didn't understand what she meant. "*Other* sources?" he queried.

"Other writers. There's a group that meets at the library on the first Monday of the month. You can get the particulars from one of the librarians."

"Thanks. I'll check that out."

"Robert, I still need you to get caught up on your rent as soon as possible."

"I will, Mrs. Scribner. I swear."

She smiled when she patted him on the arm. Lyle saw the liver spots that covered her hand. For some strange reason that made him feel like a deadbeat…this little old woman probably counted on his rent to get by. Then again, he thought, she might be richer than King Solomon. He bolted up the stairs to his apartment.

Once he was safe within his fortress, Lyle sat in his favorite piece of furniture, a reclining chair that was a couple of years past-due for a trip to the landfill, and stared at the accrued stains of years past while he tried to think of some viable way to earn some money. He snapped on the radio—the cable company had disconnected his service a month ago—and tuned it to a local news station. The commentator was giving the details of a bank robbery that had taken place not far from where Lyle lived. In fact, the branch of the Northern National Bank that had been robbed was right around the corner. When the anchorman said, "The robber walked out of the bank and disappeared..." Lyle started thinking: *Why couldn't I do something like that? Not only would it provide me with some drastically needed cash, but it could be the source of a number of viable plots—after all,* write what you know *is one of the most basic laws of authordom.* He decided to take steps to have those fifteen minutes of world fame that Andy Warhol spoke about.

* * *

When the doors of the Portland Public Library opened the next morning, Lyle was on the steps. Once inside, he made a beeline for the computer room—he had a lot of research to do.

By the noon hour he had learned that there wasn't a lot about the art and skills of bank robbery on the internet. He did, however, learn about some of the problems that one could encounter. For instance there was the dye pack. Many a robber had been arrested because they were the only person in the area who looked like a walking canvas of modern art. Lyle learned that in most cases, a dye pack is placed in a hollowed-out space within a stack of banknotes, usually $10 or $20 bills. Technology for the manufacturing of flexible dye packs make them almost impossible for a professional robber to detect by handling the stack and he was by no means a pro. When the marked stack of bills is not used, it is stored next to a magnetic plate near a bank cashier, in standby or safe mode, ready to be handed over to a potential robber by a bank employee. The minute it is removed from the magnetic plate, the pack is armed, and once it leaves the building and passes through the door frame, a radio transmitter located at the door will trigger a timer (typically ten seconds), after which the dye pack will explode and release an aerosol (usually of Disperse Red 9) and sometimes tear gas, intended to permanently stain and destroy the stolen money and mark the robber's body with a bright red color. The chemical reaction causing the explosion of the pack and the release of the dye creates high temperatures of about 400 degrees Fahrenheit (204 degrees Celsius) that further discourages a criminal from touching the pack or removing it from the bag or getaway vehicle.

There was also the problem of video surveillance cameras. He did not want to become the subject of a hidden camera video on the internet. He thought: *It would be just my luck that after robbing a bank, one of my books would become a best seller and a cop would recognize my picture on the book jacket from footage collected by the bank's security system.* He made a note to come up with a disguise that would not be attention-getting. Lyle brainstormed for a few seconds and compiled a list that he entitled: *The Last Disguise They'd Expect.* Some of the ideas were good too. Lyle listed, to name a few: a pregnant woman, an orthodox rabbi and best yet, a nun wearing a large habit.

The other fact he learned was how automated the security systems of most banks had become, gone are the days of the audible alarm. Today's systems are more along the line of a communications system. It starts with the activation of a switch. A tiny button or buttons are hidden from view of the customers and their locations are known only by bank employees. They are hidden in such a way that a bank employee can activate the switch without alerting the bad guys. Once the switch has been activated, it sends a signal to a private, third-party. The signal is transmitted to the security-monitoring vendor via telephone lines, internet or radio frequency transmissions. Upon receiving a signal from a bank, the security company performs one or more of a number of checks to make sure the signal is legitimate. These checks are not known to the public. The secrecy of their internal systems prevents the bad guys from capturing, masking, or overriding the signal's authenticity. Once the signal has been proven to be genuine, it immediately alerts the authorities, who then dispatch various teams of appropriate officers to the bank without the bad guy's knowledge.

Then there was deciding whether or not he should use a gun. Lyle had heard that bank personnel are advised not to resist any attempt to rob the bank. They are trained to give up the money and let the methods above assist the cops. He also read that the penalty for armed robbery was infinitely more severe than if no weapon was used.

He decided to test this information to see if it was true.

* * *

Lyle entered the lobby of Northern National Bank and tried to be as nonchalant as anyone who was there on business. He removed a deposit slip and on the back printed: *Put all the money in a sack and give it to me. Do not activate the alarm, I am armed and dangerous...* He slid the deposit slip under the top one and walked to a row of chairs and sat as if he was waiting for someone.

The wait wasn't long, twenty minutes at most. A woman entered the lobby dragging a loud, snotty-nosed brat in her wake. She was speaking in a low voice, trying to bargain with the miserable curtain-climber. If that kid had been his, Lyle would have introduced him to the ancient proverb, *spare the rod, spoil the child*. As he watched the woman, Lyle wondered if her name was Rosemary...she sure as hell had *Rosemary's Baby*. Unfortunately, the woman did not get the doctored deposit slip. The gentle, kind octogenarian with the walker and who had waited patiently did.

Lyle had second thoughts and left his post to head the old man off before he presented the teller with the slip. Lyle was wrong.

The old S. O. B. was anything but kind and gentle. When Lyle said, "Excuse me, may I go ahead of you?" The old man looked at him through glasses that made his eyes look ten times larger than they were, smiled as if he were about step aside and then said, "Fuck off. Wait your turn."

Lyle held his hands up in surrender and backed away. "Excuse me."

The old man turned to the desk and filled out his deposit slip. He gripped the side handles of the walker and shuffled his way to the next available teller. Lyle returned to his chair and settled back to watch the goings-on. He took out his mobile phone and started the stopwatch app.

The old fart slid the deposit slip to the teller who looked at it and then picked up a stamp. She turned the piece of rectangular paper over and her hand froze in mid-air. Her brow arched and she gave him a quizzical look. The old fool smiled at her and nodded slightly. The teller began putting money in a paper sack.

When she had finished filling the sack, the screech of brakes and the explosive entrance of Portland's finest got his attention. In seconds the unaware robber was surrounded with cops, guns drawn and aimed at him. Lyle knew that he old fart didn't know if he should raise his hands or keep them visible on the walker's handles—it took all of his will-power to keep from laughing.

In a matter of minutes, the police had the old man in handcuffs and paraded him out through the door. The prisoner was spitting, cursing and screaming that when he got done suing them, the bank, and the city, he'd be the richest man on Earth.

Lyle had stopped the count on his smartphone the moment the cops arrived. He checked the time; just under two minutes had transpired from the time the old geezer gave the teller the note until the cops were on the scene. He calculated that he would have to time himself to get in and out in less than a minute. Now, how to eliminate the dye pack. He decided that he would have the clerk hand only loose bills to him so there would be no threat that the bundles contained the explosive pack.

He stood and glanced at the teller, who was deep in conversation with plain-clothes detectives. Lyle exited the bank and walked home.

* * *

Lyle robbed his first bank a week after his test run. He handed the clerk the note and almost laughed when she expressed shock that a nun with a five o'clock shadow was robbing her. When she took out the first bundle of cash, he said in a falsetto, "Please, open the bundles and give me the loose bills, dear..." The second bundle of cash she opened contained the dye pack and he pushed it aside. Lyle knew that time was critical, so he shoved the money she had on the counter into the bag he'd brought and slid it under the habit as he fled the scene.

Once he was on the street, he cut down an alley and lifted the habit's hem, freeing his legs so he could run without tripping. Two blocks and three alleys later, he discarded the habit. Three cop cars raced by, lights flashing and sirens wailing, before he made it safely to his apartment.

That night Lyle paid Mrs. Scribner what he owed her and listened to the reports of his daring-do on the radio. He settled into a routine: writer's group every Monday, write on Tuesday and Wednesday. Once a month, usually on a Thursday, he'd rob a bank, using a different disguise each time. He kept that schedule until he'd finished another novel, this one a crime thriller, and had enough money saved up to start a business. He left Portland and came to Jemptland, where he'd been living for nine years... Lyle still wrote, but nothing serious, several online magazines had published some of his short stories.

IV

Present Day
Thomas never took his eyes from Worthington's and said, "I think that *you* are Robert Lyle."

The tavern owner wasn't sure what he did or did not know and tried to keep from showing him how nervous he was. Nevertheless, those piercing grey eyes tore through him like blazing daggers.

Hoping that his voice didn't give him away, Worthington asked, "What's your business with Lyle?".

Thomas pulled the brief case closer, flipped open the latches, and removed a dog-eared paperback that he placed face-down on the bar. Worthington stared at the picture on the back cover; it was his. It was a copy of *The Bank Robber*, the only novel he had been able to get published.

"This," Thomas said, "is possibly the best work of crime fiction I've read in years. Would you sign it for me?"

Worthington's hands shook like he had Parkinson's when he signed Robert Lyle on the title page.

Kevin St. Jarre

Baptism

Her skin was pale; it gave but didn't bounce back. It sort of stayed indented. The impression of his stick remained, whiter than the gray around it. He never knew her—the girl from the posters. He didn't know she'd be there, and he hadn't been looking for anything more than something to do. He was only looking for crayfish to catch. Going through the culvert made much more sense than climbing the bank, crossing the street, and then sliding down the gravel on the other side. When Jack Killarney and his friends came to the corrugated steel culverts, they would go through them. Their hands would stick to the spots of pitch on the inside and the air would change from fresh brook-side breeze to a stale, petroleum-based air. With their hair shorn by fathers with barber's clippers, nothing really got in it. They would waddle through the pipe, watching the stream pass between their plaid shorts and tan, bony legs. The water would darken as they went, seem to swirl more, and they wondered at the creatures that must live under the few rocks they saw. It would be dicey to lift those slick stones, because stopping forward progress might lead to falling into the water, so widely set were their feet.

But it was in there, beneath the undeveloped end of 22nd Avenue, where he found her. In the distance, backlit by the opposite end of the culvert, she could have been a clutch of branches cluttered with plastic Zayre bags.

Lying there, her body caught on a discarded car wheel, the cold rushing water pushed up her floral dress. She was bloated and, despite the current, nothing else moved but her hair. Her mouth was open, and there were bruises on her throat, purplish-brown against the gray. Marks left by the danger that so many mothers have long warned their children about; the bruises were left behind by the evil hidden in every dark basement, under every bed, and inside every windowless van. However, Jack wasn't scared, instead he was curious.

He had picked up the stick, half of the bark missing, the diameter of his mom's hair curlers and as long as his leg. It was pinned beneath the girl's right arm. He pulled and she held onto it. With a yank it came free, but the arm didn't move. Maybe it tore free.

Why didn't she smell, he wondered? Was the water washing that away? Just the odor of the pipe, and water too rich with life. Except for her.

He used the stick to stay away and yet touch her. Her skin gave, like mud under soft cloth. He wasn't nauseated, he was fascinated. The way a child might be interested with anything odd found beneath a rock or log.

Everyone knew she was missing, but she wasn't from town. She wasn't much younger than he was. He poked again, poke, poke. Why the hell was he poking her? He knew she wouldn't wake. Was he trying to push her out of his way? He was three-quarters of the way to the end. Was he poking her because he didn't want to have to walk upstream? He duck-walked closer. Her dress moved a bit on the downstream side of her. He tried to move her hand with the stick and it did lift a little, but it required more effort than he expected.

He looked at both sides of the pipe to see how he might get past her. He couldn't have both feet on either side of the brook. The water was too high up the sides. He moved closer. Could he duck-walk over her? Probably. It felt a dangerous and disrespectful thing to do, but he decided to try it anyway. Slowly, he went slowly, his steps small and echoing, mingling with the gurgling. He passed over her—her feet, her legs, her thighs. He straddled her, above her, looking down. There was a glimpse of underwear. Were they on backwards? He lifted his gaze so as not to see. Looking at her chest and throat, he could see she was ashen. As he straddled her face, he could see her eyes were not completely shut. They were like those of the fish he'd caught in the same brook, when they came out of the freezer, when his mom would fry up five or six of the little trout to make a respectable lunch for one young boy.

Her hair framed her face, but it had given up long ago. He passed over her and then realized she was behind him.

He braced his hands against the ceiling of the pipe, panicked. For the first time since he'd found her, she was looking at him, but he couldn't see her. Committing to turning around, he quickly brought both feet to one side, and then threw one foot back to where the other had been. It slipped. He fell to his knees onto the girl's left arm, and it flattened sickeningly beneath him. Putting his hands out to catch himself, he lifted his knees off her, and he sank into her middle. He reflexively let his elbows bend so the pressure on his hands would be lessened and he came down with a crash into the water. There was a burning in his arm as it ran down the rusting wheel anchoring her. His face went into the water. Downstream of her. He drank her. In his mouth, nose, and eyes.

He leapt to his feet, horrified. She was shifted now, and shaped differently. Her dress was up higher. His fault, he did that, he thought. The water, the girl-tea, ran off him mixing with his blood, and dripping from his arm and hand. Stepping backward and stumbling on a rock, he fell to one knee. He looked at her, looked down, and rose again. Turning all but his head, he felt his way out of the pipe. He stepped out into the open stream and looked up at the sky.

What was she doing there? Why did she do this to us? He looked at his wet clothing, the blood, and he stood there in the calf-deep brook. The water ran past him and into a wall of granite before turning right and heading downstream, north, beneath the tracks through another culvert to the river. When he turned back to her, the tears came. She wasn't right now—she looked horribly wronged. He had found her, and knew nothing of her, and he had fucked her up.

"I'm so sorry," he wept. "I'll get someone, I'll get someone." He almost added a plea for patience, but he thought she'd been patient enough. He scampered up the gravel embankment, with the sand beneath the larger pebbles sticking to his wet and bloody clothing and skin. Beneath his nails. Reaching the weeds and stepping out into an empty lot near where the avenue transitioned from pavement to dirt, he staggered a bit, and then broke into a run. He was drying. She was drying on him. She'd never come off.

A. J. Thibault

The Burns Family

"Honesty used to be my favorite virtue," Hart began. "With women, friends, with everyone." He remembered. "It got me places." Later all that changed. "Loyalty to a cause, to an idea, to those I loved transcended all else. That became an important issue. But now?" He stopped to reconsider. "Now, I would sacrifice any amount of loyalty to get some straight, honest answers again. Is that even possible anymore?"

If Richard Hart had the time, patience, and understanding, he might have known more than he did right now. Unfortunately, it was these qualities, these forms of friendship, the same ones that had been denied this girl by her mother and her sister that caused Erica to react so belligerently toward any man who considered himself superior to her.

If Hart had only demonstrated a subtler advance, tried a more compassionate approach toward Erica's concerns, he would have discovered that she had an older sister named Maryann. He would have also learned that from the time she was five and had shown definite signs of becoming a tomboy, Erica had been habitually called Ricky.

Having found that out, it would have taken him just one more step to piece together the importance of the dream. The dream about the mother collapsing, it was not his. It was Honey's. Somehow he was reading her mind.

The disorder Erica's mother had been afflicted with throughout her adult life was epilepsy. It was a personal problem, a family matter that in small towns knew no real cure, aside from some experimentation with various medications by the doctors who were in the beginning stages of understanding the electrochemical processes of the brain, and applying that knowledge to what one eminent neurosurgeon had appropriately tagged 'the split-brain.'

All her life, Erica harbored deep resentment toward her family. She felt like she had been discriminated against and misjudged by her mother, who thought she was a troublemaker, and by her father, who considered her odd. This eventually extended into her mind and slowed her progress in a world where she was expected to grow up quickly and come out adequately adjusted.

Maryann, her older sister, was cherished by both parents, always thought of her little sister, three years younger, as a rebel in blue jeans, a misguided brat who would probably amount to no good. Erica knew all of this from the time she could speak. With the growing resentment that built up inside her, their relationship remained strained.

Her mother didn't love her. Her father didn't care. They only loved her sister because, when all things were considered, Maryann was good, and Ricky was bad. It was as simple as that. Every fault was amplified, every wound exposed, every misfortune that descended upon the Burns household in North Carolina was attributed to and eventually blamed on little "Ricky," Erica.

Erica, the neighbors knew, demonstrated only selfishness, and more than anything else, she hated this vile and unwarranted distinction. What she also detested, and this was the leading cause of so much of the friction in the Burns family, was that her father's disappearance, which she knew was not her fault but her mother's, had always been blamed on her.

Erica caused all the family problems, she would continually be reminded. Not her mother's disease, or her lack of physical control, not her father's drinking as she was so often told, but her. For Harry and Monica Burns, Erica was an unwanted child. She was a bad seed, and the sorrow she planted infected every aspect of her parent's rocky marriage.

Frustration and anger built up inside Harry as he dealt with his wife when she collapsed publicly. To ease the guilt of her own conscience for failing him as a wife, she forced him to seek refuge in the bottle years before Erica was born. Then came the gambling to help with the medical costs and the lawsuits, and finally, the nights away, and Harry's carelessness and the rumors. It was about this time when Erica was born.

Monica was in no shape to take care of a new baby, and Harry soon found himself obligated to cleaning and feeding the infant when his wife wasn't feeling well, which was often. Monica thought she was punishing Harry for having abandoned her when she needed him most. She couldn't cope, and she relied on Harry for his strength and the reassurance and hope he gave her.

But one day, Harry grew tired of bringing Monica things and receiving nothing in return. His wife was incapable of returning his love. He had made a mistake by marrying her. But his faith prevented him from abandoning hope for a positive resolution. Till one day, when he came home early in the afternoon after selling no insurance that day, he heard Monica drifting around upstairs.

When he called, she appeared on the upper landing. She was holding ten-month-old Erica in her arms. One hand clung to the post at the top of the stairs.

"Monica, are you feeling all right?" he asked.

Harry sensed she was ill, but the booze in his blood threw him off.

"Harry," she whimpered as she relaxed her grip on the post and cradled Erica with one arm. "You did this to me, Harry. You did this to me."

Then she dropped or maybe threw—Harry couldn't tell which—Erica down two flights of stairs, ten steps apiece.

Harry scrambled to retrieve the baby screaming in pain, her arm tangled between two railings near the base. A drop of blood trickled from her tiny right ear. Harry was afraid to move her. He thought she might have a concussion, but he couldn't think about that now because just then, Monica lost her footing. She collapsed to her knees, still clutching the post with her right hand, her grip loosened. The weight of her body threw her off balance and pulled her weakened one hundred and ten-pound frame head over heels tumbling down the stairs crashing into her daughter with a lifeless moan.

* * *

Harry learned to bear up under similar circumstances, both public and private. For the next eleven years, his wife's grand mal seizures only became worse. They administered more potent doses of phenobarbital to bring her episodes under control, but this only caused her to become more drowsy and listless. She complained of constant fatigue and no appetite.

As the girls grew up, they had no time for play. Maryann and Erica were expected to take care of their mother. In most instances, the job would only get half done. They were just girls, and cooking and cleaning were pressing chores that required stamina and discipline, qualities they just didn't have.

In the end, the lot of homemaker fell to Harry. He would peel potatoes, mop the floors on Sunday, sterilize the dishes, as he referred to the process, make the meals, and bring home the bacon to boot. Harry wanted out after doing it all for eleven straight years and seeing no change on the horizon.

That fall before Erica turned twelve, Harry Burns vanished. He felt justified abandoning his family. He told himself that his girls were all grown up now, and there was nothing more he could do. He prayed God would forgive him.

When Maryann understood what happened, she let Erica know Dad's departure was all her fault. Monica's condition became worse. Ricky was responsible for this too. In her desperation and adolescent pride, Maryann couldn't come up with enough pins to stick into her little sister.

None of this helped Erica's progress through life. Unknown to the girls and Monica, each of whom knew nothing about the household finances, the little family was debt-ridden beyond belief. Every day there was a new creditor at the door.

"A poor family is not a proud family," Maryann would say as though she'd read it in a book somewhere. "The burden of the world is upon me," she would inform her little sister. And it was. She was the one who was expected to hold down the fort until Dad came back.

"It should be sometime this afternoon," she would always tell the strange men who called. She continued to hold out hope.

"Well, let me speak to your mother then," they would ask through the screen door.

"No, you can't right now," Maryann informed them as she kept one hand securely on the latch. "My mother isn't feeling well, thank you."

When Monica and Harry married fourteen years earlier, she told him that her illness was a mild case of fainting spells that a low-cholesterol diet could easily correct. This later proved not to be as accurate a diagnosis as she would have liked him to believe.

A few weeks after they returned from their week-long honeymoon in Florida, Harry and Monica were shopping at the Eastgate Mall in Charlotte. After a few hours of pricing cribs and baby clothes, they sat down to rest on a bench by Sears. Harry purchased ice-cream cones for them. Coffee was Monica's favorite flavor. At no time in her life did she enjoy it more than that afternoon sitting next to the man she had fallen in love with and soaking up the warm spring sun.

Saturday afternoon, shoppers passed by and smiled at the handsome couple. Knowing that they would have their first child, a sturdy little boy was what Harry wished for. He felt the most profound sense of contentment he'd felt in all of his twenty-seven years.

"What shall we call him?" He closed his eyes and smiled. "Steve? Tommy? Rex?"

He rolled a few more names through his mind, then he glanced at his pretty wife.

"Monica? Monica, what's the matter?"

Her head slumped between her shoulders, forcing the rest of the dripping coffee ice-cream cone up under her dress.

"Monica," Harry shouted as he grabbed her rigid arm. "What are you doing?"

A small crowd gathered and watched as Harry lifted his wife from the seat, the cone and all, pulled her dress back down over her knees and carried her back to the '57 Dodge. Everyone who passed stared at him as if they knew something he didn't, and each asked if everything was all right.

In North Carolina, the state of perfection is when everything is airtight. When Harry got Monica inside the car, she came to and told him she was okay, that everything was all right. It was just the heat.

After their marriage, Harry's career began to soar. Within six months, he started to sell more than a quarter-million dollars in life insurance policies. In two years, he would be seated at the million-dollar round table. Ecstatic about his progress, the two made plans to move out of the small apartment they were living in downtown. They started to look around for a house that would have a large enough backyard for a little boy to roam around and play in with his friends.

But before they moved in, Harry surprised Monica with the purchase of a brand new bright red '65 Mustang convertible, the same car that only ten years later would become a collector's item. The Ford was all chrome and leather and sportiness, and for a young family on their way up, was, according to Harry, the perfect automobile.

For months Monica begged Harry to teach her to drive. For months he refused. But Monica pleaded with him. She wanted to drive so much. Having grown up in Manhattan, her parents had no use for a car, so she never learned.

Harry finally told her that if she got 100% on the written test and the DMV issued her a learner's permit, he would allow her behind the wheel. She passed with flying colors, but on the application where it asked if she'd ever suffered from any lapses of consciousness, she breezed right through and checked off 'no.'

The day was calm when Harry eased the Mustang over to the side of a wooded two-lane country road. He explained the dials and the gears and told Monica that the most important thing was to keep her eyes on the road. She understood completely. Harry opened the door, and they traded places. Monica eagerly slid in behind the contoured wheel and turned on the ignition. She didn't hold the starter too long, and this pleased Harry. She placed the shift lever into 'DRIVE,' checked over her left shoulder for traffic, signaled correctly, and then crawled away from the shoulder with her foot on the brake. She was doing just fine, a little slow and overly cautious, perhaps, but that was all right.

"Give it more gas," Harry instructed. "Just a little more."

The road stretched straight ahead for miles. It was a Sunday morning, and he and Monica had just returned from church. There was no one else on the road, and that made Harry's task even more relaxed. The first hint of trouble came as they approached a gradual curve to the right. For some reason, Monica steered the car to the left.

"There's something wrong with the steering, Harry."

She tried to remain calm as she steered from the bottom of the wheel. Approaching instant panic, Harry lunged toward his wife's seat and grabbed the wheel.

In his unthinking haste, he over-corrected and did not notice the tractor that had just pulled out of a driveway five hundred yards ahead. The lumbering farm vehicle started toward them, and Harry shouted at Monica to let go.

Monica hated to be shouted at, particularly when she knew she was doing the right thing. The only way she would be able to prove anything to her nervous husband was to handle the situation and show him she was as competent as he. At least that's what was going through her mind when they were a hundred yards from the tractor. Monica wasn't sure why she did it, but she did. Everyone makes mistakes. She meant to slow down, but she hit the gas. When she noticed things weren't going as planned, she knew something was wrong with the steering or the engine or the wheels or something. She wasn't sure. That's when she froze.

A little voice told her she was out of control. She didn't believe it. It was the damned car. That was the last thing she remembered.

* * *

Harry thanked God by praying day and night after he and his wife had somehow survived the collision. The farmer wasn't hurt too badly, and Harry had insurance to cover that.

When their first child was born eight weeks later, Harry barreled into the delivery room with a baseball bat and a mitt just like he'd seen in the old movies. It was a joke. But when the nurse informed him, the baby was a girl, Harry felt betrayed. Monica had gotten her wish first, and he guessed if that's the way God wanted to play it, then "Thy will be done," he uttered under his breath.

Maryann had arrived. The next one would be his, Tommy, or Jeff, or Rick, and he'd save this glove for his boy.

When Erica came three years later, the grief and disappointment that registered on Harry's face caught the nursing staff's full attention. They assured him his little girl was healthy and beautiful, ill in no way, but Harry refused to pick her up.

God's will be done, he spat.

"Goddamnit, I wanted a boy. Why did this have to happen to me?"

He fell to his knees and begged for an answer. But all he heard along those lonely corridors late at night was the silence of his own voice. No reply ever came.

Monica's fainting spells, as she preferred to call them, progressed from petit to grand mal seizures as time passed. The atmosphere in which the Burns girls grew up became exceedingly thick and Calvinistic. They were allowed nothing. They were denied everything.

"There's a recession going on," Harry told them in the early seventies. "Don't you know what that is?" He'd answer the question himself. "It's like a depression, only you can't see it, and that makes it worse. There's gas lines. It's out of control."

Maryann and Erica were forced to miss school to take care of their mother. It was pre-ordained by God. It was a test of their faith. Harry sacrificed promotion after promotion with the opportunity to travel because he was unwilling to relocate.

The truth was, he was afraid to bring Monia to the dinners and the social functions that were a necessary part of what was required for him to advance in his field. Sales were significant, but management had always been the real goal crystallizing in the back of his mind.

While denying himself and his children, and his job, he renounced his wife and one day with no previous notice, actually late one night after heavy rain had fallen, the phone began to ring. Erica refused to answer it. She was upstairs in her tiny room, thinking things over, sorting events out. Someone had called her a tomboy earlier that day. She didn't like it, and she was determined to do something about it.

Maryann took the call and passed it along to her mother and then returned to her knitting. Erica sat alone in her room, listening to the Beatles as the rain beat against the window, following the scraping of branches on the roof with her eyes. A few moments later, she heard Maryann calling, "Ricky, come down here."

She didn't know what it was about. All she knew was that it was probably more of the same. Blame… blame… blame. Ricky did this. Ricky did that. Blah… blah… blah. Erica hated her sister. She had for a long time. Let her wait.

"Ricky, hurry!" Maryann could do no wrong. That was her problem.

Monica hung up the phone on the kitchen wall—or tried to—before her fainting spell came on. But she didn't quite make it. That was the evening that Harry Burns did not return home. And no one in the Burns family had seen him since.

Hart knew none of this.

Dane Cobain

The Case of the Missing Gnome

Jack Cholmondeley was vexed, to say the least.

"One of Mary's gnomes has gone missing," he said.

James Leipfold, who was sitting beside him in a booth at the local Wetherspoons, looked confused. "Her gnomes?" he parroted.

"Her gnomes," Cholmondeley confirmed. "She has a collection of the things. Those horrible little statues of old blokes fishing in ponds or holding tiny bloody signposts. They're her pride and joy, and now some scumbag has pinched one."

"Who'd want to steal a gnome?" Leipfold asked.

Cholmondeley shrugged and reached absentmindedly for his coffee, nudging it slightly and spilling a little without noticing. He took a sip of it and scalded his tongue.

"Shit!" he growled. He held his hand in front of his mouth and blew on it, then wiped it off on his trousers. "Where were we?"

"Who'd want to steal a gnome?" Leipfold repeated.

"Ah," Cholmondeley replied. "Who indeed? A drunk, perhaps? Some kid?"

"Perhaps."

"There's something else, though," Cholmondeley said. "Mary has dozens of the damn things, but only one of them went missing. Priscilla."

"Like the queen of the desert?"

"Exactly," Cholmondeley said. "Priscilla is her pride and joy. Her favourite gnome, if you can believe that. And I'm in the doghouse because she says I let it happen. She's making me sleep on the sofa until I find the bloody thing."

"I think I see where this is going."

"You've got to help me," Cholmondeley said. "If I don't find that damn gnome, my life won't be worth living."

Some men might have thought that Cholmondeley was overreacting, but Leipfold knew Mary and he knew what she was like.

"Tough break," Leipfold said. He thought about it for a moment. "Okay, so. Theories."

"What about them?"

"Have you got any?" Leipfold asked. Cholmondeley shook his head. Leipfold paused again. "Okay then. How about this? What if it was one of your enemies? Maybe they took it to kit it out with spy cameras? Or even something more sinister? Explosives?"

"Jesus Christ," Cholmondeley said. "You think so?"

"Not really," Leipfold replied. "But it's a possibility. You'll know for sure if it reappears again. Perhaps you should get your boys to have a look at the rest of the collection in the meantime."

"I'll do just that," Cholmondeley assured him. "Until then, I want you to put that brain of yours to use."

"I'm trying to run a business here," Leipfold reminded him.

Cholmondeley shrugged. "So what?" he asked. "You love a problem."

* * *

Cholmondeley asked his men to look at the gnomes as per Leipfold's suggestion, but they didn't find anything.

Unfortunately for Mary Cholmondeley, they also destroyed a baker's dozen of the things before she noticed they were missing and placed a panicked call to her husband. Jack was on duty and not best pleased to be interrupted by more of his wife's warbling about her precious collection. He broke the bad news over the phone and then held the receiver away from his ear as she shouted at him. He was glad that his colleagues couldn't see him.

"Listen, Mary," Cholmondeley said, trying to seize the initiative.

"I'm at work, okay? I'll talk to you when I get home."

"Oh no, Jack," she said. "Oh no, no, no. You've gone too far this time."

"What are you talking about?"

"My gnomes!" she howled. "You know how much I love those things."

"I thought we might have been in danger," Cholmondeley said, making a mental note to give Leipfold a stern reprimand. "I can't help it if I put your safety first, darling."

"Don't 'darling' me, Jack."

"I'm sorry," Cholmondeley said. "But what's done is done. At least the boys didn't find anything."

"I almost wish they bloody well did," Mary growled. Amplified and distorted by a bad connection, her voice sounded hellish, almost satanic. It sent a shiver down Cholmondeley's spine and a cold sweat to his furrowed brow. "I'm serious, Jack. I make a lot of sacrifices to support your career. I don't ask for much from you. I just want my bloody gnomes. Is that so much to ask?"

"Of course not, dear," Cholmondeley said. "I'm sorry."

"Sorry doesn't cut it," she said. "You make this better or else you're in a lot of trouble. I'm going to go and spend some time at my mother's. It'll give you some space to figure out what's really important to you."

"You're important to me, Mary," Cholmondeley said. "You are."

But she'd already hung up the receiver.

* * *

"How could you have been so wrong?" Cholmondeley asked.

Leipfold was sitting in his office, a couple of miles away from Cholmondeley's throne in one of the Old Vic's private meeting rooms. He was glad he was out of arm's reach of the man. He was clearly having a tough time of it, and Leipfold didn't want to give him an excuse to lash out.

"I'll admit it was a long shot," Leipfold said. "But it's better to be safe than sorry. Besides, I always hated those gnomes. I did you a favour."

"A favour?"

"Yeah," Leipfold said. "I knew your tech boys would destroy them if they took a look at them. Don't pretend you're not glad they're gone."

There was a pause on the phone line, followed by a sound that Leipfold interpreted as a muffled laugh from a man who was holding a hand over the receiver.

"You make a good point," Cholmondeley said. "I always hated the damn things, too. Made my front garden look like bloody Narnia. But that's not going to help my marriage."

"I can't help you there, Jack," Leipfold said. "It's not my area. But I'll keep investigating the missing gnome to see if I can find something."

"Thanks," Cholmondeley said. "I appreciate it."

* * *

Jack tried his best to make it up to Mary. He bought her a dozen roses ("they remind me of death"), took her out to dinner at a fancy restaurant ("a waste of money") and bought her a hundred new gnomes ("not the same") that were delivered two days later by a Yodel truck. But it all seemed to make no difference. Mary was in a bad mood, and Cholmondeley was still on the receiving end of it.

A couple of days later, Mary came back from her mother's, and she took to skulking around the house in a black dressing gown and refusing to shave her legs. She made her husband sleep on the sofa.

"And all over a bloody gnome," Cholmondeley said. "I don't understand it, Mary."

"Fuck the bloody gnome," she said. Cholmondeley was taken aback and stunned into silence. It was the first time he'd heard his wife swear, and it ruined the illusion. It was like he'd caught her with her trousers down in the bathroom.

"What's wrong with you?"

"Sorry," Mary said. "I got a little carried away. But damn it, Jack. You know how I feel."

Mary paused for a moment. She looked down at her lap, even though she'd done nothing wrong. "Besides," she said. "It was never about the gnomes. It was about us, Jack."

"Us?"

"You never let me be myself," she said. "I'm just poor old Mary Cholmondeley, the homely wife of the keen cop. I always knew you hated those gnomes. So did I. They were bloody atrocious. But get this, Jack. You can get rid of the gnomes, I don't mind."

"Really?"

"Really," she said. "And instead, I'm going to collect plastic flamingos."

* * *

Cholmondeley hated the flamingos even more than he'd hated the gnomes, and that did a lot to fix the rift between them. Within a couple of weeks, Mary had two dozen flamingos out front and a dozen more in the back garden. She'd even pinned a flamingo air freshener up in his panda car.

By the time that Mary bought her fiftieth, Cholmondeley had almost forgotten about them. They were just a part of life that he tried not to think about.

Then he met the kid.

He was a wiry kid, the acne-faced youth from number twenty-six who Cholmondeley knew as a menace because of what he got up to on his mountain bike. Cholmondeley couldn't remember his name— David, Dean or Derek, perhaps.

The kid approached him with a bike between his legs while Cholmondeley was setting up Big Beaky, his wife's latest addition to the family. Big Beaky was like all of the other flamingos except he was eight feet tall and weighed the same as a piece of flat-pack furniture.

"Hi."

"Hey," Cholmondeley said. "David, isn't it?"

"No," the kid replied. "It's Jacob."

"Jacob!" Cholmondeley said. "Ah yes, I knew it. How can I help?"

"I wanted to say that I'm sorry, sir," Jacob said. "I feel terrible."

"You do? Terrible about what?"

"I stole your gnome, sir," the kid said. "A couple of weeks ago. I was drunk and it was a dare and, well…"

Cholmondeley started laughing, which was clearly not what the kid had expected. He flinched and leapt backwards like a cat that had been attacked, which only made Cholmondeley laugh even more. By the end of it, he was struggling to breathe and emitting loud whistles that sounded more like a kettle boiling than a human laughing.

"What is it?" the kid asked.

"You stole the gnome?" Cholmondeley said. "That's bloody priceless. You almost ruined my marriage."

"I'm sorry," the kid repeated. "I still have it if you want it. I could bring it back."

"Why the bloody hell would I want you to do that?" Cholmondeley asked. "Good riddance, as far as I'm concerned."

"What happened to the rest of them?" the boy asked.

"They've gone, kid," Cholmondeley said. "All thanks to you."

"Jeez," he replied. "I'm sorry, mister. Is there anything I can do to make it up to you?"

"As a matter of fact, there is." Cholmondeley smiled at him, the smile of a wolf in sheep's clothing. "You see those flamingos?"

"Yeah, I see the flamingos," the kid said.

"Good," Cholmondeley replied. "Do me a favour, kid. I want you to start nicking those instead."

Sam hesitated, and then continued. "When the housekeeper arrived this morning, she noticed the front tires of Aunt Carol's car were slashed. After she discovered the body, she went to phone the police from the house phone and couldn't. The wires had been cut. She called me from her own phone because she couldn't find Aunt Carol's cell either."

"Sounds like someone didn't want Carol leaving or phoning for help. How did she die?"

"I don't know. I'll call you later, Abby. The police want to talk to me now."

* * *

Sam called me around noon while I was inoculating a Bernese mountain dog. I returned her call fifteen minutes later.

"My mother is on vacation in Aruba," she said. "I called and told her what happened. She's devastated and is getting a flight back this afternoon. Could you drive me to the airport, Abby? I don't want to be alone."

"Of course." Sam's mother was Carol's sister. A second sister had passed away three years ago.

"We need to leave my place by three o'clock."

I was only working at the veterinary hospital until one o'clock today. "I'll be at your place in plenty of time."

* * *

Sam lived in the town next to the community where Carol Judd's farm was located. When I arrived at Sam's townhouse, there were three people sitting in the living room.

"These are my cousins," Sam said, after I gave her a big hug. "Jillian, Lisa, and you know Ethan."

I'd met Ethan once before. He was in his late twenties, the same age as Sam, and they socialized a bit. I'd never met Lisa or Jillian although Sam had talked about them. I knew all three only lived about fifteen minutes from here and that they were the children of Carol Judd's late sister.

After offering my condolences, I asked Sam, "Do you know how she died, yet?"

"They'll be an autopsy. But there was no blood or bruising," she answered.

"That rules out being shot, stabbed, or bashed on the head," I said.

"I overheard a police officer say there was no sign of strangulation either. The housekeeper found her on the floor by her chair."

I digested these facts. Could it be natural causes? But the slashed tires and cut phone wires made me believe it was far more sinister. Visions of poisons floated through my mind.

I was jolted out of my thoughts as Lisa rose from the sofa and said to Sam, "I need to be going." She glanced at her watch. "And I guess you need to be leaving soon to pick up your mom."

Jillian and Ethan said they would leave now too.

Sam wiped a tear off her cheek. Jillian's eyes were red and puffy as if she had been crying too. Lisa and Ethan seemed more composed.

Once they were gone, I asked Sam how she was doing.

"Not well. It's worse than you think. When the police talked to me, the questions they asked made me feel like a suspect."

* * *

As we sped along the highway on our way to the airport, Sam told me that she would be helping out with the horses at Carol's farm until everything was settled.

"The groom, Manny, is perfectly capable of running the place by himself, but I know Aunt Carol would have wanted a family member involved," she explained.

"What about your cousins?"

"They know nothing about horses. They couldn't tell a stallion from a mare." She grinned. "Well, they probably could tell that, but you get the point."

"Do you know what will happen to the horse farm?" I asked.

"Aunt Carol planned on leaving it to my mom."

I nodded. Sam's mom was an avid horsewoman—just like her daughter.

"Aunt Carol's stock portfolio will be divided among the rest of the family—Ethan, Lisa Jillian, and me."

I said nothing. Silence can work magic.

"Her investments are worth close to five million dollars," Sam added.

I let out a low whistle. "That's more than one million apiece. People have been known to kill for less."

"I know." She sighed. "The police want to talk to me again tomorrow. They'll be talking to my cousins for a second time too. Luckily, my mom was out of the country, so she won't be subject to this."

"How did your cousins get along with your Aunt Carol?"

"As far as I know, fine. I was probably the closest because of our mutual interest in horses, but Ethan and Lisa stopped by quite a bit. Jillian got along well, but I don't think she visited much."

"Do you get along with your cousins?"

"I do, but we're not particularly close even though we all live nearby. Ethan is the same age as I am, so I see him socially on some occasions. Lisa is fifteen years older and married with kids. I basically see her at family functions."

"Jillian moved back from the west coast less than two years ago. I had her over for dinner once, but she never reciprocated. She's also lives far more extravagantly than I do. She likes to go to expensive dinners and high end clubs that I can't afford on my writer's salary."

Dozens of questions squirreled though my mind, but there was one that kept popping to the front.

"Sam, you were planning to ask your aunt a favor last night. What was it?"

My friend was silent for a moment.

"Aunt Carol was thinking of selling the horse farm," Sam finally said. "She had gotten an offer she claimed was difficult to refuse. And although she loved her horses, she said it was time for something new. She wanted to travel."

Sam paused. I waited for her to speak up again.

"Last night, I begged her to sell the place to my mother and me," Sam continued. "We couldn't match the offer, but I didn't think the money was that important—Aunt Carol had plenty. We could scrape up enough for a substantial down payment and then get a loan."

Sam was a freelance writer and her mom a retired teacher. They could easily manage the horse farm. But coming up with enough money to buy it was a different matter.

"What did your Aunt Carol say?"

"She said she would think about it. I'm sure she would have ultimately agreed."

I didn't respond. But one thought popped into my mind and wouldn't leave.

Now the horse farm would belong to Sam's mom.

* * *

It was two evenings later, and my house smelled of garlic. I stepped into my kitchen where my fiancé, Jason, greeted me. He was preparing shrimp scampi for dinner.

"Perfect timing," he called out. "Dinner will be ready in fifteen minutes. I have a lot to tell you."

I wanted to question him now, but I knew I'd have to wait while he concentrated on his culinary masterpiece. An attorney by profession, he was a serious amateur chef.

I set the table and poured two glasses of white wine. Once we sat down and began eating, Jason said, "The autopsy on Carol Judd is finished."

Jason was an assistant district attorney and had access to this information.

"How did she die?" I asked.

"Poison," he said. "Strychnine."

I took a deep breath. "How did it get in her body?"

"The police found an espresso cup on the end table next to her chair. Since they suspected poisoning, they had the cup tested. It contained traces of strychnine. That's why the medical examiner checked for it in the body."

"Do they know when she died?"

"Judging by the rigor of the body when she was found, along with the fact that strychnine doesn't kill immediately, it had to be before eleven at night."

"Sam said she left her aunt around seven. That means the poison had to be administered between those hours."

Jason frowned.

"What's the matter?" I asked.

"I don't know if I should say this, but the police have a suspect in mind."

"Who?"

"Sam."

I almost choked on a shrimp. "That can't be."

"She was the last person to see Carol alive."

"The last person that you know of," I reminded him. "You said the time of death was before eleven. The killer could have visited her any time between seven and then."

"Sam has motive," Jason argued. "All three cousins told the police that Sam wanted the horse farm. While Carol was alive, Sam was free to come and ride as often as she wished. And her mother was inheriting the property. But according to her cousins, all this was changing because her aunt planned to sell the place."

"Not true. The night of the murder, Sam talked to her aunt about the farm. Her aunt was reconsidering."

"You only have Sam's word on that. Before the housekeeper left, she overheard Sam and her aunt fighting about it."

I swallowed hard. Sam had made it seem as if her aunt had readily agreed to rethink selling the horse farm. Sam never told me they argued about it.

Jason shrugged. "Maybe in the end, her aunt did agree to reconsider. But maybe she didn't. No one knows. The point is they had a fight the night she was murdered and—"

"But strychnine? Sam knows nothing about poisons."

"Have you kept up with her writing career?"

"Yes. Sam usually sends me a copy of her work. I usually receive it a few weeks after it is published."

"Then you're a little behind. Sam had an article come out last week in a mystery magazine. It's all about the poisons Agatha Christie used in her books."

I groaned. "What about the cousins? They will each inherit more than one million. That's motive too."

The police are still investigating. But Sam has motive, means, and opportunity."

* * *

I was meeting Sam at our favorite pub, *The Hedge and the Hog*. When I stepped through the door, I spotted her at a booth in the back. I bee-lined for the table.

Sam looked terrible. Her face was ashen, and her usually lustrous auburn hair hung limply over her shoulders. As I slid into the seat facing her, I noticed she had bitten her nails to the quick.

"An old boyfriend of mine who is on the police force contacted me," she said. "He told me I'm the prime suspect, and he advised me to get a lawyer."

I nodded. Although the evidence was circumstantial, Jason had reminded me that most convictions were based on circumstantial evidence.

We remained silent as the server dropped off menus and took our drink order—two white wines.

"Who do you think killed your aunt?" I asked as soon as the server left.

"I don't know. There was no break-in, which means Aunt Carol opened the door for the killer. It had to be someone she knew."

"Your cousins will each be inheriting a good sum of money," I stated bluntly. "They have motive. Do you know of anyone, besides them, who would want to see your aunt dead?"

"No." Sam shook her head.

"What about Manny, the groom, or Ruth, the housekeeper?"

"Both adored my aunt, and both have airtight alibis that have been verified by the police. Manny left early that afternoon to attend a birthday party in New Jersey for his niece. Ruth was participating in a bingo tournament."

"Then I think we should concentrate on your cousins. Do any of them have an immediate need for money?"

Sam furrowed her brows as she appeared to think about this. "Lisa and her husband own White Wolf Nursery. I imagine they are doing well."

"A nursery," I said. "Strychnine can still be found in some products that kill garden pests." I made a mental note to find out what I could about White Wolf Nursery.

"Ethan is teaching at Braxton College," Sam went on to say. "He finished his doctoral degree a year ago." She smiled.

"Why are you grinning?"

"About two years ago, he got this crazy notion about ditching his studies and opening a brewery."

"But he didn't, did he?"

"No. Thank goodness he couldn't raise the money for it." Sam shook her head. "This was a pipe dream. I'm sure he's over it. He's not a business person. He's a science nerd and an academician."

"What does he teach?"

"Chemistry."

"That's another cousin with knowledge of poison."

"Actually, there are three," Sam said. "Jillian's a nurse."

We paused as the server delivered our wine and jotted down our dinner orders.

Sam continued, "I don't know if she has money problems. She lives well. She has a gorgeous condo, a luxury car, designer clothes, and she travels a lot. She just returned from visiting friends in Las Vegas."

Living well didn't always mean you had the money to support your lifestyle. I wondered if she was living beyond her means.

"What about alibis?" I asked.

"Lisa was home with her husband the night of the murder. He backs her up. It was only the two of them. Her son was at a sleepover."

"A husband might lie," I said. "What about the others?"

"Ethan taught a course until eight in the evening. After class he worked at the college chemistry laboratory until almost eleven. Then he went home. Braxton College is almost an hour away from the horse farm, so if his alibi held up, he couldn't have murdered Carol."

"Did anyone witness his time in the lab?" I asked.

"Sam nodded. "Another professor stopped by at about eight-thirty and saw him."

"But you only have Ethan's word that he stayed until eleven. Maybe he left right after his colleague saw him. What about Jillian?"

"Her alibi seems solid. She was at a fundraiser for the hospital. It was a cocktail party and auction held at Fox Lair Caterers—"

"Fox Lair Caterers is only a ten minute drive from the horse farm," I interrupted.

"The event started at seven and ended at midnight. Several guests vouched for her being there throughout the night."

Our dinners arrived. Before we began eating, Sam said, "There's going to be a memorial service for my aunt this weekend. They'll be a small gathering back at my house afterwards. I'd like you to come."

"Of course."

While paying my respects, I would dig into the motives and alibis of her three cousins.

* * *

The day before the memorial service, I did some research. I discovered there were no video cameras in the chemistry lab at Braxton College and the cameras in the parking lot by the building had been out of order the night of the murder. After the witness saw him at eight-thirty, Ethan had no proof that he was at work.

* * *

Early Saturday morning, I drove to the White Wolf Nursery. I figured Lisa and her husband would be getting ready for the memorial, and I wanted to poke around when they weren't there.

About five miles before the turn-off for the nursery, I drove passed one of the big box stores—the kind that sell all sorts of home improvement supplies including plants and gardening equipment, usually at discount prices. I remembered reading the newspaper when this mega-store opened two years ago. Several shops in the town, such as the local hardware store, were afraid it would run them out of business. I was afraid that might be true. The place was bustling.

Upon arriving at White Wolf, I noticed a few cars in the parking lot, but not many.

I began wandering through the spring plants, when I was beset upon by a salesman.

"May I help you?" he asked.

"Just looking. I thought more people would be here today. I passed the store down the road. It appeared packed."

He frowned. "Everyone wants cheaper prices. Small independent companies can't afford to compete."

"Think they'll run this place out of business?"

"I did think that, but not anymore." He smiled. "Studies have shown that the small business can survive if they host events, especially children's activities."

"What do you mean?"

"Pumpkin carving contests in the fall, hayrides, haunted corn mazes. In the winter classes on making bird feeders—we sell bird seed. Then in the spring, an Easter egg hunt with prizes—"

"That's great. Have you started with any of these activities yet?

"No. These things cost money to do. With the loss of business from the box store, we had no extra cash—we were in the red. But that all changed." He grinned. "The owners are coming into some money. They can pay off what they owe and put some into events and advertising."

I bought a daffodil plant that I would bring to Sam's house. I said good-bye and headed to the car.

* * *

The memorial service had a decent crowd, but I didn't know most of the people or how they were connected to Carol Judd.

After the service I drove to Sam's townhouse for the reception. I was greeted by Magnus, the Maine Coon cat, who rubbed against my leg, purring.

I grabbed a glass of wine and started to mingle. I spotted Jillian standing in a corner with two other people. I hadn't been able to find out much about her, so I headed in her direction.

She introduced me to her companions. They were co-workers from the hospital—Paul and Amanda.

"We were talking about last week's fund raiser for the hospital," Amanda volunteered.

I realized this was the perfect opportunity to ferret out information. I had viewed the schedule for the fundraiser on the hospital website. Seven to eight was a preview of the auction items. Eight to ten was the cocktail party. Ten to midnight was the auction. The question that squirreled through my mind: Was Jillian present the entire evening?

"Were you at the fundraiser?" I asked Amanda.

"Oh, yes," she said. "In fact, Jillian and I both bid on the same item—a basket of expensive wines."

"Who won the bid?"

"Jillian. At one point I thought I had it, then, at the last moment, she called out a higher bid."

"I should have warned you, Amanda," Paul said, laughing. "I saw

Jillian lingering around the wine basket during the preview."

Jillian sneezed.

"You should do something about that cold," Amanda said. "You've had it since the auction."

"I didn't notice it then," Paul said. "And we were sitting together during the cocktail party."

I sighed. It appeared Jillian had been at the preview, cocktail party, and auction. I needed to turn my attention elsewhere. From the corner of my eye, I spotted Ethan. As I made my way toward where he stood, I noticed Magnus brush against him. He pushed the cat away.

I guess he spotted the frown spread across my face. "I don't like cats," he said as I approached.

He had a beer in his hand, which provided me with the opportunity to segue into what I needed to find out.

"How's the beer?" I asked.

"Good. I do like craft beer."

"Sam told me that at one time you wanted to open a brewery."

"Still do," he said.

"But you're a professor."

"Several professors at Braxton have businesses on the side. I love teaching, but it doesn't pay much. I have a friend who is willing to partner with me. He'll cover the place while I'm in class or at the lab. I think we're going to do it."

* * *

I came home to bad news.

"I heard from a contact in the homicide division," Jason said. "It appears Sam's arrest is imminent."

"But she didn't do it. Her cousins also have strong motives. Lisa and Ethan have weak alibis, and even Jillian might have slipped out of the fundraiser at some time."

Owl, my calico cat, jumped up on my lap, and I stroked her. She didn't stay long. She appeared to have spotted something out the window and quickly hopped off. I looked down at my navy blue skirt. It was covered in cat hair.

"She's in full shedding season," Jason said.

"Yes. But some of this hair is also from Sam's Maine Coon..." Suddenly, I knew who murdered Carol Judd.

I grabbed my phone and punched in Sam's number. I told her what she needed to do.

* * *

"What did you give as an excuse for our stopping by?" I asked Sam the next morning. We were driving to Lisa's house. Ethan and Jillian would be there.

"I told my cousins that although my mom inherited the horse farm, including the house and its contents, she wanted each of us to take a memento. Aunt Carol left mom an inventory of her *treasures* and I'm bringing that list with me today."

Sam pulled into the long driveway of Lisa's colonial-styled home.

We hopped out of the car, and I grabbed the crate containing Magnus from the back seat.

Lisa let us in and led us to the living room. Ethan and Jillian were sitting on the couch. As soon as Jillian saw us, her smile faded.

"What's he doing here?" she asked, pointing to the cat carrier.

"I'm taking Magnus to my veterinary office for a thorough exam," I lied. "I didn't want to leave him in the car. You don't mind, do you?"

It looked as if she was about to say she did mind, but instead she frowned and asked, "Why are you here? You're not part of our family."

"Abby and I are meeting another friend later and are traveling together," Sam said. "This is a stop along the way. After we drop Magnus off at Abby's veterinary office, we will head to the friend's house."

I smiled. "Don't worry. I won't interfere."

"Just be sure you keep that cat in the crate," Ethan added. "I don't like cats."

"Abby and I do have to be going soon so let's get started," Sam said. Lisa served coffee, while Sam distributed copies of the inventory to her cousins. As they discussed the items on the list, Jillian's eyes became puffy and began to water. Then she sneezed.

I sent out a quick text, then sat back and sipped my coffee. A few minutes later, after each cousin had chosen a memento, I spoke up.

"Jillian, you have a cat allergy, don't you?" I said.

"Yes."

"I noticed you had a reaction at Sam's house yesterday."

"You knew I had an allergy, and you bought that cat here today. What kind of sick joke—"

"No joke. I needed to be sure. Now that I am, I have proof you killed your aunt."

"What!" Jillian exclaimed. Ethan spilled his coffee, and Lisa opened her mouth in surprise. Sam smiled at me. I'd told her my theory earlier.

"The day after the murder, you had a mild reaction at Sam's home—"

"Sam hadn't taken the cat yet," Jillian argued. "It was still at my aunt's house."

"You're right. But reactions from cat allergies can last more than a day. You had an encounter with Magnus the previous night—when you murdered your aunt."

"That's why in the two years since you moved here you rarely visited her," Sam said. "The first time you went to her house was last week when you killed her."

"This is preposterous. I was at the fundraiser. There are witnesses."

"You left, murdered Carol, and came back," I said. "Again, your allergy is proof."

"What do you mean?"

"Your co-workers, Amanda and Paul, both provided alibis for different times. But Amanda, who saw you late in the evening, asked about your cold. Paul, who was with you earlier, said he didn't think you had one."

I sipped my coffee and continued. "That's because it wasn't a cold. It was an allergic reaction. And it didn't occur until after you slipped out during the cocktail party and went to your aunt's house."

"Paul was with me during the cocktail party. We sat together—"

"You weren't seated for the entire time. I know how these things work. You get food from the buffet, sit and eat, then get up and mingle. It was a two-hour buffet. That gave you plenty of time to disappear. The horse farm is only ten minutes away."

"My fiancé is an assistant district attorney," I continued. "He spoke with the homicide detective on the case. You live beyond the means of someone on a nurse's salary. The detective checked you out and discovered you were heavily in debt. "

At that moment, I hear sirens. I looked out the window and saw two police cars pull up.

"Once I was sure my theory was correct, I texted the homicide detective in charge of this case," I said. "He's coming up the walkway now. It's all over."

S. Lee Manning

Choices

Kolya hadn't been home for almost two weeks. Well, technically, it wasn't his home anymore; he shared an apartment with three other associates close to the law firm in lower Manhattan where he'd been working for the past month, but the two-bedroom apartment in Brooklyn where his cousin Rivka had raised him from the age of fourteen still felt like home. He'd wanted to visit, but he'd been working sixteen hours a day, including weekends. He only had the day off because the partner he worked for had settled the case on Friday night, but starting Monday, he'd be on a new case. It wasn't just the hours—he felt no sense of accomplishment or pride in what he was doing. He'd already reached the conclusion that this was not how he wanted to spend his life—which was why he'd sent an application in to the FBI.

Seated at the table in the kitchen, Rivka was crying. She looked even thinner than the last time he'd visited, a scarf wrapped around her head in a manner that reminded him of the Orthodox women who populated the neighborhood. But she wasn't Orthodox.

Alarmed, he crossed the room and bent over to kiss her. "What's wrong? Did you hear something from the doctor?"

She pulled a tissue out of her pocket and wiped her face. "No, no, Kolya. Nothing from the doctor. Everything is as it was. I'm not crying for myself."

He sat next to her and took her hand.

"It's my friend. Nina. You remember Nina? She was killed yesterday."

"What? Who would have killed Nina?" He was shocked and angry.

Nina had been a regular fixture on Saturdays in his teenage years. A regular attendee at the reform temple where Rivka had dragged him during adolescence for a token visit on the Jewish High Holy Days, Nina would drop by after Saturday services and spend much of the afternoon kibbitzing with Rivka. She almost always brought cookies or rugalach, homemade and delicious. Once the sun set and Shabbat was over, she would perform Havdalah—a ceremony that marked the end of the Shabbat and the beginning of the week—and then encourage him to play some of his favorite jazz pieces on the piano.

He later realized that Nina, widowed, twenty years older than Rivka and the mother of two grown sons, was also quietly offering Rivka advice on parenting a teenage boy.

"She was hit by a stray bullet when two *mafiya* gangs started shooting at each other on Brighton Beach Avenue." Rivka put her hand up to her face and wept. Calming again, she wiped her face as Kolya fixed her a cup of black coffee with sugar, her favorite. Even though it sometimes made her sick, she still wanted it. He set the cup in front of her and seated himself again.

"Did the police catch the *kozyol yobannity* that shot her?" He resorted to his native Russian to express his indignation.

She shook her head. "You know how it is. No one saw anything. No one's going to risk it."

"*Yob tvoyu mat.*" He quietly spoke his favorite Russian curse, but she had heard it. She smacked his hand.

"Stop saying that. You sound like a Russian thug."

"Well, it's what I am, isn't it?" Or at least what he would have been had Rivka not adopted him from the abusive boys' home in St. Petersburg where he'd spent five years after the death of his mother. But his intent was to divert her, and he succeeded.

"You absolutely are not. You're a lawyer, a musician. Not a gangster." But at least the tears had stopped. "Have you had lunch? Can I fix you something?"

"Why don't I make both of us scrambled eggs and toast?" He could have cooked something more elaborate, but toast and scrambled eggs were what she could keep down. He mentally cursed the chemo, the breast cancer, along with the unknown men who had killed Nina.

Eating lunch brought a semblance of normalcy. He told her about his job, omitting how much he disliked it, and she told him the neighborhood gossip. After the meal, he washed the dishes, and she asked him to play the piano for her. He preferred jazz, but like his mother who had taught him to play piano almost before he could walk, Rivka loved Mozart. He played Mozart's 11th piano sonata, while she curled up in her favorite chair, eyes closed.

At four, he kissed her goodbye.

"You're going to have dinner with your friend? The one from Russia who called the other day?" She clung to his hand.

"Dmitri. Yes, we're meeting at The Ukraine in Manhattan." Dmitri had been his best friend at the boy's home, but Kolya hadn't even known Dmitri was in the country until the phone call two days earlier. "I'll come see you next weekend. I'm sorry I missed a week." He'd do it, even if he had to compensate by working through the night.

"I'll be here." She smiled at his look of concern. "I'm going to beat this, Kolya. Women in our family are strong."

Neither of them was being completely honest, but he decided to let it go.

* * *

On his way to the subway, he passed the Blue Parrot, one of his favorite piano bar restaurants. The owner, Avram, a former resident of Moscow, had invited him to play jazz with other musicians when he was a teenager. Kolya had continued to jam at the Blue Parrot in the summer during his college years.

But today, the Blue Parrot was barred and shuttered.

It should have been open. On weekends, Avram usually opened for lunch and stayed open until one o'clock the following morning.

Puzzled, he entered the small grocery store next to the bar. The owner of the store, Masha, a wiry woman in her sixties, nodded a hello but didn't look up from the newspaper she was reading. When he'd first arrived in Brooklyn, Kolya'd stolen some candy bars and magazines from the store. Rivka had found the illegal booty in his bedroom, and he'd confessed. She had marched him back to the store, where he'd apologized, and Rivka had paid for the items. Then after school for the next two months, he had put in several hours sweeping and cleaning. Since then, Masha had been friendly when he dropped by.

"Why is the Blue Parrot closed?" he asked her.

She looked up from the newspaper. "How is Rivka? I haven't seen her recently."

A deflection.

"Okay. She's okay." Although she wasn't. "Upset about Nina."

"Nina's not the only one dead. Eight people have been killed in the last two weeks. That's not counting the criminals killing each other off. Eight good people. You didn't know?"

"I haven't been following the news." And Rivka had only mentioned Nina. "I had no idea that this was happening."

"Well, it is."

She returned to her newspaper. He waited for another minute. She looked up again. "You're not waiting around to steal candy bars again, are you?"

"I pay for them now. The Blue Parrot?"

She rustled the newspaper. "What did I just tell you?"

"Avram? He was killed?"

She nodded.

He felt a surge of grief. He'd liked Avram. "Did he get caught in a crossfire, like Nina?"

"No. He refused to pay protection money. Because he was a stubborn fool. So they killed him."

"*Yob tvoyu mat.*" He spoke softly, but like Rivka, Masha had keen ears. Unlike Rivka, she didn't object.

"You can say that again. Those bastards will destroy every business in Brighton Beach."

He felt a level of fury that he hadn't felt for several years. "You?"

"I pay them. Because I'm not a stubborn fool."

"Someone should do something. The police."

She laughed softly. "I thought you were Russian. You should know that the police won't do shit to stop organized gangs. Not in Russia. Not here."

He had known about the gangs in Russia, about the dangers of simply walking down the street in the 1990s. Still, he'd thought America was different. Maybe he was wrong.

He picked up a 3 Musketeers candy bar and held it up for her to see. Then he handed her a twenty-dollar bill. She offered him change, but he shook his head.

"It's interest. From ten years ago."

"You paid that back and then some."

"Consider it lagniappe." He doubted she knew the Creole term for something extra given during a business transaction, but he liked the phrase. He'd learned it during a trip to New Orleans his senior year in high school to hear Ellis Marsalis, Jr.

Whether she knew the phrase or not, she accepted the money and waved him off.

* * *

At six, he arrived at The Ukraine, a popular restaurant in the East Village serving Ukrainian and Russian specialties. The inside of The Ukraine almost glowed with pink. Pink ceilings, pink walls, and pink tablecloths. Kolya didn't really care for the decor, but he liked the food. It brought back memories of his early years in Russia, of his grandmother who'd fled Kiev and who had loved to cook. And he was looking forward to seeing Dmitri again, even if it would be a little strange. The brief conversation on the phone to arrange the meeting was the only contact they'd had in ten years—except for a few letters Kolya had written that had gone unanswered.

He had no trouble recognizing Dmitri, seated at a table in the corner, his back to the wall. At twenty-four, Dmitri still resembled the boy who'd taught him how to defend himself—round face, slightly unkempt brown hair, although the haircut appeared to be an expensive one and the unkempt appearance, a deliberate affectation. At the sight of Kolya, he stood, and the two men embraced.

"Good to see you, you son-of-a-bitch." Dmitri seated himself again, and Kolya took the empty chair. "You look good." He spoke in Russian, and Kolya responded in the same language.

"So do you."

Dmitri looked more than good. He looked rich. At the law firm, partners regularly sported hand crafted suits from London, and Dmitri's outfit had that expensive feel. Kolya also noticed the diamond pinky ring.

"So you're a lawyer now?" Dmitri signaled a waiter, who rushed over to take their order—herring, hot borsch, and a bottle of Absolut vodka. The waiter departed and Dmitri turned back to Kolya. "You like your job?"

"Not particularly." He thought of mentioning that he'd applied to join the FBI, but for reasons he couldn't articulate, he held back.

"I would have thought you'd become a musician."

Kolya shrugged. "I still play. But it's hard to make a living at jazz." He'd enjoyed the challenge of law school, the analysis of cases, the building of arguments, but the practice of law was quite different. "And you? You look like you've done well."

"I'm a businessman now. Doing some real estate. Buying and developing properties." The waiter returned with the vodka and two glasses, unusually fast service for The Ukraine, Kolya noted. Dmitri poured, and they clicked glasses. "*Za zdarovye.*"

"Do you ever see any of the gang from the *dyskeii dom*?" Kolya asked.

"Sometimes," Dmitri said. "Misha is in prison. Arkady is married and has a kid. We meet for dinner when I'm in St. Petersburg. We've considered paying a visit to Yelseyev, the bastard. But we decided that you should be with us."

"I don't have any interest in seeing him," Kolya said.

"He probably remembers you. But not fondly. You did break his nose."

Kolya didn't want to revisit the incident—the time when Yelseyev, the director of the boys' school, had tried to rape him, and the maneuver that Dmitri had shown him, palm slammed upward against a nose, had saved him. One of many bad memories from those years.

"I was thinking of breaking more than his nose." Dmitri grinned at the memory. "You still remember how to fight?"

Kolya inclined his head. "I studied Krav Maga and mixed martial arts in high school and college. But I only use it for self-defense. I'm not going to go hunt down Yelseyev."

"I get it. You are respectable now."

"More or less. And you aren't?"

"I'm more or less respectable. But I'd still like to give Yelseyev what he deserves for molesting defenseless kids." Dmitri poured another shot for both of them.

"Hard to argue with the sentiment." Kolya clinked glasses again. "Here's to someone, but not us, beating the shit out of the old bastard."

The borsch and herring arrived. They continued to drink through dinner, while talking about the past, about music, about America versus Russia. Dmitri spoke of his years in the boys' home after Kolya had left; Kolya spoke of growing up as a Russian Jewish immigrant in America. By the time they finished eating, Kolya had drunk enough to describe a woman he'd fallen in love with in law school, but who regarded him as a friend.

"Why not tell her how you feel?" Dmitri asked. "Maybe buy her an expensive necklace."

Kolya drank another shot. "Not a great idea."

"American women don't like jewelry?"

"American women who've made their lack of interest quite clear want their opinion to be respected."

Dmitri grinned. "Boring, *moi droog*. I like America a lot, but this I don't understand. So, you're not fucking anyone?"

"Of course, I am. From time to time. Nothing serious though."

"Doesn't have to be serious to be fun."

"No. But caring for the woman does enhance the experience."

"It can." Dmitri signaled the waiter and held up the empty bottle of Absolute vodka. "It can be very nice. There's this ballet dancer—Katrina—back in St. Petersburg that I really like. I'm thinking of asking her to come to New York and move in with me. What she can do with her legs. Amazing."

The waiter appeared with a new bottle.

"So, let us get down to business," Dmitri's voice was warm, if a little slurred from the vodka. "I'd like you to come to work with me. I can make you rich, my friend."

"Work with you? I don't know anything about real estate."

Dmitri chuckled and poured himself more vodka.

"What's funny?" Kolya asked.

"What you know about my business isn't the point. I need a second in command. Someone I can trust. Someone who is like a brother."

"This is the first time you've seen me in years."

"I still trust you."

"But not completely." Kolya remembered their first meeting. He'd been hiding from Yelseyev under a piano in an empty auditorium when Dmitri found him. They had struck a bargain, Dmitri offering to teach Kolya how to fight in exchange for music lessons. Then, instead of shaking hands, Dmitri had knocked him down and explained that Kolya should never trust anyone completely.

"Maybe not completely, but I trust you more than anyone else I know."

Kolya poured another shot and regarded Dmitri, taking in again the expensive suit, the diamond ring, the chair strategically placed in the corner. He glanced around the room and realized that there were two men seated at a table fifteen feet away, watching them. He thought of the waiter, hurrying to provide the best service, unlike other times he'd dined in the restaurant.

"Those men are watching us." Kolya indicated with his head. "Do you know them?"

"They work for me," Dmitri said.

"They work for you?"

"Yes. And they're doing their job right now."

Kolya had graduated with honors from Columbia Law School, but he'd been slow in putting together the obvious. Maybe because he didn't want it to be true.

"You have muscle protecting you, Dimi? I thought you said you were in business."

"Well, I *am* a businessman. North American representative of Vladimir Rzaev. You've heard of him?"

"Of course. We used to talk about running away and joining him." And Rzaev was a gangster, one of the biggest.

"He has an import/export business these days. That's what I do. Import/export."

"There have been a number of shootings in Little Odessa in the past few weeks. People I know have been killed."

"I'm sorry to hear that. Some people think I'm cutting into their businesses, and they act stupidly."

"Stupidly? You call starting a gang war acting stupidly?"

"Yes. And I didn't start anything. They started it. And sometimes bad things happen to the wrong people. No one you were close to got hurt, I hope."

"No, but I knew them." Technically, not a lie. He had liked both Nina and Avram, but he hadn't been close to them. Not the way he was close to Rivka. He thought of her crying at the kitchen table.

"I'm sorry that people you knew got hurt. I tell my people to be careful of by-standers, but some of them are idiots and a little trigger happy."

Kolya glanced at the two men watching them. "What are you importing/exporting?"

"What does it matter?"

"You asked me to work for you. I'd like to know what I'd be doing."

"We import/export whatever the market demands—or what Rzaev tells us to do. It's very simple. I also am diversifying into real estate. Buying rundown properties, fixing them up, and flipping them. Very profitable."

"And you'd want me to do what?"

"Watch the business, keep track of the men working for me, of the money coming in and going out—you;re smart. Also, now that you're a lawyer, you can help me navigate the American legal system."

"I'm just out of law school. You'd need someone with more experience to help you with legal problems."

"I need someone I can trust." Dmitri downed another shot. "That's more important than experience. I can hire a lawyer to do the actual legal work. I need you to supervise. Besides, my friend, you don't like your job much. You just me told me so."

"No, I don't like it. I am thinking of leaving. Although the job I'm considering pays less, maybe fifty thousand." Specifying the job that he'd already applied for was out of the question given what he now knew about Dmitri.

"If you're earning fifty thousand, how will you get your cousin the best possible medical care?" Dmitri held up a hand. "Yes, I checked on you and on her. I know about her cancer. With the money you'll make working with me, she can have the best doctors in this country. I remember you crying when you first arrived at the *dyskeii dom*, just after you'd lost your mother."

"I was nine."

"Still, do you want to go through that again? Lose your cousin who's been a substitute mother to you?" He leaned on the table, speaking low. Maybe not wanting his bodyguards to hear. "You'd be making millions, not some crummy fifty thousand. Think of what you could do for your cousin with that money. And we'd be together again. Doesn't that have any appeal, my friend?"

Kolya thought of his conversation with Masha. Of playing piano at Avram's bar. Of Rivka at the kitchen table, ravaged by the cancer and the treatments for it, weeping over Nina. Then he thought about Rivka's bills that were starting to pile up now that she could no longer work. He'd applied to the FBI, but it would take some time to get in.

If he got in. Meanwhile, he would be working on the new case he'd be assigned at his law firm on Monday—another corporation suing over nothing that fucking mattered—and as a new associate, he'd get all the shit work. Then there was the fact that he'd be lucky to see Rivka even once a week, given his job.

He had the possibility of a different path, one directly opposed to what he had thought he wanted. Instead of being in law enforcement, he'd be a criminal. Or at least, helping a criminal enterprise.

Would he have even hesitated if he had stayed in Russia? There it was hard to tell the police from the criminals. Or maybe they were the same. Was America really different? He'd always thought it was, but was he wrong?

Dmitri was the closest he'd ever had to a brother. Despite everything, he liked Dmitri, and Dmitri was offering him friendship and riches. A life that would allow him to take care of Rivka.

He might not have survived the boys' school without Dmitri. Did it matter that "sometimes bad things happen to the wrong people?" Did it matter that Rivka would hate his becoming a member of the *vorovsky mir*, the gangster world?

Did it matter that Dmitri was turning an American neighborhood into a hell for its residents?

He made his decision.

"I'll resign on Monday."

Dmitri grinned with genuine warmth. "Great. Then you'll start Tuesday." He pulled out a card. "My office in Brooklyn."

Kolya accepted the card.

* * *

On Monday morning, he went online to check for a response to the email he'd written over the weekend. Then he handed his resignation letter to human resources, packed his up personal items, and arranged with his secretary to have the box shipped to his apartment. He left the building, located in the Wall Street area, and walked to the Jacob Javits Center, arriving a little before one o'clock.

After going through security, he approached a receptionist. "I have an appointment. Bob Smith. One o'clock." He gave his name.

Despite the appointment, he had to wait twenty minutes before being ushered in the office. Bob Smith, a large man who looked elegant in a suit despite his size, stood and offered a hand.

"Are you sure about this?" Bob motioned him to a chair in front of his desk.

"I wouldn't have emailed you otherwise." Kolya seated himself.

"You should know that this is dangerous. If you go through with it, there'll be no going back. And you'll be a marked man. A hit can be arranged even from prison."

"I am aware."

"And he's your friend?"

"Childhood friend. Best friend."

"Mind if I ask why you're doing this?"

"People are getting killed." He would find some way to take care of Rivka, but he would not disappoint her by making choices he knew she would hate. Whether she ever knew what he was doing or not. "It has to stop. This isn't Russia."

"No, but it ain't paradise either."

Kolya smiled at that. "I'm aware of that as well." America was not perfect, far from it, but it was his country, and he owed it a debt for the opportunities that it had offered him. And he paid his debts.

Making the decision was the hardest thing he'd ever done, but Dmitri and his gang would continue to hurt innocent people. It was the right thing to do.

"Okay, then." Bob's tone became brisk and businesslike. "Just so you know, your application materials have already been processed, and we were going to offer you a position as a special agent anyway. I admit to being impressed that you didn't even ask about your application before you volunteered to take down your friend Dmitri. Welcome to the FBI, Kolya Petrov."

Catherine Dilts

Cindy's Storm

"Hey Cowboy, looks like a storm's brewing."

Clouds boiled up over the mountains at the end of the valley. Wind jostled pine branches above Cindy's head, sending a delicate spray of snow down her neck. She shivered and tugged her hood up, tucking loose strands of her red hair inside.

"It's moving in sooner than the fella on the radio predicted," Cindy said. "Maybe we should hunt closer to the truck."

"We'll be fine."

Herb arranged fallen pine boughs on the ground, then spread a thin survival blanket on top. He leaned his bolt-action .30-06 rifle against a tree, eased his backpack off his shoulders, and plopped down on the blanket.

Cindy frowned. Not that Herb would notice. Between her hood and a camo balaclava covering her face from the nose down, only her angry eyes were visible. Herb wasn't paying attention to her eyes. He was too busy glassing the meadow, sweeping his spotting scope from one side to the other, hoping to spot an elk cow.

The final day of hunting season. So this was how it would end. The trip she'd hoped would reignite the waning spark in their marriage. They'd only been hitched four years. It hardly seemed fair the honeymoon phase should end so quickly. And now, that flickering flame was about to be doused by a blizzard.

Cindy shrugged out of her gear and sat beside Herb on the blanket. An entire week, alone with her husband, and she'd failed. If the blizzard froze them both to death, she'd count it as a mercy.

* * *

The night before hunting season began, a glowing blue light filled the motel room. Cindy picked up the TV remote and clicked it off.

"Honey. I finished my shower."

Herb didn't stir.

Cindy slipped between the coarse sheets. She eased across the saggy mattress to Herb's side, pressing her bare skin against his back.

A rattling snore erupted from her husband.

"Herb!"

She gave his shoulder a gentle shove. It was no use. He was out cold.

Cindy had spent a year preparing for this trip. She took her hunter's safety class, went target shooting, and entered the draw for a license. She got in shape. It hadn't been easy, but now she had more energy than she'd had since Ruth's birth a year ago.

Cindy rolled away from Herb and grabbed the novel she'd brought at the last minute, assuming she'd be living a romance, not reading about one. Several chapters in, she dozed off.

* * *

"We're going to be trapped by the blizzard," Cindy said.

Herb squinted at the sky. "We'll be okay."

"Okay?" Cindy asked, her voice squeaking in panic. "That storm's headed our way. We'll freeze to death!"

Herb turned toward Cindy, grasping her forearms gently through layers of his gloves, and her down coat, long-sleeved T-shirt, and thermal shirt.

"Do you trust me?"

Unsure, Cindy held her tongue.

"That weather guy is wrong." Herb shook his head. "It might snow hard across the valley, but it'll blow over this mountain fast. If we head back to the truck now, we'll get caught out in the open. Here we've got shelter, water, food. Fire if we need to start one, but let's consider that a last resort."

"Last before what? Death?"

Herb's emotions played across his face with the speed of the changing weather. He looked startled, then hurt, settling on a hearty laugh. He wrapped Cindy in a bear hug.

"We're not gonna die, Babe. Trust me."

* * *

Day one of hunting season, the clock radio burst into a country western song. Cindy sat up, disoriented. Herb was not on his side of the bed.

She groped the clock for the button to silence a cowgirl wailing about love gone wrong. She finally succeeded, then noticed the time.

"Five thirty?"

Herb emerged from the bathroom, a steamy cloud following him briefly before dissipating in the cooler air of the motel room.

"I thought I'd let you sleep in the first morning." He rubbed a towel over his short red hair. His high school football player physique had gone a little soft around the middle, but his arms were more heavily muscled than the hero on the cover of Cindy's novel. "I already made coffee. As soon as you get dressed, we can hit the road."

Cindy felt queasy. No human should get up this early, unless tending to a sick child. Or fleeing her flame-engulfed home.

She wasn't home.

The motel room was shabby but clean, with indoor-outdoor carpeting Cindy imagined being washed down with a garden hose instead of vacuumed. The bath towels were rough cotton terrycloth. One crowded corner of the room had a mini-fridge, microwave, coffee maker, and a two-burner counter top stove.

The room was what Herb considered a compromise. They could have saved money by camping in his outfitter's tent. Cindy had jumped at the chance to have hot running water.

Coffee was essential. Much easier to brew in a motel room than on a propane stove in a tent. She poured tap water into the glass carafe.

"Babe, I already filled the Thermos."

"I know how you make your coffee, Cowboy," Cindy said. "Strong enough to melt a spoon." She abandoned coffee preparation and heaved her suitcase onto the bed. "I'll grab a cup on the way."

"There's nothing open at this hour."

"That's right. No sane person is awake this early."

Herb reached for Cindy's arms, stopping her from disemboweling her suitcase.

"Babe, you can stay here. Go ahead and crawl back in bed."

"Really? You wouldn't mind?"

"No, I suppose not." The disappointment in his voice was clear.

What would she do all day in the tiny mountain town? This wasn't a ski resort or tourist destination. The economy was based on agriculture, hunting and fly-fishing. She could watch TV on one of three cable channels. The shopping choices were the feed and seed or the dollar store.

Cindy's plan didn't involve spending the day separated from her husband. She pulled on her camo slacks, happy she had to purchase a smaller size. They fit her curves nicely. Herb raised an eyebrow. Maybe he finally noticed she had shed serious pounds.

"Those look too tight for long johns."

"I don't need long johns, Cowboy. These are insulated." Cindy patted her hips. "I'm actually smaller than this."

He returned his attention to stuffing gear in backpacks.

"Today we'll be mostly scouting around, but you never know. We could get lucky."

Lucky as in shooting an elk? Because Cindy sure hadn't gotten lucky last night.

* * *

This was it. The final day of the season. Cindy endured the entire week, not once yielding to the temptation to stay alone in the motel room. Heavy snowflakes blew into her face, coating her eyelashes. They splatted against the pine trees.

"Next time, let's go on a tropical cruise." Cindy huddled into her jacket.

"This was your idea."

"Hunting was the only thing that convinced you to take a week off work."

White flakes coated Herb's stubbly red whiskers. The layers of hunting clothes make him look twenty pounds heavier. This might be what he'd look like in a few decades. Still handsome.

Still obstinate. So focused on his goals, he was like a racehorse wearing blinders.

"Herb, it wouldn't throw us too far off budget to take a break once in a while."

"Vacations cost money. Only a few more years, and I'll have the money to start my own shop."

He dreamed of owning a maintenance and repair business, working on snowmobiles, ATVs, and boat engines.

"When you start the business, you'll have even less time off. Not like when you're working for someone else."

Herb frowned. "It's seasonal."

Cindy had noticed other mechanic's shops stayed busy year-round.

"It scares me how fast time's goin' by," Cindy said. "Our fifth anniversary will be in exactly a year." She stopped to let that sink in. "One. Year. Exactly."

Herb's mouth opened like he was going to say something, then closed.

Thick dark clouds raced across the far valley, nearing the meadow.

* * *

At 6:15 that first morning, Cindy unscrewed the lid of the Thermos, releasing the teasing scent of liquid caffeine. Herb geared the truck down and turned. Pouring hot coffee while bouncing down a dirt road was not a good idea.

"I hope you're ready for this," Herb said. "It's gonna be a long day."

"Unless we get an elk right away."

Herb nodded. "It could happen."

How would they spend the rest of the week? Lounging in the motel? Cindy cringed at the thought. Going home meant picking up the kids from her folks. Either alternative was a far cry from her romantic dream getaway of lounging on a tropical beach and sipping a fruity umbrella-adorned drink while bathed by a warm ocean breeze.

Herb shoved a topo map at Cindy. "See if you can find logging road 204."

The map was a worm's nest of squiggly lines. Cindy couldn't decipher the altitude markings from the barely distinguishable road lines.

"Can you stop for a minute?" she asked.

"Never mind," Herb said. "Here's the turn."

A small green sign indicated the turnoff. Herb shifted the truck to 4-wheel drive and aimed for the rutted tracks.

"That's not a road."

She reminded herself she had suggested this trip. Herb hadn't been hunting since Matthew was born. With both of them working, spending weekends laboring on their fixer-upper house, and raising two kids, there wasn't time or money for a visit to a tropical paradise. Faced with the reality that they couldn't financially justify a real vacation, she had suggested a hunting trip. Stocking their freezer with meat had appealed to Herb.

The engine growled as the tires dug into dirt. They bounced over rocks that pitched the truck at frightening angles. Cindy covered her face with her hands.

Dear Lord, I hope this trip was worth dying for.

Herb pulled onto a narrow bulge where the road leveled out, and turned off the engine. He opened his door and hopped out. Cindy reluctantly pushed her door open.

The cold was so intense, it sucked the breath right out of her lungs. Stars glittered against a velvet black sky. Leafless brush wore a cloak of snow.

"Don't forget your blaze orange."

Herb handed Cindy a loose fleece vest. The added layer of clothing erased any suspicion that she had a womanly figure. But there would be other hunters in the forest. Cindy wanted to be highly visible to anyone with a gun.

"I can't lift this." Cindy attempted to heft a day-pack onto her shoulders.

Herb held it while she slipped her arms through the straps. When he released his hold, Cindy felt like a donkey in a mine, burdened with a heavy load of coal.

"Do I really need all this stuff?"

"You'll be glad if you need something from your pack," Herb said. "It could save your life."

"Maybe I'll just sit in the truck."

"After you did all that working out to get in shape?"

"I didn't think you noticed."

Herb pressed his lips to Cindy's cheek. "I noticed."

As Herb locked the truck, Cindy remembered she hadn't gotten even a sip of coffee.

"We should make it just in time." Herb spoke in a hushed voice. "If we hurry."

He headed up a trail, his boots crunching through the snow. Cindy staggered under the weight of the backpack and her rifle. She tried to keep up, but his long strides and fast pace were impossible to match.

Fortunately, Herb made frequent stops to watch and listen, although it was doubtful he could hear anything over Cindy's panting as her frosty breath poured from her lungs in a cloud.

There was no top to the hill. Every time Cindy thought they had reached the peak, there was another, farther slope to climb. Despite the frigid pre-dawn temperatures, she felt sweat dampen the inner layers of her clothing.

"This is it," Herb whispered.

He leaned his rifle against a pine tree and lowered his pack to the ground. Cindy gratefully did the same. Her shoulders ached from the pack's straps.

Herb grabbed a fallen pine limb and shook off the snow. He placed it in front of a log and motioned for Cindy to sit. She sank onto it, resting her back against the log.

"I should have carried the Thermos," she whispered, "Hot coffee right now would be pure heaven."

Herb shook his head. "The smell would alert the elk that humans are near."

"Maybe the elk would appreciate a shot of caffeine on a cold mornin'. It might draw them in."

He ignored her suggestion, and settled onto the pine branch. Cindy snuggled close to him. As close as she could get, considering a dozen layers of clothing separated them.

"A sleeping bag would be nice," she whispered, then yawned. "I could almost take a nap, if I wasn't afraid I'd freeze to death."

"Hush, Babe. Sound carries out here."

The sky lightened with the coming dawn. Their perch on a hill faced a meadow that dropped off to a wide valley. Sunlight burned a golden path down the slopes of the far mountain peaks. The sunlight surely looked inviting.

Herb pulled his pack close. He unzipped a pocket and dug out a protein bar.

"Want one?"

Cindy had never been a fan, but this morning, the bar tasted like a gourmet meal. Their hike up the hill had burned a lot of calories.

Finally, the full light of the sun bathed Cindy head to toe. She unzipped her coat several inches.

"Who knew thirty-five degrees could feel so warm?" she whispered.

Herb pulled out his spotting scope and glassed the slope below them.

If this was hunting, Cindy didn't understand what the big deal was. The only danger was getting bored. Maybe tomorrow she'd bring her novel. If there was a tomorrow. It was only eight am. They could see elk at any moment.

Seeing elk required having your eyes open. Cindy's lids refused to cooperate, drooping low, until she gave into the pull of unconsciousness. She dozed for twenty minutes before Herb jabbed her arm.

"Over there," he whispered.

Cindy held the scope to her eye and aimed in the direction Herb pointed. Two dozen elk cows followed a narrow trail below a ridge. Cindy felt a rush of adrenalin.

"Are you gonna to take a shot?"

Herb shook his head. "Too far away. Even if I hit one, how would we get it up this hill? We'll wait for a better shot."

The herd moved farther away, not closer, finally disappearing into a creek bed thick with leafless scrub.

"Nothing's happening here." Herb stood and stretched. "We might as well move around."

As Herb helped her put her pack back on, Cindy considered all the good it did to rise at five am. She could have slept in. But this was her first trip. Maybe hunting was like marriage. A slow, boring climb up impossibly steep hills, with brief glimpses of goals that vanished before you had a shot.

They circled around the hilltop, Herb pointing out animal tracks or other signs of wildlife. It was fun, for a couple hours. Then exhaustion settled on Cindy. Her boots dragged through the snow.

"Here." Herb motioned to Cindy. "Look."

She trudged to his side. Churned-up snow mottled a sun-bathed hillside. Dark droppings scattered between distinct hoof prints.

"Tracks," she whispered. "Lots of them. Elk?"

"A whole herd."

She took a step toward the area. Herb held her arm.

"They've been bedding down here. If we walk around, they might catch our scent. We'll hang out nearby, in case they come back tonight."

Tonight.

The word sounded like an alarm in Cindy's head.

"We can't hunt at night."

"Thirty minutes before sunrise, and thirty minutes after sunset," Herb said. "Those are our boundaries."

As she followed Herb in pursuit of a suitable hiding spot, Cindy calculated the length of the day. Five a.m., up and out the door. Drive up the logging road. Hike up a mountainside, then wander around in pursuit of elk. Sunset wasn't until six. Add thirty minutes. The hike back to the truck. Then the drive to the motel.

Cindy might have cried at the thought, but tears would likely freeze to her cheeks, and her skin already felt wind-chapped.

They settled on a spot. Despite her insulated pants and down jacket, after an hour the cold seeped through to Cindy's bones. She shivered.

"Can I get up and move around?" she whispered to Herb. "My toes feel like ice cubes."

"Sure. That'll get your blood circulating."

Cindy wandered from their hiding spot, careful to memorize the landmarks. The wind had blown the snow thin on the hilltop. She couldn't count on following her tracks back. For a moment, she became disoriented. A sickening feeling filled her stomach as she considered she might be lost. Then she glimpsed Herb's blaze orange.

When she sat down in the shade of the blue spruce, Herb handed her a packet.

"Toe warmers," he said. "Put them in your boots. You'll feel better."

Taking off her gaiters and boots was a laborious process. Cindy stuck the packets beneath her toes. She tugged her boots back on, then strapped on the gaiters that kept snow from getting inside her boots.

"Better?" Herb asked.

"Heaven," Cindy said.

Although not as heavenly as a hammock on a tropical beach.

Now would be the time to initiate a conversation with Herb. Spark some talk about where they were at, and where they wanted to be. Hopes and dreams stuff. But Cindy was too tired.

"Babe, wake up." Herb nudged her shoulder.

Cindy opened her eyes. "I wasn't—"

She reached for her rifle. Herb held up a hand.

"Mulies," he whispered. "We don't have tags. I thought you'd enjoy seeing them."

Cindy tamped down the wasted adrenalin rush. Mule deer. Something she saw on a regular basis, living in the Colorado mountains.

Sunset was amazing. Blazes of orange and red lit up the sky. Was it red sky at morning, or at night, that was a warning to sailors? Did that apply in the mountains?

By the time they reached the truck, it was dark. Cindy was glad, because she couldn't fully see the terrifying road they bounced down.

At the motel, Herb set the alarm.

"The good news is, it doesn't make sense for us to get up any earlier than five."

All thoughts of romance, real or fictional, were erased from Cindy's mind as she collapsed face down on the bed.

* * *

The last day of the hunting trip, Cindy wasn't any nearer her goal. She crossed her arms and frowned. Herb wore a deer-in-the-headlights look.

"Happy anniversary?"

Cindy's cheeks stung with tears sluggish from the cold. When Herb reached for her gloved hand, she didn't have the energy to jerk it away. Besides, there was nowhere to move in their shelter that didn't involve sitting on fresh snow. The thin survival blanket at least kept the seat of her insulated pants dry.

"Four years, Herb. Is this how you imagined our marriage? Endless work and chores and adulting, with no breaks? Do you realize our last anniversary we didn't even celebrate?"

"My folks gave us a gift card." Herb lifted a dried pine twig from the snow and slowly plucked off the needles, one by one. "They offered to watch the kids so we could take off for a long weekend. I was offered overtime." He peeled off the bark. "We didn't go." He tossed the stripped twig into the snow. "My fault, I'll admit it. In my defense, we did go out to dinner."

"With the kids," Cindy said.

"Matthew was acting so squirrelly, I was sure the restaurant manager was going to make us leave."

"He calmed down once the basket of bread came," Cindy said. "Then he filled up on bread, and didn't have room for dinner."

"The manager heard it was our anniversary." Herb grinned as he stared up at the underside of the pine branches. "He must've thought we were too poor to afford a real celebration. Remember? They gave us that little cake for free?"

"How can I forget? Ruth ate too fast, and threw up chocolate cake all down her dress."

"Wasn't much of an anniversary." Herb eased his arm around Cindy's shoulders. "Maybe we're just no good at celebrating our marriage, but I'd say we're pretty darn good at living it."

* * *

The second and third days of hunting season alternated between boredom and death-march hiking. The fourth day of hunting, Herb prepared to take a shot at a cow. Cindy had a bull tag, so she watched and waited. She couldn't see any reason to lower his rifle, but Herb whispered there were trees in the way. He didn't want to risk wounding the elk, and having to follow it who knew how many miles to finish it off.

On the drive back to the motel, Herb veered into a parking lot.

"Let's celebrate."

"But you didn't take the shot."

"We finally got close enough to consider taking a shot," Herb said. "Besides, I'm tired of microwaved leftovers."

Cindy had cooked ahead for weeks, freezing meal portions for their trip to save money. She didn't argue, though.

The mom-and-pop restaurant served American style meals in American style portions. Herb ordered a steak and baked potato. Cindy had worked too many months to shed pounds. She ordered a chef salad.

Men at a nearby table struck up a conversation. Got anything yet? Seen any sign? One man had harvested his elk. Cindy asked why he hadn't gone home after taking his animal to the butcher. He was staying on to help his buddy.

"This is my wife's first hunt," Herb said.

"Congratulations," one said. "I'm impressed, ma'am." He tipped his cap.

"I can't get my wife interested in anything outdoorsy," another complained.

"Cindy's one of a kind," Herb said. "I'm lucky to have her."

When the waitress asked them if they wanted dessert, Cindy began to reply no. Herb stopped her.

"You lost a lot of weight this year. You deserve a treat."

The waitress went to retrieve them pie a la mode.

"I didn't think you'd noticed," Cindy said to Herb. "That I've lost weight."

"Sure I did. It's just, there's always some crisis popping up. I suppose there's a lot of things I don't say that I should." He reached across the table for her hand, gave it a squeeze. "I guess you know I—"

The pie arrived, and the moment was gone.

* * *

The rest of the week passed, bringing them to this final day. The last day of hunting season. The last chance to fill their tags. Cindy felt melancholy. Not because they hadn't gotten an elk. There were other things left undone.

The circle of bushes and pines provided a natural blind. Animals might not notice them, but the gusting wind found its way through a thousand gaps between branches. Cindy was amazed at how much abuse the human body could take. That was one thing she'd learned during this grueling week. She had never felt so strong, so confident.

Until she saw the storm, bunching up like a cat about to pounce.

Herb grabbed his rifle. Cindy reached for hers, but her husband lowered his barrel.

"Just a buck."

Cindy watched the male mule deer step cautiously into the meadow. He nibbled dried grass, then raised his head and sprinted across the field.

Rays of sunshine, bounded by the dark clouds above, shot across the meadow briefly, lighting up the distant mountain peaks. Cindy grabbed her cell phone, snapping photos.

"Pretty, huh?" Herb said.

"I've never seen anything so beautiful," Cindy whispered. "You can feel God's presence."

Minutes later, the sun lifted above the ceiling of clouds. The yellow light vanished, turning the meadow back to dull shades of gray.

And then the storm hit.

Snow rushed in on a fierce, bitterly cold wind. Cindy jammed hand warmer packets into her mittens, but that didn't stop her shivering. Herb pulled a cheap plastic rain slicker out of his backpack and held it over their heads. Just in time. Snow sloughed off the branches above, dumping onto them.

"You're shivering." Herb dug one-handed in a pocket of his backpack. "I was saving these. You'd better eat them now. Might help." He handed Cindy a packet of chocolate-covered coffee beans. "Seeing as how you never reached your caffeine quota this week."

Cindy tore open the package and poured beans into her mouth. She tried to chew slowly, to enjoy every moment, but she was too hungry. And tired. And thirsty. She swallowed down the gritty, chocolatey deliciousness with a swig of ice-cold water.

"Want some?" She held the packet out for Herb.

"Nope. Those are all yours. Consider it your anniversary present." Herb directed a lop-sided grin her way. "Sorry, Babe."

The wind howled through their shelter, tearing at the rain slicker.

"Herb, there's so much more I had to say. And now I might not get the chance."

"Yeah, me too. I feel bad about forgetting our anniversary."

"That's just a date on the calendar." Cindy felt warmth easing into veins in a slow-motion caffeine rush. "What's more important is here and now."

"I'm happy with how things are," Herb said. "You know I love ya, Babe. And I'll make up for this anniversary next year."

Well, at least he said The Word, even if it was in an offhand way.

"We don't have to wait a whole year," Cindy said. "Why should we celebrate our marriage only one day a year?"

"Because the rest of the time we're just too busy getting by?"

"That's it, then. You get married, have a couple kids, work, and die? What kind of life is that?"

"Most people's lives. And that's not for nothing. Establishing your family is carving out your legacy in this world." He chuckled. "Some legacy. Our kids are a mess. But they'll grow up. Start their own families. Like in that lion movie, the circle of life."

"I agree, Herb. That's what's most important. Family. Have you thought about more kids?" Cindy asked. "Two just doesn't feel done to me."

"That's a lot to juggle with your job."

"Here's the thing," Cindy said. "That fella at the rock shop offered me a job. The place with the donkeys? It doesn't pay as much, but he'd be flexible with the hours."

The wind tore at the trees. They creaked and groaned as they scraped against each other. Cindy huddled closer to Herb. If a tree fell on them, or their shelter blew to pieces, would anyone find their bodies before the spring thaw?

"We're both working full-time," Herb said, "and we barely make ends meet."

"We can manage on less money. You don't need to work all that overtime. I want you. Not the leftover scraps of you at the end of a hard day. I want more and better, but not things. Life."

Herb nodded, as though he was beginning to grasp her complaint.

"You want more moments like this," he said.

Facing imminent death huddled under trees in the middle of a blizzard wasn't quite what Cindy had in mind.

"Times where you feel real," Herb continued. "Not like a hamster on a wheel."

"It doesn't have to be hunting," Cindy said. "We can take the kids camping, or canoeing on the reservoir."

The wind slowed. The trees resumed their upright stance. A gentle snow drifted down as the dark clouds moved east. Herb was right. The storm blew over quickly.

"I can probably get a long weekend off here and there," Herb said.

"And a couple weeks a year for a real family vacation." Cindy felt like she was in negotiations.

A dreamy look filled Herb's eyes. "Florida in the winter. I've always wanted to catch one of those big fish." The look twisted into a defeated expression. "Heck, I can't even get an elk, and the hills are full of animals."

Their intense conversation about hopes and dreams dwindled. Cindy's caffeine energy faded. She was dozing when she heard Herb chambering a round.

He was on his knees, the rifle at his shoulder, the barrel resting on a sturdy pine branch. A herd of elk cows moved across the meadow, plowing their way through the new snow. Cindy started to pull out her phone to snap pictures, but she was afraid she'd spook the animals.

A gunshot exploded from Herb's rifle, echoing across the hills. At first, all the elk bolted for the trees, but then one faltered. It fell to the snow.

* * *

Cindy had never imagined dressing and packing out an elk would be so much work. It was midnight when they parked in front of the motel, dead tired, their clothes bloody and dirty.

They showered and ate one of Cindy's frozen meals. Herb texted photos to his brother, father, and a couple friends of his successful hunt. Finally, exhausted, they crawled into bed.

The trip had been a success. They had an elk, and they'd had a heart-to-heart talk.

Cindy snuggled close to Herb, seeking body warmth. She wondered if she'd ever completely thaw out.

"Were you serious about having more kids?" Herb asked.

"Circle of life," Cindy said. "Right, Cowboy? We might not leave this world sittin' on a pile of money. But we can darn sure be rich in family."

"Babe," Herb mumbled, "I should be too tired." He rolled over. "But it seems a shame to waste a perfectly good stay in a motel."

Karen Hanson Stuyck

The Day of Reckoning

She was making a mistake, a terrible, irreversible mistake. Alexandra Sinclair sat bolt upright in her bed. Why had she not realized it sooner?

The house was packed with sleeping relatives, who would be only too happy to awake and have a chat with her. Alex tiptoed to the wardrobe and slipped into a loose dress that did not require a corset. She picked up her half boots, which she would put on once she was outside. Her slippers would be quieter on the stairs.

The light seemed to indicate it was barely past dawn, though the grayish sky might also be a result of the light rain running down the window. How very appropriate: dismal, gray, and wet, a reflection of her mood.

Alex crept down the stairs and was heading toward the front door when a voice from the kitchen stopped her. "Good morning, Alex."

"Good morning, Aunt Violet." Drat! If only her early-rising aunt had chosen this morning to sleep in.

"Going out for a walk?"

Aunt Violet, bless her, was not one to ask probing questions. A result, Alex always thought, of never having children. "Yes, just a short walk."

"Grab an umbrella," her aunt advised. "They are in the pot near the door."

Alex hurried to the front door, changed into her half boots, grabbed an umbrella, and got out. Even the least intrusive of her relatives might start asking questions if Alex lingered too long.

Outside it was cooler than she expected. A shawl would have been welcome, but she didn't want to risk returning to the house to retrieve hers. Walking would warm her up.

She stood on the front porch, taking in her surroundings. The house was at once so familiar—she'd spent nine years of her life here—and yet somehow alien. Perhaps she had seen too many newspaper photos of the place. The sprawling, three-story wood building looked as if it had been built for function rather than aesthetic pleasure. The headlines associated with those photos still made her stomach churn: *Refuge Founder Killed By Runaway's Husband.* *"I Only Wanted My Wife Back," Husband Yelled When Hauled Away By Constables.* The newspapers called her grandmother "Edith Sinclair, the notorious philanthropist and founder of The Refuge, a home and school for abused wives and their children."

Alex was not on the premises when her grandmother was strangled when she refused to let an enraged husband retrieve his badly injured wife. The wife's screams had brought help before her husband could abduct her. The man was arrested and eventually hanged for the crime.

Alex had been devastated by the loss of her beloved grandmother. She still grieved for her. When her own parents had died, her grandmother had taken her nine-year-old granddaughter to The Refuge to live with her. Alex lived there for the next nine years.

All of her father's remaining relatives—Grandmother, Aunt Violet, and Aunt Emily—had done what they could to comfort the newly orphaned little girl, to let her know she was loved. But Grandmother had also provided Alex with a purpose. "The most important thing we can do with our lives, Alex, is to aid people less fortunate than ourselves. Think how glorious it is to help women who for years have felt trapped and helpless to climb out of their misery and build happy, independent lives for themselves and their children."

For a long time Alex could not imagine anything more satisfying. Her grandmother had nurtured her strengths and given her numerous opportunities that girls her age seldom received. At fifteen, she had begun teaching the younger students at The Refuge's school. She was encouraged to speak up at staff and resident meetings, and her opinions were respectfully considered.

Although Grandmother had never asked it of her, Alex had expected to continue working at The Refuge. After her grandmother's murder, she was even more convinced that this was her calling: to devote her life to continuing Edith Sinclair's work. But Aunt Emily had insisted that Alex have her come-out and her season as a debutante, in which she would be introduced to eligible men at balls, parties and social events, before she decided to dedicate her life to The Refuge. Aunt Emily wanted Alex to see the other options open to her.

Alex had hated her year in Society. She was repulsed by the shallowness and maliciousness of so many aristocrats, by the exorbitant cost of the dozens of necessary ball gowns, and by the frenzied rush from one vapid social event to another. The men she met bored or infuriated her with their not-so-subtle probing of how large her dowry actually was. When she politely refused their marriage proposals, her suitors told her what they really thought of her. She was "unnatural," a bluestocking, a "sharp-tongued vixen."

Alex counted the days until her twenty-first birthday, when she would come into her substantial inheritance from her father. Her disappointing foray into Society would be over. Alex intended to use her money to continue the work of The Refuge. The place had been closed after her grandmother's death. Vandalism and arson had burned down many of the outlying buildings. Alex would see the buildings restored and Grandmother's program expanded. Eventually she wanted to fulfill her grandmother's longtime dream of building other Refuges for suffering women around the country.

Then Alex had met her cousin's friend, Benedict Nash, who was unlike any other man she had ever met. In a matter of months, all her expectations, her very life had been upended. She, who had always known she would never marry, who viewed the institution of marriage as a socially approved prison for women, was now going to be doing just that—*today*.

She had chosen The Refuge for her marriage celebration. After the ceremony at the village church, guests would return here for the wedding breakfast. If, of course, Alex did not call the whole thing off.

She opened her umbrella and started walking to the back of the property. New grass was starting to grow where previously only ground had been visible. Some foundations remained, but a row of new cottages had been built, and more were being constructed. Alex and her aunts, the trustees of The Refuge, had finally reopened the facility. They had raised funds and contributed some of their own money to repair what was salvageable and replace what was not. They had hired a very competent manager, a former employee who came with a carpenter husband, to run the place. Strictly speaking, The Refuge did not require Alex's daily participation.

Nevertheless, this morning she had awoken with the nagging suspicion that the new manager did not have the passion and determination for the very difficult job—traits that Alex had in abundance. How long would it be before the inevitable community attacks on The Refuge began again? Not just the broken windows and blood-red messages—WIVES, OBEY YOUR HUSBANDS—painted on the walls of the main house, but vicious assaults in the press and from the pulpit. Preachers would thunder to their congregations that marriage was a covenant made with God, and just as sacred as a woman's promise to obey her husband and stay with him forever. "No matter that he broke his wife's ribs and let his children starve because he spent his entire pay drinking at the pub," Grandmother had always pointed out. How long before someone else tried to burn down The Refuge or another irate husband murdered a staff member trying to protect his injured wife? Alex had been trained to fight for the oppressed. She knew the price required. Could the new manager say the same thing?

The rain picked up, no longer a drizzle. Alex decided to take shelter in the nearby school building. The first room held rows of small desks, with a larger desk in front of the class. Here was where Alex had taught the younger students how to read and write, how to add and subtract. She settled into the chair behind the teacher's desk. Perhaps in her old seat she could make sense of her roiling emotions and plan her next step.

It was not as if she hadn't considered the problems of this marriage before; she was not, after all, an idiot. But today she felt as if she was no longer the person who had said yes to Benedict's proposal. Today she saw her life more clearly, devoid of the lovely, warm emotions Benedict elicited in her. She had not changed her assessment of him. He *was* a wonderful, kind man, smart and funny too. Also handsome. It was not her choice of groom she was questioning.

This morning she had come to realize how Benedict's charm had lured her into overlooking the greater issue: She should not get married. She was not meant to be a wife, and certainly not the wife of a titled aristocrat.

Marrying Benedict Nash, the Viscount Litton, would make her a viscountess. During her interminable Year of the Debutante, Alex had learned the myriad rules of Society and decided she was not cut out for a life among the social elite. She had nothing to say to the insipid ladies and bored gentlemen she met, who only spoke of their recent purchases or gossiped about the new couple they had seen driving through Hyde Park. Everything Alex was interested in made their eyes glaze over.

No, she definitely was not viscountess material. Somehow her affection for Benedict had blinded her to that fact. It was only a matter of time before her new husband would reach the same conclusion, while the person Alex had intended to be, the woman carrying on her grandmother's innovative ideas for helping poor women and their children, would have died. Alex Sinclair, social crusader, would be wiped out by Lady Alexandra Nash, Lady Litton.

"Alex!" The voice from outside was Aunt Emily's. Her footsteps sounded nearby.

The school room door opened. Her aunt eyed her sitting at the desk. "I thought you might be in here."

Alex tried to smile. "My old classroom. I was remembering how much I liked teaching, seeing the little ones' faces light up when they first managed to sound out a word in their readers."

Her aunt nodded. "You are an excellent teacher. You even managed to get Tommy to understand fractions when no one else could. But it is time to come inside now. It is freezing in here. You need a hot bath and some food inside you." Aunt Emily was the aunt who had children. She was used to giving orders.

Alex did not move. "What if I want to call off the wedding?"

"That is your right." Aunt Emily looked unfazed by the question. "You can write Benedict a note or go talk to him in person <u>after</u> you have a bath and breakfast."

Despite herself, Alex laughed. "I can cancel the wedding, but not the bath?"

Her aunt smiled. "I won't have you catching pneumonia. The wedding is your decision."

Alex followed her aunt into the house.

By the time she finished soaking in the hot bath water and eating her eggs and toast, she felt warmer, less hungry, and a bit calmer. But she still had not decided her next step, a rather crucial decision, since the wedding was scheduled to begin in less than two hours.

"This just came for you," Aunt Violet said, handing her a note in Benedict's writing.

Everyone around the breakfast table watched her. "What does it say, Alex?" Tommy, her youngest cousin, asked.

"None of your business, pipsqueak," his older brother answered.

Alex picked up her cup of tea and excused herself. She would read her letter in her bedroom.

What if Benedict was calling off the wedding? The thought of it brought tears to her eyes, though, rationally speaking, she should be relieved to have the decision taken from her hands. She sat on her bed and opened the letter.

> *Alex, darling, I imagine you, my fierce warrior for justice, making a mental list of everything you hate about the institution of marriage. A woman loses her independence, her rights, her very name, you will be telling yourself. Perhaps you are also wondering if you would be accomplishing*

more good in the world if you used your many talents to continue your grandmother's work at The Refuge rather than to marry me.

I cannot argue against that reasoning. I can only argue <u>for me</u>. I love you, Alexandra

Sinclair, and my life is so much better with you at my side. I love your quick mind, your sharp wit, your compassion for everyone who is suffering, and your determination to help them.

I want you to remain the strong person you are in our marriage, as I intend to stay the same person I am. We will not be the pretty, dutiful wife and strong, protective husband of the storybooks. I want you to use your compassion, skills and fierceness to convince four small orphaned children that we, all of us, are now a family, <u>their</u> family.

I am so happy that you agreed to become my wife.

With all my love,

B

Alex read it a second time, her tears blurring the words. He knew her so well. And he loved her anyway.

There was a soft knock at the door, followed by Aunt Emily poking in her head. "Have you made up your mind?"

Alex nodded. "I need to start getting ready."

"Benedict must have written a lovely letter," her aunt said.

"He did. Besides telling me how he felt about me, he said how much his little nieces and his nephew needed us to build a new family."

Aunt Emily hesitated. "Alex, I know how you feel compelled to help anyone who is hurt or suffering. But sweetheart, that is <u>not</u> a sufficient reason to get married."

Alex shook her head. "Oh, no, that is not why I am marrying Benedict. He just reminded me that impoverished children and abused wives are not the only ones who need my help."

Her aunt smiled. "Good. I am glad you decided. Let us get you dressed for your wedding."

Within minutes Aunt Emily's maid Margaret arrived, carrying Alex's dress draped across her arm and a crown of flowers that Alex had not seen before.

"I was planning on wearing my new bonnet," Alex told her.

"This is much more festive," Margaret stated. "I saw one just like it in a magazine."

"It is very pretty," Alex admitted. A variety of fresh flowers had been assembled and then apparently been sewn together by some kind of hidden thread. The flowers were mostly white or pastels, but she spotted a few blue ones. "You even have some blue ones, my favorite color."

"The blue goes with your dress," Margaret said, though she did seem pleased that Alex liked the piece. "We brought the flowers from London and I sewed them together last night." She started to lace Alex into her corset.

"Not too tight, Margaret," Aunt Emily warned. "We don't want a fainting bride."

In quick order the maid pulled the pale blue silk dress over Alex's head.

"Lovely," Aunt Emily said with a sigh. "That is the perfect color for you, Alex, and the dress's clean, simple lines are so elegant."

Alex glanced at her reflection in the full-length mirror. The dress, indeed, was beautiful. Aunt Emily had insisted on buying it from a well-known dressmaker, but Alex had picked out the material and approved the design.

Margaret had her sit down so she could put on Alex's mother's pearl necklace and matching earrings.

As the maid began to fuss with Alex's hair, Aunt Emily pulled something from her pocket. "Your mother's pearls are perfect. I have a gift that you might also wear."

Alex unwrapped the cloth protecting a glittering brooch. She gasped. A dark blue evening sky was dotted with dozens of sparkling stars above a grassy hill. Upon a closer look, she realized the sky was composed of sapphires and the stars were small diamonds. The grassy hill was made of emeralds. "I have never seen something so lovely."

"That was what I thought when Mother gave it to me on my wedding day." Aunt Emily blinked several times. "As a child I always loved to lie on the ground at night and count the stars. Mother used to say I should give each of the stars one of my dreams for the future. When she gave me the brooch she said my marriage to Paul, a wonderful man who loved me, was what I had always dreamed of."

"That's lovely, but rather surprising, coming from Grandmother."

Her aunt laughed. "That is exactly what I thought. Over the years I heard so many stories of monstrous husbands who beat their wives or stole their money. And, of course, Mother's own marriage had not been a happy one. But when I mentioned that, she said that unlike her, I had got to know my husband before I married him, and I managed to pick a man who was not merely handsome and charming, like Father, but also was a kind, faithful man who cherished me. She said that marriage had never really been her dream; she just got married because it was expected of her. But it was _my_ dream, she said, and choosing my own path took as much courage as the path she chose to take."

"Courage." Alex grinned. "'Courage, child,' that's what she always told me."

Aunt Emily laughed. "That's what she told all of us. In fact your father said he could see a C in the pattern of the stars of the brooch. Probably when Mother realized it wasn't big enough to spell Courage, he said, she decided to make do with the first letter."

Alex peered at the brooch. "I don't see any C."

"Neither do I. Your father just had a vivid imagination."

The maid took the brooch. After consideration, she pinned it over Alex's left breast.

"Above your heart." Aunt Emily smiled.

The maid shrugged. "Do not lift your bouquet too high for everyone to see the brooch."

The carriage to the church included Alex, her two aunts, and Uncle Paul. The cousins and other members of the household had left earlier.

"You look breathtaking, Alex," Uncle Paul said. "I wish your parents were here to see the woman you've become. They would be so proud."

"And your grandmother," Aunt Violet said. "How she would have loved to be here."

"Now don't make her cry," Aunt Emily scolded. She handed Alex a handkerchief. "I was going to point out that the rain has stopped and the sun is finally peeking out."

Fortunately the atmosphere lightened considerably when they entered the church. The minute Benedict's three little nieces caught sight of Alex, they ran over to show off their flower girl dresses. Rebecca, the youngest at three, twirled in a circle to allow Alex to take in the full effect of her pale pink dress with darker pink sash. "Pretty!" she announced.

"You look very pretty indeed," Alex agreed. "As do you, Samantha and Elizabeth." Samantha, six, was dressed in pale green while Elizabeth, eight, was all in lavender.

Samantha, the artist of the group, moved closer to inspect Alex's brooch. "The colors are so beautiful and the stars sparkle in the sky."

Elizabeth studied the pin. "The stars form a C."

"That's what my father said," Alex told her. "But you and he are the only ones to see it."

"Perhaps the C stands for something. Perhaps 'congratulations.'"

"Very good!" Alex made a mental note to consult the girl's governess to ensure she received challenging lessons. And artistic Samantha would undoubtedly enjoy drawing lessons.

"You do look lovely, Alexandra," Benedict's grandmother, the formidable dowager viscountess, observed. It had taken her longer, walking with her cane, to follow her great-grandchildren. "Your grandmother had a magnificent sapphire and diamond necklace with stones of that brilliance," she told Alex, as she studied the brooch. "Your grandfather gave it to her as a wedding gift. The man had his faults, but he had exquisite taste in jewelry."

Aunt Emily and Alex looked at each other. Grandmother had dismantled that magnificent necklace to make a wedding present for her daughter.

Aunt Emily's son John appeared in front of them. "Toby says once Alex arrived, I must get everyone seated." Toby was Aunt Emily's oldest son and Benedict's best man.

Aunt Violet took her nephew's arm. "You may escort me to my seat."

Benedict's grandmother was issuing instructions to the girls. "Don't walk too fast, Elizabeth. A stately pace is best." Seeing Rebecca's look of confusion, she told the little girl, "Just follow Samantha, Rebecca, and do not run. I know you all will be on your best behavior today because you want to make your Uncle Benedict proud."

All three girls nodded, looking solemn.

When John returned to escort the dowager viscountess to her seat, Uncle Paul whispered into Alex's ear, "Should I tell the girls they can smile?"

Alex chuckled, and the girls turned around to see what was funny. "Thank you all for being in my wedding," she told them. "That means a great deal to me."

"You are very welcome." Smiling, Elizabeth walked into the church at a stately pace.

Samantha followed and then Rebecca, at a less stately pace, but not running.

Then it was Alex's turn. Taking Uncle Paul's arm, they started down the aisle.

There were more people in the church than she expected. Alex was pleased to see that many of the staff from The Refuge, her colleagues and dear friends, had come.

Nearing the altar, Alex only had eyes for Benedict. He was watching her too, looking so handsome in his black superfine coat, immaculate white shirt and cravat. And a robin's-egg blue waistcoat! How had he learned the color of her wedding dress? Or had he simply chosen that waistcoat because he knew blue was her favorite color?

As she got closer, she could see the warmth in Benedict's eyes, the sheer joy in his smile.

Alex smiled back, knowing, with total conviction, that she had made the right choice.

Lara Tupper

Go Fish

Monhegan Island, Maine

1.

The locals said *off island* when they wished to leave. (*Going off island to see the new* Star Wars.*)* Anything beyond the island was off.

Edie went off island for interlibrary loans and cappuccinos. For T.J. Maxx. (She supposed she was a Monhegan local now, five years in.) She taught K-8 in the island's one-room schoolhouse. She had to be vivacious and alert. She could say the wrong thing and they'd shift on a dime. *Spinster*, one boy whispered. She didn't correct him. When the workday was done, she belonged to herself.

In the schoolhouse she double-checked the algebra of the oldest. She inflated plastic Letter People for the youngest. She kept the subsidized milk pints floating in ice water. She tacked their art projects to the lowest wooden beams.

A first grader had painted the word *beautiful* in bright orange, a tricky word for one so young. The little girl was beautiful—she'd heard this word from grown-ups, no doubt. She had eyes that were dark and wide, as if they were trying to make sense of things.

Edie saw herself in the girl. Not the beautiful part but the *trying to make sense of things* part. She wrote this down in her ledger so she wouldn't forget.

It happened like this. Words floated up as she went about some mundane task. (Sharpening pencils or popping straws into milk cartons.) The trouble was stringing the phrases together, before they solidified. Like candle wax, hardening. She was supposed to make something before they got too stiff to mold.

After school, Edie crossed the lawn to the island library. It was part of the gig, teacher/librarian. She liked the quiet there. No one asked her how to spell things. She could rearrange spines on shelves and play with the due date stamp. She watched the rough waves of the harbor through the panes and thought of her mother, still in the family home in New Harbor. She had offered Edie's old room, should she want to get off island for good.

Thanks, but no, she'd replied.

She'd found the ledger in the back room of the library, tucked under stacks of old *Portland Press Heralds*. It was a clerk's list from the general store, money owed for eggs and apples and flasks over a century ago. *Bread, 10 cents. Fish hook, 5 cents.* There were plenty of blank pages for Edie to fill.

There will be time, there will be time, she thought. (Who wrote that? She'd look it up.) One library shelf featured books about famous islanders: Rockwell Kent, the Wyeths, Zero Mostel. Maybe someone would stare at her book on a shelf someday and feel similarly defeated.

2.

In colder months, when the children were slow to fasten shoes and jackets, Edie sometimes delayed the library opening by ten minutes, fifteen. Certain regulars dumped their paperbacks on the wet doormat before she arrived. Inside, no one noticed her display on smelting. They exchanged one Stephen King for another and left.

Come spring, things melted. That's when the woman from Bay Harbor dropped off her books.

"Making a donation," she said. She dumped the cardboard box on the porch and nodded through the torn screen door.

It was past closing but Edie hadn't locked up. She was trying to finish the sentence she'd started.

The woman, Molly Townsend, stood there like a tower. Her shirt was blue flannel, faded. She looked incapable of falling down.

"Appreciate that," said Edie.

"Good riddance," said Molly. The books, she meant. She lifted her hand in a little salute and walked away.

Ten oversized monographs. Edie would have to clear space next to the Wyeths. There were bare breasts on the covers of two and inscriptions in all, *For Pete. Love, Molly.* Christmases and birthdays. There were notes in red ink in the margins in a different handwriting, Pete's, she supposed. Which the regulars wouldn't like. *Not a charity case out here*, they said of the battered books left behind by day-trippers.

Edie read all the scrawls in the margins there at her desk until it was too dark to see without a lamp. This Pete (Molly's husband, she guessed) wasn't too chipper. But he seemed to like Paul Gauguin an awful lot.

She began to feel the shape of her story creep in like a rich, smelly tide. Not at all based on facts, but quite enticing, at least to her. She'd call it *Off Island*.

3.

By mid-June, Edie's duties were daily but few. Only two island children had signed up for summer school. The grown-ups on Monhegan were outside all the time, healthy bastards, fishing or painting. Bookless. The library was quiet and dark in the afternoon.

She opened the ledger. *Write what you know.* That's what *Writer's Digest* said. What did she know about Paul Gauguin in Tahiti? It was hot. There was sand. Maybe she'd have to go there, research.

She laughed out loud at the thought.

Make it up. She knew about hot weather. At her desk she summoned a day at Funtown as a child. She went on the water slide, her bathing suit riding up. It was before she cared about what she looked like in a suit and, not caring, the water was glorious. There was a whole summer of swimming ahead and a Rocky Road cone her father had promised for later.

Someone sneezed. It was Ollie in the back, on the web.

"Don't you have a job this summer, Oliver?"

"Next summer, probably," he shouted back. A few minutes later he shuffled past her desk, red faced.

She hoped it wasn't porn again.

"Stern man, probably," he said. Then he went to sit on the porch.

Gauguin on Monhegan? Was it possible? Gauguin had lied a lot, particularly to his wife, Mette. So who knew exactly where he'd been?

Maybe he'd sailed to Monhegan sometime before he died in 1903. No one would have known him. Just another tourist from Europe, come to paint. Heard about the famous artist colony off the coast of New England. Maybe he left a painting or two behind.

She scratched at a mosquito bite, drawing blood, and thought: *pigment*.

The painter drew blood, warmth on fingertips. He smeared the canvas and this was how he began, letting his own stuff start the picture.

Too much?

Last month's *Digest* had encouraged her to "start with sensory details." She'd read it as *sensual* details and wondered why this was necessary for books that weren't about fornicating. Then she got it. Sensory. The senses.

She scribbled quick lines through all of it, ripped the page from the ledger, dropped it in the pail. *What would Gauguin do next? Shit on a paintbrush and call it ochre?*

4.

In late June, as luck would have it, a Published Author sent his flier to the Post Office, where it hung on the bulletin board next to a year-old ad for pottery classes. He'd lead "convivial workshop meetings" for $300 per person. Mr. Leavitt the Post Master nodded as Edie mailed her latest submissions. He'd already signed up.

They met at the Author's rented house on Lobster Cove Road, which everyone knew went for $1000 a week. Edie looked around and did the math—one week paid for and then some. They were on the porch sipping Old Fashioneds, which Edie had brought in a pitcher. (Convivial beverages.) Island Ink, they were called. The Author had thought it up.

The first batch of comments wasn't terrible.

"Visceral," said the Author out loud, on the porch. *So many secretions,* he wrote in the margins.

"It's historical fiction, right?" said Edie's former student, June, now the island yoga instructor. "It's not the same as actual history."

Which was what Mr. Leavitt from the Post Office was constructing. Family history. A narrative family tree, he called it.

Leavitt asked how it was possible that a French artist who'd gone to Tahiti, died in Tahiti even, had ended up on an island in the Atlantic.

"Because it's fiction," said Edie.

"So he didn't actually leave his wife and go to Monhegan," said Larry McFadden from the general store.

"He left his wife," said Leavitt. "That part is real. He just didn't come to Maine."

It was a dumb idea, Edie decided.

"Wait," Larry said again. "So he didn't really come to Monhegan?"

"What if it's a random, unknown painter?" said Leavitt. "Does it have to be Gauguin?"

"Yes," said Edie.

"*Historical fiction,*" said June.

"Right," said Edie. Her articles on ice harvests and smelting had been published in online journals, she reminded them. *Librarian's Corner* and such. But this was a fair point about Gauguin. There were gaping logistical gaps.

She looked to the Author, who wasn't saying much anymore. He seemed a little droopy, the empty Old Fashioned glass at his feet. The silence grew and puffed itself out until he managed to stir himself.

"It's a brilliant idea, Edith," he said, slipping a little over the 'th.'

"A prologue would clarify these questions. And read Maugham's *The Moon and Sixpence*. Based on the life of Gauguin."

"Of course. Thank you," said Edie, beaming at him.

Mr. Leavitt frowned.

5.

Gauguin would hear about Monhegan from his friend and art dealer, Schuffenecker. They'd worked together at the bank, Edie read in Molly Townsend's books, before Gauguin quit to become a painter.

Maybe Schuff had traveled to America. Maybe he took the day trip from New Harbor himself and found the island charming, quiet.

The light, he'd tell Gauguin. The locals would surely leave him alone. The other European artists, if there happened to be any, would admire his use of color.

Gauguin wouldn't be hard to convince. He'd have to tell his wife he was leaving again; her face would get stony and stay that way. (Or maybe not. Maybe Mette wanted him to go.) The painter's children would beg to come along. Gauguin would promise to bring back conch shells.

But why? his wife would ask later, once the children couldn't hear.

"Because I like islands."

Mette would think *Tahiti* because that's where he'd gone before. She'd never suspect New England, a place her husband had mocked. *Rebels*, he'd called them. *Misfits*. He'd have to bring his children the shells of clams.

6.

Prologue

Paul Gauguin (1848-1903): banker, painter, transmitter of syphilis—

"Is one a transmitter of syphilis or a carrier?" said the Author. "Or both?"

Edie made a note.

...*Once the painter had set sail again, the wife, Mette Gad, felt a complicated relief.*

"Relief?" said June.

"Yes, relief," said Edie.

"Okay. America," Mr. Leavitt conceded. "But does it have to be Monhegan?"

7.

Did it have to be Monhegan?

Edie stared at the Rockwell Kent coffee table book, propped by the library window for tourists to gawk at. On the cover, the view from Lighthouse Hill: the grassy lawn, the round, hot sun over nearby Manana Island. *Sun, Manana, Monhegan,* the painting was called.

She'd picnicked on that field, spotted the Barter girl and the Calhoun boy by the raspberry bushes once. (She'd coughed and they'd rolled apart lightning-quick.)

Gauguin had a *Fields* painting too. A similar view. Water beyond the land.

Close enough, she thought when she found it in Molly's book. *Fields By the Sea,* it was called. Painted in Breton, but that fact could be ignored. There were small figures of women in funny hats, but take them out and it could have been the same Monhegan view (the curve of Manana Island poking out, like a still, solid whale). Like the one Kent had painted.

It would do. She photocopied enough duplicates for all of Island Ink.

On the porch, she passed the copies around.

"The Gauguin painting," Edie read aloud, "called *Fields By the Sea,* was found under the floorboards of a crumbling fish house on Monhegan."

"It was?" said Larry. "Really?"

"No," said Leavitt. "Not really."

"But does it seem plausible?" Edie asked the Author. "A painting left behind on Monhegan?"

"It was probably a copy. Some painter trying to paint like Gauguin," Larry said.

"There was no painting," said June. She touched Larry's arm.

"It was painted in Breton," said Leavitt. "Right? Those curvy women in hats he loved so well. All that rugged earth."

The Author decided to speak. "Much like your own seaside. And people," he said.

Curvy? Edie thought.

"Rugged," said the Author. "Sturdy. Monhegan looks much like that part of France."

"It's a great idea," June reminded her.

"I've decided to stay on through August," said the Author, as though he'd just decided. "If you'd all like to carry on, that is."

Edie wrote him a check after class.

8.

Gauguin stayed on the northern island longer than he meant to, a full month longer. How had Maine become an enticement? How had America?

He kept track of the incremental shifts from drunk to sober. He stopped on the dirt road, his breath loud in his ears, the loose rope of a sailboat clanging somewhere in the black harbor. He looked at the stars, something to enjoy and pick at for a while. Like a tall piece of corn.

"Corn?" said the Author.

He looked at the stars, wanting to be pulled away from himself. The stars were always there, even in daylight. At night, when he could see, they were a slippery kind of gift.

His skin was prickly and hot on the island road, despite the ocean air. His thighs chafed against his wool trousers. He wanted to take them off, to be naked in the road at night, as he'd sometimes done during the hottest weeks in Breton.

His trousers. The landlady, naked. Just a bit of distraction in the night.

"Is it offensive to painters?" Edie asked the Author. "The assumption that they're quite often randy?"

Larry blushed. Leavitt got up to refill his glass.

There were so many opportunities for fondling, Edie meant. All the naked models, posing.

The Author ignored this and said, "What's the story's central question? Why is this a story that needs to be told?"

She thought about this. Later, she told her ledger, *It's a story about why people leave. They just can't help it sometimes.*

Edie had been the one to leave. She was not, in fact, a spinster. There was a husband. Still her husband, technically. Not a painter, not carrying a flask everywhere, not falling down drunk, but an educated man, a social, daily drinker. He'd been a teacher off island, just like her. It was a familiar tale. He could be very, very charming until he wasn't.

The loneliness now was not overbearing. She was glad they no longer shared utensils and sheets. She'd forgotten, for the most part, about his smells, his skin. She didn't care for someone else's DNA on her clean linens anymore.

I grow old, I grow old, she thought. But not that old. The schoolhouse boy also called her *old maid*, which made her think of the card game, the ugly cartoon characters of ladies with hair buns and warts on their noses. The point was to get rid of the old maid card—to be left with it meant you lost. *You're an old maid!* the winner said to the loser.

She'd never liked card games. Though Go Fish was alright, she supposed. *Go fish!* said the winner. It sounded like the opposite of being an old maid.

9.

"Could there be a dead body in the woods no one claims?" Larry asked in workshop. "Or a woman Gauguin gets pregnant? The landlady?"

"Maybe," said Edie, "she'd have the baby, then keep it locked up in the attic." She grinned.

"Why would she do that?" said June.

"It's Maine," Edie said. "Stephen King."

For once, Leavitt agreed. "There's no end to the twisted, irregular things people do to each other. How regular they can look on the surface."

They were all quiet on the porch for a while.

Then the Author moved on to Larry's piece, about a dog named Sandy who talked to humans.

In the library, Edie finished a bag of Doritos and made a list.

Things to Google:

1. Doughnuts. Did they exist in 1903? (Gauguin should eat them.)
2. Did zippers? (Re: Gauguin undressing the landlady.)
3. Research the floating house.

She underlined the word house. She drew a house with a chimney and a little plume of smoke beside it.

She got up to find the house book and saw Ollie on the porch again, cradling a cat the size of a raccoon.

"Oliver," she called through the screen. "Want to earn a dollar?"

"Mowing?" he said. The cat leapt from his arms, still agile.

"Not mowing, no. I need a doughnut from McFadden's." She gave him two dollars.

"But doughnuts are two dollars," he said.

She wasn't sure they were, but she gave him another bill. "Did you know," she guessed, "in 1903, you could buy a doughnut from the store for a nickel."

He turned to go.

"Hold on," she said. "What would the change be?"

"No change. It's two bucks. I told you."

"No, in 1903."

He looked at her. "Same. Almost two bucks back—dollar ninety-five."

"Right you are," said Edie. Maybe she was an okay teacher.

She looked for the book, *Monhegan: Her Houses and Her People*. There was a man related to her—a great-great-great uncle. He'd built his house on the mainland, a small but sturdy thing with a shingled roof and a timber frame, and he'd liked it so much he decided to take it with him, all the way across the bay to Monhegan. He'd waited for the highest tide of the year and prayed the barge would land by dark. He winched it up the beach somehow, inch by inch.

How it had actually worked out, Edie had no idea. But he was a man who knew what he liked and brought it with him. Like a turtle. Which was why everyone had called him Turt.

She settled back at the desk to find out more.

'Turt' Brewer kept an eye on the sea—the tides and the storms—and brought his house to Monhegan in 1880. How? By manpower, by capstan, inch by inch up the beach. He wasn't one to give up on an idea and so he didn't often fail.

Ollie reappeared, let the screen door bang, and placed a greasy napkin on her desk.

Edie made some notes about the size, smell and the color. *Chestnut?* The boy sat on the floor and watched her scribble.

"Take it," she said when she was done.

"Sure," said the boy. He balled the napkin and crammed half the doughnut into his mouth. He tore a small piece for the cat.

A house on a barge. A capstan, as seen on a ship. It would have required one body per spoke to push the lever around. A *Spiral Jetty* in motion.

(She Googled Robert Smithson's *Spiral Jetty*.)

What had all the people on Fish Beach thought? The house was coming *to* them. Like the *Macbeth* scene—*Macbeth*?

(She Googled this.)

Yes. Like Birnam Wood marching up to Dunsinane Castle.

Turt and his house, marching up the beach. He'd planted himself right where he wanted to be.

10.

The Author folded his hands and beamed at her. "I find it quite postmodern in its use of pastiche."

Go fish! The Old Maid laughed and laughed inside. She unfurled her bun and let her hair fly wild, just like the shampoo commercial.

"I find it a stretch," said Leavitt. He looked angry about this. "No offense."

Edie assigned one-page papers on doughnuts and zippers for her two summer students. She told them not to use Wikipedia.

On Wikipedia, Edie read some more about *Spiral Jetty*. Which somehow led her to a site called Marvels of Our Time, where she found the most marvelous thing: a man who was pregnant. For a few valuable moments she felt a sail of excitement flap open—what this would mean! And then she saw that it was a hoax. The kind of thing even Ollie would know to laugh at, right away.

Sometimes, when she saw the children of day-trippers (children she didn't know), she felt a distant stirring. She had an Old Fashioned and the feeling went away.

"The very first doughnuts were made by Hanson Gregory, age 15," the Brewer girl reported. "His mother baked lots of sweets. Like cakes. If they were mushy in the middle, Hanson just dug the center out. And, ta-da, doughnuts were born in 1847."

"Very nice, Abby."

The following week, Edie asked, "How old would a person—an artist, say—have to be in 1903 to have descendants living now?"

"Doesn't that depend on how old they were when they mated?" said Abby.

"Yes, good. That would definitely be a factor."

"Because if you're too old, it's harder to reproduce," said Jonathan. "If you're female."

"Yes, true."

"My mother is only forty-five but she's already going through the change."

"Hmm."

"But the man can be wicked old and it doesn't matter," said Abby. Her father was wicked old.

"Not *wicked* old, though," said Jonathan.

"So assuming all parts are working just fine and both parents are under forty, how many generations would it take to get to present day from 1903?"

"Four generations," said Abby. "If the males were slow to marry and spawn."

"Thank you," said Edie. So somewhere, in the Monhegan of her novel, there could exist a bastard great-great grandchild of Gauguin.

"You can't choose your relatives," Jonathan said.

"True that," said Edie.

But you could choose to keep them at a distance.

11.

Leavitt dumped a stack of *New Yorker*s on her desk.

"Hi there," said Edie, closing her ledger fast.

"They're for you," he said. His maroon windbreaker had been on sale in the North Face catalog, which he'd dumped on her desk last month.

"To peruse," he said. "Literary fiction. Maybe it will help you figure out what you're trying to say."

He wasn't trying to be an ass, she realized.

Once he left, she started reading a story about a tax auditor in his cubicle. *When is he going to get out of his cubicle*? Edie wondered. But it wasn't enough of a question to make her finish. The font was annoying. She read the cartoons, then "I Will Not Be Sad in This World," a poem that made her weep a little.

"An epitaph," she said at Island Ink.

"Epi*graph*," said the Author. "But yes, it does seem apt."

"Thanks, Leavitt," she said to him after. "For the *New Yorkers*, I mean."

He studied his Gore-Tex boots, still pristine. "I'm glad you found what you needed."

12.

More on Mette, please! wrote the Author.

Paul Gauguin had married Mette Gad because she was a practical, grounded sort. Edie's father, an offshore fisherman, probably married Edie's mother for the same reason. She had to be prepared to go it alone if the sea took him away.

Her mom snapped one summer and insisted the house be put in her name. If he was going back on that god-forsaken boat. Last time he came back from Georges Bank, money bulked in his back pocket, he'd taken his sweet time coming home. "An indirect route," her mother said.

Everyone in town liked her mom. She was full of piss and vinegar, with her cackle of a laugh and her hair falling down and the way she called her oldest daughter Stinky, even when she became a teacher and had a husband of her own.

The mothers were in charge by the sea. The mothers spoke and things happened.

Mette Gad Gauguin was like that in Copenhagen with her five kids and no husband around. She would not be sad in this world.

Edie's mother wanted her to be plucky. Not sad. For this reason, Edie tended to avoid her mother. She didn't want the sadness to leak out of her, unexpectedly. She didn't want to be a disappointment.

Edie found Molly Townsend on Facebook and thanked her again for the books. "Sure thing," Molly replied, and that was all. It was a comfort to know she could be found.

Edie would polish her Gauguin story next summer. It was too hard to concentrate on the whole thing with Letter People and milk to organize. But she kept drafting pieces in a haphazard way. At the library, when she heard the phrases come.

The Author had said to keep in touch. She should feel free to send her chapters by email. For comments, free of charge.

Which she did, for many months. (She thanked him repeatedly.) Until the email messages began to bounce back.

13.

Nine months later, on a trip off island, Edie caught her breath in Bookland.

The Clam and Six Bucks: A Mainer's Retelling. An old picture of the Author on the back, when he still had hair. Edie's story inside.

She paid for the *New Yorker* she was gripping and then tore it into very small pieces in the parking lot. There was no wind. On the tar, the pieces looked like slippery, colored snow.

She could find a lawyer. She had her ledger. She had witnesses in Island Ink, plus Molly Townsend. Proof.

She went back inside. She had to admit, it was a wicked title. Some clever bookseller had placed *The Moon and Sixpence* right beside it.

At the café she bought the most expensive cappuccino and a stale chocolate biscotti, then settled in to read her published book. She found her red pen and began to write in the margins.

He'd started with "The Mother," the last chapter she'd sent. He'd pay, but she could live with that. He'd made it Mette's story.

Mike Befeler

Jennifer Jacobson, Private Eyeball

Katherine Milo put the back of her hand to her forehead and moaned. "Ugh. I'm bored out of my mind."

Jennifer Jacobson sat up, flipping her pony tail. "How in the world can you be bored? Only one week before school starts. Then look out. Seventh grade, here we come." Jennifer adjusted the towel she sat on, listened to the sound of splashing in the swimming pool and sniffed the aroma of sizzling burgers.

Katherine yawned. "School sucks. But at least we're turning thirteen soon."

"Yeah, then you can actually blame how grumpy you are on raging hormones." Jennifer elbowed her friend. "And after all the grief my parents give me, I'll start getting back at them. They've never been through this before—I'll make sure I drive them crazy. I can't wait."

"Enough about parents," Katherine said. "Nothing's happening for the last lame week of vacation. We need something fun and exciting—now!"

At that moment, a teenage girl in a blue tank top near them screamed, "Ach, someone stole my phone!"

"That's Marcie's friend," Jennifer said. "Marcie's in the red swim suit and on my swim team. Let's see what's up."

Jennifer and Katherine scrambled up and approached the two older girls who frantically searched through towels and blankets, throwing them around as if they were trying to escape from spiders.

"It was right here. Now it's gone!" the girl in the blue tank top shouted. "Omigod. My mom's gonna kill me if I've lost that new phone."

"Mine's right here," Marcie replied, holding hers up.

"Hey… um… do you want any help?" Jennifer asked.

Ms. Tank Top spun around. "Ri-i-ight. Like some little kid can do anything."

Jennifer wondered why someone as nice as Marcie had such a jerk for a friend. "Is the missing phone turned on?"

"Well, duh, I always have it on," Ms. Tank Top said with a sneer.

Jennifer had the urge to stomp on the girl's phone if she saw it on the ground, but clenched her fists to control her anger and turned to Marcie. "Try calling it."

"It's the first number on my speed dial." Marcie tapped the keys. "It's ringing."

"What's your ringtone?" Jennifer asked the girl in the tank top.

She threw a towel down on the ground. "What else? For Marcie, I set it for the theme from the movie *Jaws*."

Jennifer resisted the temptation to reset the dingbat's jaw. "We'll look around. Maybe we'll hear the phone ringing. Keep calling her number."

Jennifer grabbed Katherine's hand and gave a tug. "Come on, let's start in the clubhouse."

As they got out of hearing range of the two girls, Katherine asked, "Why did you offer to help that stuck-up girl?"

Jennifer shrugged. "She's Marcie's friend. Marcie was my 'big sister' when I first joined the swim team and has always been nice to me."

Inside the clubhouse, they halted to listen. Several tennis players were speaking in a low tone and the sound of tennis balls smacking the courts could be heard in the background.

Jennifer cocked her head to the side. "Did you hear that?"

"No," Katherine replied.

"This way. The locker room."

They dashed inside and stopped.

From one of the lockers came the sound, "*Bum, bum… bum, bum… bum, bum…*"

"There." Jennifer pointed at a locker,

They headed back outside where Marcie and her friend stood by the pool.

"Are you going to tell that snotty girl where her phone is?" Katherine whispered to Jennifer.

"We should make her suffer a little, I guess, but I want to get back to sunbathing."

"No problem. You tell her the good news."

Jennifer cleared her throat and eyed Ms. Tank Top. "We found your phone. It's in locker forty-two."

The girl turned the same shade of red as Marcie's swimsuit. "Oops. That's my locker."

As Katherine and Jennifer returned to their towels, Katherine said, "Nice detective work."

"I had lots of practice helping my grandpa."

Katherine wiped a bead of perspiration from her forehead. "Yeah, I like your grandpa, but we still need something cool to do this last week of vacation."

"I have an idea." Jennifer gave her friend a Cheshire cat grin.

"Like something totally crazy?"

"Definitely," Jennifer said. "We could start a private investigation agency."

Katherine smiled. "Good idea. You start the detective agency, and I'll be your assistant investigator."

"Elementary, my dear Watson." Jennifer punched her right fist into her left hand. "All settled. We have a plan for the rest of vacation. We can't let you get bored."

* * *

That night, Jennifer sat down at her computer. She felt excitement surge through her body at the thought of her own detective agency. She would solve mysteries all over her neighborhood. But first she needed to get word out. She limbered up her fingers, bit her lip and started designing a logo for the detective agency. She made a large eye and underneath typed in, "Jennifer Jacobson, Private Eyeball."

She tapped away, adding her address and phone number. At the sound of footsteps behind her, she jerked her head around.

"What are you working on?" Jennifer's mom asked.

"Katherine and I are starting a private investigation service. We even practiced today by helping a girl at the swimming pool find a missing cell phone."

"You'll have to be quick with your detective work. School's just around the corner. And you better get some sleep."

"In thirty minutes. I need to finish designing my business card."

"The clock is ticking." Her mom pointed at her watch and left the room.

Jennifer reduced the size of the logo, changed the font for her contact information and constructed a business card. Finally, she pasted fifteen copies in a full-page format, printed out two pages' worth and with scissors cut them out.

She viewed the results and nodded with satisfaction and said to herself, "Nothing'll escape the eye of Jennifer Jacobson, Private Eyeball."

* * *

The next morning Jennifer traipsed around her room, assembling a detective kit, which consisted of a notepad, pencil, cell phone and small magnifying glass. She raced out the front door, slamming it just as her mother said, "Don't slam the door." Outside she looked up at the bright blue Colorado sky, adjusted the rubber band holding her pony tail, and galloped from house to house distributing her new business cards.

Several people chuckled when she explained her new business, and at houses with no one home, Jennifer left her card in the door. She continued for several blocks and approached the Fishers' house.

"Are you going to sell me more Girl Scout cookies?" Ms. Fisher asked.

"No, ma'am. I'm here on another mission." She held out her card.

"What's this?"

"I'm starting a private detective agency. Let me know if you need anyone or anything tracked down or investigated."

"Just like your grandfather."

Jennifer exhaled loudly. "Actually, he learned how to solve crimes from me."

"I don't doubt it. Well, Jennifer, the only mystery I have to figure out is a missing gardening glove."

Jennifer took out her notepad and pencil. "Tell me what happened."

Ms. Fisher gave a dismissive wave of her hand. "I'm sure I just misplaced it. I put my gloves down on the table on my patio yesterday and this morning could only find one of them."

"Why don't you show me the crime scene?"

"I wouldn't call it a crime scene, but let's go out back, and you can see the one glove."

They walked through the house and exited the back door. Under a patio overhang, a gray garden glove rested on a redwood table.

"There it is."

Jennifer ran over and extracted her magnifying glass from her pocket and inspected the glove and surrounding area. "I see some scrape marks on the table."

"Probably from when I put my trowel down. I just don't know what became of the other glove."

"I'll keep an eye out for it, Ms. Fisher. Any other things you need investigated?"

"I don't have anything else for you to solve right now, but you might try Ms. Jensen next door. Her cat is missing."

"Thanks, Ms. Fisher, I'll get right on it."

Jennifer hurried over to Ms. Jensen's house and rang the doorbell.

A frazzled woman in a housecoat came to the door. "You're the girl who sold me three boxes of cookies."

"Yes, but I'm not here on Girl Scout business today. I'm Jennifer Jacobson, Private Eyeball, and I understand you have a missing cat." Jennifer handed her a business card.

"My goodness, do you think you could find Pandora?"

"I'll try."

"What do you charge?"

Jennifer realized she hadn't given that aspect of her new business any thought. She had charged her grandfather a Beanie Baby for every crime she helped him resolve. "When I return Pandora you can pay me a plate of cookies."

She chuckled. "That sounds fair."

"When did you last see Pandora?" Jennifer asked, taking the notepad out of her pocket.

"I let her out at eight this morning. She's always gone for about thirty minutes and then returns, but today she disappeared. I called for her and rattled cat treats, but no Pandora. I asked all the neighbors, but no one has seen her. I'm so worried."

Jennifer bit her lip, wrote furiously on her notepad and then looked up. "Describe Pandora."

"She's a gray and white Persian."

"Do you have a picture of her?"

"Why, yes. Come inside."

Jennifer entered the house and gazed at one living room wall. "Holy cats. You have a lot of pictures."

"Each one is Pandora. From kitten to last week."

Jennifer selected one large pose of Pandora sitting on a chair with her tail sticking out, aimed her phone and snapped a photograph of the picture. She checked to make sure it came out. "Good, now I know exactly what she looks like."

"I hope she's all right," Ms. Jensen said, wiping a tear from her eye.

Jennifer had an idea. "You mentioned that you rattle cat treats to attract her attention. Could I borrow some?"

"You can have the whole jar." Ms. Jensen went into the kitchen and returned with a small plastic jar of Pounce moist tuna flavored treats. "Just shake this and Pandora can hear it a mile away. Well, except for right now."

"Thanks, Ms. Jensen. By the way, you haven't seen Ms. Fisher's lost gardening glove, have you?"

"Why no. But I'm missing a flip-flop."

"Ah, ha. Another possible crime." Jennifer licked her pencil. "Tell me what happened."

"I left a pair of flip-flops on my back porch two days ago. Yesterday, I could only find one."

"Let's take a look."

Ms. Jensen led Jennifer out the backdoor and showed her where a solitary flip-flop rested on a doormat.

Jennifer bent over and examined the doormat. "Hmm. Looks like some marks on the mat."

"Probably from my husband's golf shoes."

"I'll add this to my list for investigating. But Pandora has top priority."

Jennifer dashed home and called Katherine. "We have our first case. Come right over."

When Katherine arrived, Jennifer grabbed the cat treat jar with its pink label and purple cap and dragged Katherine out the door and down the steps.

"Whoa. Don't be so hyper."

"We have to find Ms. Jensen's missing cat Pandora."

"How're we gonna to do that?"

"We'll go through the whole neighborhood shaking this jar of cat treats to see if the sound attracts her."

"No way."

"Yes way." Jennifer said. "It's the best approach to start with. We'll go to Ms. Jensen's house and then search from there."

The girls trudged through the neighborhood for two hours, shaking the jar but finding no Pandora.

"Do you think a fox got Pandora?" Katherine asked. "I saw one just last week running through the Anderson's front yard at night when we were returning from a movie."

"I don't think so," Jennifer replied. "Foxes aren't usually out in broad daylight in the morning."

"I wonder where they live."

Jennifer smiled. "I remember seeing them going into the drainage pipe by the park near our school once."

Katherine's eyes widened. "Maybe Pandora was catnapped."

"More likely she could be stuck somewhere. Cats are curious and sometimes get themselves in trouble."

"This is getting old, and I'm starving," Katherine said. "Time for a lunch break."

"Soon. Let's try one more block."

Jennifer kept rattling the jar. She came to an abrupt halt and put her hand out to stop Katherine. "Did you hear that?"

"What?"

"It sounded like mewing."

"I didn't hear anything. How come your ears are so good?"

"Detectives have to use all their senses." Jennifer put her finger to her mouth. "Shh."

The girls stood perfectly still, but a car drove by. Jennifer waited until the sound of the car disappeared. Then she shook the jar again.

"I heard it!" Katherine shouted.

"Hush. Let's figure out where the sound's coming from."

Jennifer rattled the jar, and the girls stood completely still.

"It's coming from the O'Kelley's place." Jennifer pointed to a wooden two-story house.

The girls entered the yard and Jennifer rattled the jar again.

"*Meeew...*"

"There." Jennifer pointed. "That drainpipe."

The girls hurried over, and Jennifer bent down to find a gray and white tail sticking out of the drainpipe. Handing the cat treats to Katherine, she took out her cell phone and brought up the picture she had taken earlier.

"Yup. That's the same tail. We've found Pandora."

"How are we going to get her out?" Katherine asked.

"I'll try to pull her out." Jennifer tugged but the cat was wedged in. Next, Jennifer took a picture of the drainpipe with the cat's tail hanging out, and then she marched to the front door to ring the doorbell. In a moment, a woman using a cane came to the door.

"Why it's the Girl Scout cookie girl."

"I'm sorry to bother you, Ms. O'Kelley, but a cat crawled into your drainpipe."

"I thought I heard an odd noise this morning." She turned her head back inside. "Charles, come take a look."

A man with pure white hair shuffled to the door. "What seems to be the problem?"

"There's a cat stuck in your drainpipe," Jennifer explained.

"That's unusual. Let me get my toolkit." He returned in a minute, and they all went outside.

"There's a section of pipe that can be taken off," Jennifer said, noticing screws holding it together.

"I'm not as agile as I once was." He handed Jennifer a screwdriver. "See if you can detach the lower section of the drainpipe."

Jennifer removed two screws, and the piece of pipe came off with Pandora's head sticking out. The cat struggled forward until Jennifer was able to grab her under her front paws and extract her. She calmed and petted Pandora, who even started to purr. "Rescue complete. And, Mr. O'Kelley, have you seen a lost gardening glove or flip-flop?"

"Why, no. But I'm missing a sock."

Handing Katherine the cat, Jennifer popped out her notepad. "Tell me what happened."

"I got mud on my socks while gardening a few days ago. I took off my socks, washed them using the hose and left them to dry on my patio. The next day I could only find one sock."

"Describe it."

He chuckled. "It was one of my St. Patrick's Day socks. White with green shamrocks on the ankles."

"I'll add it to my list of missing items," Jennifer said

Katherine and Jennifer waved goodbye and headed to Ms. Jensen's house, cat and treats in hand.

"What's with the question about a glove and flip-flop?" Katherine asked.

"There's a mysterious thief in our neighborhood. Earlier this morning Ms. Fisher and Ms. Jensen told me they lost those items. Now Mr. O'Kelley also has a missing sock."

"Maybe it's Randy Buchanan or Teddy Bishop from school," Katherine said. "I saw them skulking around our neighborhood last night."

Jennifer jotted on her notepad. "Good. Our first suspects."

They arrived at Ms. Jensen's house and knocked on the door.

Jennifer held up the cat.

"You've found Pandora!" Ms. Jensen gave the cat a hug.

The cat yawned.

"Come on in. I owe you girls a reward." She disappeared into the kitchen for a moment and returned with a plate piled high with chocolate chip cookies.

They each ate two, and Ms. Jensen put the rest in a paper bag to take with them.

"Thank you so much for rescuing Pandora."

"All part of the service," Jennifer said with a grin on her face. "Tell all your friends about us. We're also on the case of your missing flip-flop."

As they strolled away, Jennifer waved her half-eaten cookie. "We rescued the cat, but we still have the other mystery to solve. Who's stealing gloves, flip-flops and socks?"

* * *

Jennifer pounded on Katherine's door before eight the next morning.

Ms. Milo was just getting ready to leave for work. "Come on in, Jennifer. Katherine should be down in a minute."

Moments later Katherine stumbled down the stairs, rubbing her eyes. "What's all the noise?"

"We need to get on the case right away."

"What case?"

"We need to see if we can find any clues for the missing glove, flip-flop and sock."

"At the crack of dawn?"

Jennifer clicked her tongue. "The day is a-wasting. Finish getting ready."

* * *

For the first block no one else was out. Then they saw one man picking up the newspaper in his front yard. He disappeared back into his house. "Nothing suspicious here," Jennifer said.

On the next block, they spotted Randy from school putting something behind a bush.

"Do you think he's hiding the missing glove, flip-flop or sock?" Katherine asked.

"It's possible. Let's go check it out."

The girls snuck up on Randy who had his back to them. Jennifer tapped him on the back.

He jumped. "Yikes!"

"What are you hiding, Randy?" Jennifer asked.

"Nothing,"

Jennifer peered behind the bush and saw a T-shirt. "Have you been stealing things from backyards?"

Randy turned red. "No. That's Teddy's shirt. We're having a treasure hunt before he starts his first day of weeding at the Matherbee's where he'll be working the rest of the week."

Jennifer pushed her index finger into his chest. "Have you stolen a glove, flip-flop and sock?"

"Nope. Now leave me alone. Teddy will be coming shortly to see if he can find the shirt."

As the girls walked away, Katherine whispered to Jennifer, "I think he's lying."

"We'll have to see if we can find more evidence. Randy is definitely suspect number one."

* * *

Early the next morning, Jennifer went out on the deck to retrieve her tennis shoes left out to dry after she had stepped in a mud puddle the day before. She looked down. Only one shoe.

She raced inside. "Mom. Did you take one of my tennis shoes that I left out to dry?"

"No, what's wrong?"

"There's only one shoe out there."

"You're not getting like your grandfather and forgetting things, are you?"

Jennifer put her hands on her hips. "Mother, I left two shoes out there yesterday, and now there's only one. I remember fine. Something happened to it."

Her mom chuckled. "Don't get so exasperated. Maybe the wind blew if off the deck."

Jennifer went back outside with her dog, Max, following her. She checked all around the deck but could find no trace of the shoe. She strolled out in the yard, looked in the bushes and returned to where the one shoe rested, all alone.

Max ran around in circles, sniffed the deck and woofed.

"Max, the thief took my shoe just like what happened to Ms. Fisher, Ms. Jensen and Mr. O'Kelley. Do you think Randy or Teddy stole it?"

Max cocked a white ear and looked at her. Then he woofed again and pawed the deck.

"I wonder..."

Jennifer retrieved the magnifying glass from her room and went to inspect the area around the one remaining tennis shoe. She got down on her hands and knees and looked carefully. Sure enough, she found a few splinters of wood sticking up from the deck.

* * *

Later that day, Jennifer received a phone call from her grandfather and told him, "I have a crime to solve. Someone has been stealing footwear and gloves from backyards."

"You're sure they're not people like me who forget things?"

"Nope. One of them is me, and I have a great memory. Yesterday, I left my tennis shoes out to dry. This morning one of them was missing. I'll have to keep working on it."

"I'm sure you'll solve the mystery."

"I hope so. You take care, Grandpa. I miss you."

* * *

First thing the next day before any other investigating activities, Jennifer decided to check on Teddy Bishop. She grabbed her cell phone, dashed out of the house and jogged over to the Matherbee's. She saw the newspaper still out on the front sidewalk. Surveying the surroundings, she found a good surveillance spot across the street where a hedge rested alongside a small vacant lot.

Jennifer crossed the street and sat down next to the hedge. Teddy should be coming from the opposite direction, so she felt confident she could remain there undetected.

Fifteen minutes later Teddy strolled up the street, kicked a pebble off the sidewalk, hocked a loogie into the shrubs and picked up the newspaper. He disappeared behind the Matherbee's house and emerged in a few minutes carrying a dandelion digger.

Just as I suspected. Jennifer peered more closely from her hiding place.

Teddy set to work weeding the next section in the yard, whistling as he dug up dandelions.

After half an hour, Teddy stopped and wiped the sweat off his forehead.

A squirrel hopped down the trunk of an ash tree in the Matherbee's yard.

Teddy leered, grabbed his dandelion digger and stalked the squirrel like he was a big game hunter. As he got close, Jennifer snapped a picture from across the street. Just then the squirrel scampered away.

Teddy shook a fist at the tail that disappeared into the tree. "I'll get you next time."

Jennifer decided she had enough evidence. She stood up and crossed the street.

Teddy was digging with his back toward her and whistling the tune, "Heigh-ho," from Snow White.

Jennifer looked around and picked up a piece of branch that had fallen out of a tree. She tiptoed up behind Teddy and stuck the end of the branch in Teddy's back. In a deep voice she said, "Reach for the sky, mister, and don't look around."

Teddy yelped and dropped the dandelion digger.

Jennifer continued in her deep voice. "Did you steal a glove, flip-flop, sock or tennis shoe from yards in this neighborhood?"

"N—no," he stammered.

Jennifer decided he could be lying but pulled the branch away from Teddy's back. "Turn around."

He did as commanded, and his eyes widened. "Oh, it's you, Jennifer. You surprised me."

"Look me in the eyes. Did you steal a glove, flip-flop, sock or tennis shoe?"

"Wh—why would you think that?"

"I've seen marks near where the items were stolen that look like dandelion digger scrapes."

"I only use the dandelion digger in the Matherbee's yard."

Jennifer still couldn't tell if he was lying or telling the truth. "I'll be watching you."

* * *

Late that afternoon, Jennifer retrieved Katherine and they continued to scour the neighborhood for clues to the missing items. Jennifer mentioned how her own tennis shoe had been added to the list of missing items and how she had confronted Teddy Bishop.

As they turned the corner, Jennifer came to a halt, pointed and whispered, "Look."

At the end of the block a hunched-over man in a trench coat and dark hat trudged away from them. He held a package in his hands.

"Just an old man," Katherine said.

"He looks very suspicious."

"No way. He's only taking a walk."

"I think something's going on. We better check him out."

"Jennifer—"

Jennifer grabbed Katherine's hand and hauled her after the man.

"We need to stay back fifty feet or so and step carefully so our shoes won't squeak," Jennifer whispered.

The man turned the corner, and Jennifer pulled Katherine along after him.

"What do you think he's carrying?" Katherine asked.

Jennifer's eyes grew large. "Maybe he has the stolen glove, flip-flop, sock and tennis shoe. No innocent person would be dressed in a trench coat on a summer day." She snapped a picture and jotted a note on her pad. "Now we have another suspect besides Randy and Teddy. Do you think they're a crime gang working together?"

"You're freaking out for no reason."

Jennifer put her index finger to her mouth. "Shh."

The man turned another corner, and the girls kept him in sight. Then he paused in front of a small one-story house and stumbled up the walkway to the front porch. He slowly bent over and set down his package.

"He's leaving the stolen items near the door," Jennifer whispered into Katherine's ear. "Don't let him see us."

They scurried behind a hedge and watched as the man returned to the sidewalk and continued on his way. Once he disappeared, the girls tiptoed up to the house.

"Do you think we should call the police?" Katherine asked.

"Not yet. Jennifer Jacobson, Private Eyeball, will investigate first." Jennifer led the way up to the package. It was a brown paper bag with the top folded over. "Stand back." Jennifer waited until Katherine took two steps away. Then she bent over, unfolded the top of the bag and peered inside.

Jennifer gawked at what she found. "Peaches."

* * *

Back at Jennifer's house, the girls grabbed some grapes for a snack and went out onto the back deck, Max trailing behind.

Katherine and Jennifer wouldn't share the grapes with Max since they are poisonoius to dogs, so he curled up under a chair while keeping his eyes on the girls just in case something new to eat appeared.

"That guy in the trench coat certainly looked suspicious," Jennifer said with a frown.

"Goes to show that you can't always tell by someone's looks. Just an old, geeky guy who probably has dressed that way for years."

"I thought he could have the stolen items. Maybe he really is the thief and the peaches were a diversionary tactic."

"I don't know, but you sure got sucked in." Katherine giggled. "It was pretty funny with you sneaking up and finding a present he had left for someone."

Jennifer scowled. "We can't let this out. It would reflect poorly on our detective agency."

"I'm good. You still have an excellent track record. You figured out the lost cell phone on Sunday and then recovered Pandora. Max likes to play with things. Maybe he hid your shoe."

Hearing his name, Max came up and scratched his paw on the deck.

Jennifer stared for a moment and snapped her fingers. "Of course. That's the answer. Katherine, we can solve the mystery right now. We'll test my hypothesis on who took the missing items."

* * *

Jennifer stuffed an empty trash bag in a pocket of her jeans, then reached up and took two flashlights off the shelf. She handed a flashlight to Katherine, grabbed her hand, dragged her out the door and led her through the neighborhood toward the park near their school.

"Why are we here?" Katherine asked.

"At several of the crime scenes, there was one thing in common. Scratch marks." Jennifer snapped on her flashlight and aimed the beam into the large drainage pipe.

She hunkered down on her hands and knees and crawled inside the pipe. Along a recess in the side, she found gloves, shoes, flip-flops, socks, a pile of clothes and even a wallet. Then with Katherine's help, they picked up all the items and placed them in the trash bag. They lugged the bag back to Jennifer's house and emptied it in her front yard. She found her missing tennis shoe, Ms. Fisher's gardening glove, Ms. Jensen's flip-flop and Mr. O'Kelley's white sock with the green shamrock on it. While Katherine continued to organize the items, Jennifer went inside and produced a poster on her computer and printed out copies, which she planned to staple to telephone poles throughout the neighborhood. It read, "Our neighborhood foxes have been stealing clothing items left outside. If you are missing an item, stop by Jennifer Jacobson's yard to retrieve it." She gave her address.

Afterwards Jennifer and Katherine sat in the kitchen and munched on cookies.

"Man, am I tired," Katherine said with a yawn.

"It will be good to get back to school to relax after this strenuous last week of vacation."

Katherine smiled and looked at her friend. "And the mystery is solved thanks to Jennifer Jacobson, Private Eyeball."

J. K. Knauss

Lady Of Bureba

County of Castile, Kingdom of León (Spain) 964 A. D.

In later years, Justa would recall the first time she saw Lambra as looking into an enchanted mirror in which every feature appeared a little more sharply defined, a touch haughtier. They met each other in front of the stone house by the river, neither taller than the other, both with clear blue eyes and gold-blonde hair parted down the center and plaited on each side. Lambra's dress was a richer crimson and the apron was fastened with heavy gold buckles Justa could never dream of owning, but to the casual observer, the two could have been sisters, if not twins.

At the time, neither of them had completed six years, and Justa was conscious only of holding tightly to an adult's hand—any adult's hand—while those adults spoke together about things like fostering and serving. They must've told Justa what had happened to her parents, but she didn't understand. It only mattered that they couldn't take care of her anymore. Lambra and her parents were all Justa would ever have.

The blonde girl with the silky ribbons seemed to like what she saw. Lambra took Justa's hand and led her to a field of blossoming daisies. "I had two brothers and two sisters, but they all died. You can be my sister now, and we'll play together every day, forever."

Sitting in the soft grasses, Lambra finger-combed and re-braided

Justa's hair and made her a daisy wreath. Justa tried to make one for her new friend, but her unpracticed hands were destined for failure.

"It's all right," said Lambra, pulling Justa up to explore the rest of the estate of Busto de Bureba.

Justa barely heard Lambra's chattering descriptions of the buildings and people over a buzzing sensation of good fortune. They ran around the slaughterhouse, teased the stable boys, and looked at the river as if they had never been a day apart in their lives. Justa remembered the sun shining down on them, gentle and bright, in stark contrast to the darkness she'd been living through over the past few days. She wanted to wade in the river and throw stones.

A fish popped out of the water, splashing back in among the reeds. "May we catch some fish?"

"No," Lambra said. "We're ladies, and ladies do not catch their own fish."

Justa recognized that this new place to live and especially this unexpected friendship required specific behavior. From the first night, the girls slept on the same straw pallet near the fire and often ate from the same plate, so she was in the right position to learn the new rules. They turned out to be simple: not to do anything that Lambra said not to; not to suggest activities if Lambra would never think of them herself; not to touch Lambra's dolls unless specifically instructed; and—this was the difficult one—not to do anything that would anger Lambra, lest she hiss about how ungrateful Justa was and how her parents didn't have to care for her and how everyone in Bureba barely tolerated her.

Justa timed her childhood days according to the bells of the new church, which tolled across the fields with a comforting regularity. She did the chores Lambra wouldn't deign to carry out, such as gathering wild herbs for the cooks, fetching water from the river when she was strong enough to hold the bucket, collecting firewood, and checking the sites of the tread traps near the edge of the forest to see whether an animal had sprung them.

Such work gave Justa a satisfying sense of her importance to the running of the estate. For her utter obedience to the painfully discovered rules and to the doting adults, Lambra and the rest of Bureba rewarded Justa with a warm place to sleep, delicious, sustaining food, and a constant companion.

In the springtime of their tenth year, Lambra caught a fever while her parents were away helping the Count of Castile with some political task. Justa nursed her under the maids' supervision until she fell ill herself.

Lambra recovered first. She sat at Justa's bedside for half the day, playing quietly with an elegant doll that had hair made of flax strands. Justa's body ached, and she struggled to breathe, but she was not so delirious that she even considered asking to touch the doll. The presence of her companion gave her somewhere to direct her attention besides the anguish and heat, and she was grateful. When Lambra began to stir, Justa made a huge effort and raised her arm to keep her friend there.

"Don't leave," she whispered.

"No, I won't," Lambra said. "I'll be right back." She skipped off, Justa knew not where, and didn't return to sleep by Justa's side that evening.

"Make me a bed on this side of the hall." Lambra's voice addressed the nanny somewhere far away. "I don't want to be too close to Justa's humors and get sick again."

The maids had made special electuaries for Justa and lovingly covered her with cool cloths. But she reached across the vast emptiness of the pallet where Lambra should be and knew herself to be more alone than the condemned Cain she had heard about in church. She didn't sleep, but fainted, her feeble energy drained by the demons that ran through her mind, tormenting her with her own solitude and worthlessness.

Justa woke the following morning breathing freely. She stretched her limbs to find that they weren't in pain so much as they'd been inactive too long. The nanny leaned over her and smiled. She handed her a bowl of cucumber-tasting borage mash, and Justa could finally feel her body responding to its medicine.

She closed her eyes with enjoyment as the nanny washed her for the first time in days with water warmed in the cook pot and soap fragranced with spearmint. Justa was so glad it was a new day that she went immediately to the river with the water bucket, but found that she had to stop and concentrate on breathing normally. Perhaps a different activity today.

Lambra came up behind her from nowhere, causing Justa to startle and double over coughing. She spat globs of mucous on the ground.

"Are your humors balanced yet?" asked Lambra.

"I have too much phlegm." Justa wiped her mouth.

"Let's dry you out," said Lambra.

They sat in the freshly sprouting millet fields under the gentle morning sun, and Lambra set to work tidying and braiding Justa's hair. As Lambra ground her expensive overdress into the soil, Justa's hands began to itch in anticipation of working with lye to get the stains out. But soon, a soothing sensation spread throughout her body and tamped down any protests.

She had the distinct impression that she and Lambra had always done this, since the beginning of time, and that sense of everlasting friendship was well worth any scrubbing Justa would have to do later. When Lambra said she was satisfied with her friend's appearance, they lay back and watched the wispy clouds sail above them.

"I might marry the Lord of Miranda, or perhaps my parents will find me someone of the royal blood of León or France. Bureba is a rich enough territory that I can really have my pick of matches," Lambra mused.

Justa had only recently regained her friend and now she was talking about leaving Bureba altogether. "When will you go?"

Lambra laughed. "Not for a few years. We still have to become women."

"Will I go with you?"

"I think my parents can find you nearly as good a match as they find for me. Your kinfolk weren't exactly serfs, you know."

Justa remembered almost nothing about her parents. Lambra's

parents had taken up residence in her heart, as if they were the same blood. When they had said farewell a few weeks earlier, Lambra's father had embraced her and then patted her on the head as if she were his own daughter. Lambra's mother had choked back tears for both girls in what seemed like equal measure to the foster child.

"Then we'll both have our own households, and be able to travel and visit each other whenever we want. Not like now, when my parents can go wherever they please and leave us babies here," Lambra continued.

Justa understood that Lambra's parents traveled out of obligation to their vassals and, this time, out of loyalty to the Count of Castile. She let Lambra prattle on while her imagination ran with the new possibility laid out before her.

What kind of husband would they find for her? She hoped it would be someone like Lambra's father, who was the highest-ranking man she'd ever met. Much younger, of course, but with kind eyes and a parcel or two of land. She would willingly tend to animals and even hoe the rocky earth, as long as her husband accepted her and let her contribute to the estate. It might be nice to see Lambra now and again, but her family would occupy her day by day. Better if her husband didn't have a lot of obligations to higher lords, so they wouldn't have to travel. And now that the Moors were farther to the south, there shouldn't be any wars to take her husband or her sons away, either.

So it was settled. Justa sighed with contentment in spite of her congestion and decided that the previous night's demons had been the last test God or Satan had seen fit to put her through. She was preparing to return to her duties as a friend and listen to Lambra for a few more hours when the nanny's voice reached her ears, muffled below the green millet.

"Lambra! Justa! Where are you?"

The shrillness in the normally gentle voice moved Justa to sit up immediately.

"Ah, what does she want?" said Lambra before she sat up, too.

The nanny stood at the door with several men, scanning the horizon for the girls and shouting in every direction. Justa stood up out of a deep-seated need to end the woman's distress, but Lambra remained mostly hidden in the sheaves. Justa took Lambra's hands and tugged, but was too weak to overcome the girl's lack of urgency.

The nanny must have seen them, because she came running toward them and the men followed. Justa punched Lambra's shoulder as hard as she dared and the reminder of noble propriety spurred her friend to stand up, stretching and dusting herself off.

The nanny embraced Lambra and then Justa too tightly. "Oh, my beautiful girls, so alone!"

Lambra struggled and broke free. "What's happening?"

The men, who walked more deliberately, arrived to bow before Lambra. There were five of them, and though their ages varied, they all wore richly colored tunics under their traveling mantles and their shoes were worked with gold filigree.

"These are some of the knights who were traveling with the count and your parents, Lambra," said the nanny. "They bring news." She dissolved into sobs.

The knight with the grayest hair lowered himself slowly until he knelt before Lambra. "My lord and lady, your parents perished on the southern roads three days ago when the Moors ambushed us. They had no other heirs, so the count has sent me to pledge my fealty to you, Doña Lambra." He took her hand and kissed the back of it ceremonially.

Lambra made no move to react until each knight had knelt and pledged his loyalty in a similar fashion.

"Very well," she said with a shallow sigh. "We must tell the news to everyone on the estate. Send them all to the main house immediately."

She started toward the house, and Justa nearly stayed behind in shock. When the nanny stayed where she was, repeatedly wiping tears from her cheeks, Lambra said, "Stop crying. There's too much to do."

Justa recognized Lambra's command humor. She was well accustomed to withstanding it for the short duration it had always lasted before. Lambra thought she could be the lady and run the estate, but she was only a girl, and even amidst the tumult of feelings and thoughts, Justa hoped they could soon find someone else to take care of them.

Lambra didn't give up her superior position even to weep over her parents' shrouds. They arrived a few hours behind the messenger knights in a cart pulled by enormous black horses that made Justa tremble.

A silver-haired knight parted the tight cluster of new arrivals when he held his arms out to Lambra. She glided toward him, holding out her hands the way she used to when her father had presented her with gifts.

Justa looked on in awe as the old man swept Lambra up as if she were a baby. "Lambra, I've failed you terribly," he said, planting a kiss on her forehead.

The girl didn't respond. He set her on her feet and smoothed her hair. A younger man came to stand by his side as the old knight continued, "Even though your parents are gone, you'll never want for anything. I've made sure every man in my domain will acknowledge you as the Lady of Bureba, and when I'm gone, my son will uphold your rights against any challenge."

Justa felt the thrill of recognition. This must be the Count of Castile Lambra's parents had been traveling with.

"I'm sorry to meet you under such sad circumstances," the younger man said.

"My grief has blinded me—forgive me," said the count. "You don't know each other. This is Prince García. You ought to have met sooner. He's your cousin, after all."

Lambra bowed gracefully, but her cousin took her hand and kissed it, raising her back up before he placed his even whiter hands behind his back.

In the carts, the shrouds of tightly wrapped, coarse cloth looked too small to hold Lambra's mother and father, whose kindness and generosity loomed large in Justa's mind. And yet Lambra had the knights work the wrapping loose around the dead faces and said in turn, "This is my mother," and "This is my father."

Justa wanted to see them, too, to catch a last glimpse of the people who had taken her in only to leave her in so much uncertainty.

"Their spirits aren't in the shrouds, sweet child," the nanny told her. "They're somewhere far away, with our Savior and his saints. Only empty shells are inside the cloth."

Justa buried her face in the scratchy wool of the nanny's apron and wept with her.

"Are you crying?" said Lambra behind them. Justa wiped her face in time to see Lambra instructing the knights.

"There's a parish church beyond our fields there. Take them in and tell the priests to prepare a funeral." The knights looked all about, their eyes landing on the count, the highest authority in all Castile. He nodded gravely.

"What are you waiting for?" asked Lambra. "I'm the lady here, and you have to do as I say."

The knight looked at her as if she were an impossible combination, like a talking dog, or a horse with wings, but she met his gaze, and he was the first to look away.

The following morning at Prime, the priests sang mass for the dead. The count, his son, and their noble retinue departed the church, bound surely for a town where they could threaten the murderous Moors. Doña Lambra, wearing one of her mother's dresses that dragged the straw along the compact earth floor, pointed out the exact spot near the main altar where she wished her parents buried. She engaged in a long discussion about what the funerary stone—which would make up part of the church floor once the remains had wasted away to bones—should have written on it.

Justa marveled at the way Lambra took on all the responsibilities without ever breaking down. She would have liked Lambra better if she did.

"They were the noblest and bravest lord and lady Bureba has ever seen," Lambra concluded.

The priest seemed to think it over before he replied. "Even a great lord, like the Count of Castile or the King of León, would rest under a humbler marker. We wouldn't want to risk their appearing proud at their judgment."

"My parents gave the money for this church's completion. Do you think you would have all these smooth-cut blocks and timber to stand under, or the paint to decorate them with, if it hadn't been for them?"

"Doña Lambra," the priest replied, wincing, "we mustn't tempt your parents' souls to stay close to Earth with such flattering commemoration."

"My parents were great enough to merit eternal memory, and I want this stone to identify them at the Last Judgment." She turned away without waiting for a reply.

Justa wondered who would verify whether her wishes for the stone were carried out properly, as Lambra hadn't learned to read, and probably none of the servants could, either. She must not have heard the nanny and the priest explaining that the souls were already in their eternal glory and the flesh and bones no longer mattered. There was ample space for Lambra's mother and father in the churchyard, where they would rot and make way for more of the loyal people of Bureba.

A tremendous ache inside Justa demanded that she sob and wail and ask all the saints at the heavenly banquet how they could have allowed something like this to happen, but each time she showed the merest sign of her sorrow, Lambra corrected her mercilessly. Earlier that morning, she'd even slapped Justa across the face. The violence spoke loudly enough to keep Justa from ever speaking out of turn.

She looked forward to the nighttime, but doubted whether she would be able to keep her weeping quiet enough for the new Lady of Bureba. She hadn't had time to balance her humors properly, and she wheezed more often than not, making breathing to Lambra's satisfaction the most difficult task Justa had ever taken on.

They walked around the fields back toward the main house in a sort of procession with Lambra at the head. Justa stumbled along behind her. She nearly twisted her ankle several times on the stones in the path and grabbed hold of the nanny's hand. A lock of hair fell into her face, because no one could get the braids as tight as Lambra. Justa longed to sit together like that with her old friend again.

When the main buildings were already in sight, Lambra took a sudden stumble, a cat darted into the field, and Lambra was on the ground in a heap of heavy fabric.

She didn't try to rise before she ordered the nearest man, "Find that cat and kill it. That's the last time it will get in my way."

Heart pounding, Justa darted to Lambra to help her up, expecting the man, who tended the horses in the stable, to go running after the animal. But he stood where he was. Justa left the dusting off to the nanny and stared at the man. His name was Marcial and he had served Lambra's parents since long before Justa had come to live with them. He was one more of the permanent fixtures in Busto de Bureba, like the buildings, the river, and the nanny, that Justa loved dearly, even while she took for granted that they would always be there.

"Lambra, you know we need that cat to catch the mice and rats. It's time you rested and left the decisions to someone with a clear head," Marcial said.

Lambra wrested herself out of the nanny's grasp and picked up a stone. She hurled it with all her ten-year-old strength at Marcial. He caught it in his hand and dropped it back on the ground.

He said nothing, but Lambra didn't let the silence condemn her. "I would have him stoned," she said to all the members of the household.

Justa astonished herself by looking for rocks to use in the service of Lambra's request. Such was her fear of the Lady of Bureba.

No one else made a move until Marcial turned abruptly and started back toward the church. Without stopping, he looked back to see if anyone would join him.

No one followed. Justa knew he was right to leave, and felt as if something were tugging on her dress, urging her to flee with him. But even aside from Justa's obligations to Lambra as the foster child of her parents, she knew she couldn't leave Busto de Bureba. She had nowhere else to go.

A cat's head peeped out from between the short stalks of the field. Lambra whipped around to face Justa, who lied, "That's not the cat that tripped you, my lady."

Lambra nodded and started forward again, bringing the household behind her as if they were tied together.

Relief cleansed Justa's burning temples while the wind ruffled the leaves. She gazed in the direction Marcial had gone, then followed her old friend and new mistress home.

BJ Magnani

Lily Robinson and an Ab-breve-iated Mission

I'm not as cold and clinical as you may think. Tragedy sometimes stirs the best in us, or in my case, the worst. I felt responsible for the loss of my child, and since I couldn't protect her, I try and save the rest of the world. My job? I'm a physician by training, working at an academic medical center, but that's not where I help most people. No, I'm an assassin who works deep undercover with a government team charged with eliminating terroristic threats. The yield is bigger, and the price, reasonable—one life—mine. I know what you're thinking. How could I defy the Hippocratic oath and kill my fellow human beings? I, too, have struggled with this question, but I've come to accept that the good of the many outweighs the good of the one. Many governments approve of—but don't admit to—sanctioned assassinations. Plausible deniability. Think about it. You know it's true. Assassinations of political rivals, terrorists, or game-changers often make the news—and then again, some never do.

Chad's the operative for our small team and hands out assignments when he receives the information from Intelligence. Before I left Boston, he met with me and asked that I take on this short mission.

"Dr. Robinson, I have that info for you," he said, moving wisps of brown hair over his head to cover some of the baldness. His hazel eyes move down from my green eyes and land on my stilettos. "What kind of shoes do you have on this morning?"

"These?" I say nonchalantly, "These are my black lizard peep-toe heels." I smile, pushing my raven-colored hair behind my ears.

"Those are your favorites since you wear them so often."

Accurate, but I refocused the conversation.

"Thanks, Chad. What's the current situation?"

"Yeah, sorry. To clarify what's happening. We have information that your target has already sold some of NATO's defense strategy to the Russians. And he's about to do it again. He must be stopped and now."

"Jesus, Chad. Why not just arrest the guy and charge him with an international crime? Why kill him?"

"We could, but that might feed into the rhetoric that's going around about how NATO is no longer serving the best interests of the United States. Rather than take him into custody, our security sources feel it would be better if he were just eliminated. It would have to appear like a natural death, or there could be repercussions. I know that you understand this. Clearly, this is why we called you in."

"Yes, Chad. I know the drill. So, what can you tell me about his existing medical conditions?" This information always makes my job easier.

"Right, Robinson. Our traitor has a history of some chronic illnesses; it's all in the file," he said, and then handed me the dossier on my target. How they get this information, I'll never know. I quickly thumbed through the pages until my eyes landed on a solution for our problem. "Chad, will you be able to get me into NATO headquarters?"

"I think we can use diplomatic status to make that work. You have an idea?"

"I do. But I need to make a quick trip to the cottage first to retrieve my poison of choice, one that will bring our traitor to his knees."

My seaside cottage is located off the coast of Massachusetts. That's where I keep my poison garden, and some other toxins I like to use. This sacred place contains the plants I favor—those that cultivate toxic leaves, fruits, and tubers—deadly molecular packages whose products defy detection by routine chemistry. How do I know this? Because I'm a pathologist who specializes in toxicology, and I work in a laboratory. My encyclopedic knowledge of poisons is why the government has forged this unholy alliance.

After Chad's instruction, I went to the cottage and found what I was looking for. The plan was set in motion, with Europe my next stop. As the plane lands at Luchthaven Zaventem, I prepare to meet another operative who will work with me on this assignment.

The headquarters for NATO, the North Atlantic Treaty Organization, is in Brussels—the historical setting for the capital of Belgium. An ancient metropolis with roots back to the Stone Age, its rich history resulted from the influence of many European nations. In the city, both French and Dutch are spoken, and while my French is fairly good, my Flemish is non-existent. I have always appreciated the compromise, signs in both languages, and accommodations for those who speak English.

Having cleared customs with my diplomatic passport, I find my hotel in Brussels, and get ready for the luncheon that the traitor will be attending. My mission's simple. My handler has asked me to assassinate a man who's about to betray NATO's 'collective defense'. An attack against one nation is an attack against all, but in this case, the traitor's someone within the organization who will reveal NATO's strategic plan.

Thoroughly prepared before I find my mark, I've memorized his face, know his medical history, and have found his Achilles heel. I'm introduced to the company of men as a visiting diplomat from the United States. As previously arranged, the round man with light brown hair and brown eyes is seated next to me. We engage in telling conversation. The NATO Secretary General joins in and discusses the importance of strengthening transatlantic ties. The time is right. I lean into my target and whisper in his ear, our closeness enabling the scent of my perfume to be inhaled. Within minutes he begins to wheeze as his airways start to tighten. The traitor moves his hand to his chest.

"Are you all right?" I ask.

Those sitting at adjacent tables, alarmed by the scene, now focus their attention on the man. Their forks rest on their plates, and their faces show raised eyebrows and pursed lips. My target struggles—more wheezing and coughing.

"Do you have an inhaler with you?" I ask.

He nods yes, and points to his jacket pocket. I reach deep inside and pull out his inhaler, uncap it, and place the device in his hand. I watch as he inhales deeply, trying desperately to get a breath in, and out. I can see his nail beds turn blue, and his skin turn from white to gray. Oxygen is not getting into the bloodstream—the treatment is not working. My target's nose runs, his eyes tear, and finally, he collapses to the ground. I continue to give him puffs of the inhaler but to no avail.

The Secretary General has already requested medical backup. We wait. By the time help arrives, it's too late. The traitor is dead—an unfortunate asthma attack. I close my eyes and look away, reflecting the callousness of the moment. I leave once the commotion stops and go back to my hotel for a short debriefing.

"Robinson, I can see the sting in your eyes, *mais* this was necessary," the dark-haired man says in his smooth French accent. He puts his hand on my shoulder as a sign of solidarity. "How did you do it?" He had watched the scene unfold from an adjacent table. "I could not see."

I let out a sigh, the guilt like a boomerang returns to my chest. I like healing better than killing. "That was the idea; make it seamless," I say dispassionately.

"*S'il te plaît*, explain."

"I knew from reading his medical record that he was a severe asthmatic and was sensitive to odorants. I triggered his asthma attack by wearing a strong floral perfume. When I leaned in close to him, he inhaled the scent that started the cascade."

"So your perfume was the poison?"

"No, the perfume just initiated the attack, and once he started wheezing, I knew he would look for his rescue inhaler. The medication contains albuterol, a beta-agonist."

"What is that?"

"This beta-agonist drug opens up the airways by relaxing the smooth muscle that surrounds them. It allows the patient to move air in and out of the lungs. With an asthma attack, the airways constrict, and the person can't move oxygen in or carbon dioxide out."

"But the inhaler did not work."

"That's because when I reached in his pocket to grab it, I swapped it for an inhaler I had tampered with. Of course, before he left the scene, I put his inhaler back in his jacket pocket. With all the attention on the patient, no one noticed—not even you, and you were watching me."

"Clever, Robinson; so what was in the inhaler?"

"Brevetoxin. It's a marine toxin produced by the dinoflagellate, *Karenia brevis*. These are small algal organisms and are one of the culprits that cause red tide. Blooms of organisms in the Gulf of Mexico and along the coasts of Florida and Texas are responsible for this neurotoxic shellfish poison. Crashing waves have been known to aerosolize the toxin allowing beachgoers to inhale the poison, so I simply followed nature's blueprint."

"*Mais oui,* you *are* the queen of all poisons," he says with a smile. Then looking at his watch, he continues, "It has been a long day. We should make our plan to pack our things so we can head out to the airport." His overnight bag is open on the bed, waiting to be filled.

"Oh, so soon?" My voice echoes the unbottled urges that spill over the top.

Adrenaline still circulates in our blood, coursing from the tension and excitement of our mission. Guilt is buried and replaced. I move into him and look into his blue-green eyes and craggy face. My lips cross space and touch his, and his arms surround me in return. I sense his warm breath on my neck, followed by soft kisses, and I feel his hardness grow. Those hormones that rise with danger also stimulate passion, and push us together, reaffirming life after death. With both our hearts racing, we fall onto the bed knocking the overnight bag to the floor.

"My Lily. I believe we have a little time before we need to catch that flight."

I thought so.

Matt Cost

Mainely Trapped

"Nobody is going anywhere." The man stood in the middle of the top-floor-outside deck of the Pelican Perch. He had on a mask and casually held a rifle aloft that looked to be a semi-automatic. "Welcome to Mystery Dinner Theater's Escape Room."

"You didn't tell me about this," Chabal said. They'd been invited to a charity fundraiser in Port Essex, a bit less than an hour from home, and had decided to turn it into a weekend trip. "That's a fun surprise for our anniversary." She was more than a foot shorter than Langdon's 6'4", with blonde hair cascading to her shoulders like a brook in the wilds, hair that was now dyed to offset the graying of her mid-fifties.

"They're real actors from Maine State Music Theater, or the interns at least. Happy anniversary, babe," Langdon said.

Two people were led over to their high-top table by the hostess. "I think we're sharing the table with you," the man said. "Clay Wolfe, and my partner, Baylee Baker." He held out his hand and shook first with Langdon and then Chabal, his partner following suit.

"Name is Langdon. This is my wife, Chabal."

"Sorry, we're running a bit late. Did we miss anything?"

"We were told that we're trapped," Langdon said.

"So, we're trapped here with good food and a bar?" Clay asked. He was a shade under six feet, well-dressed in a waistcoat and expensive shoes. His hair was a mussed blonde and his eyes a rare greenish blue.

"Somebody will be murdered here this evening," the man in the mask said. "To avoid a similar fate, you must apprehend the guilty party before," he paused, looked at his watch, and said, "ten o'clock."

That gives you two hours. Those with masks like mine will be your tour guides. If asked the right question, they'll supply helpful information. The initial clues will be discovered with your meals at your tables. Upon completion of the meal, you'll have one hour to mingle with the other guests and exchange what you have learned to fill in the strokes of the canvas to showcase the masterpiece that is this murder."

"I've heard of you," Langdon said to Clay. "You're a PI right here in Port Essex. Had some pretty high-profile cases lately."

Clay chuckled. "Like the blackmailing of a U.S. Senator?"

It was Langdon's turn to laugh. He was about twenty years older than his fellow PI, rumpled and casual where this other man was pressed and neat. "I was thinking more like heroin and cults, but each to their own," he said.

"You own that mystery bookstore down in Brunswick, don't you?" Baylee asked. "We stopped in there a while back but the only guy in there was this crusty old fellow. Got a few good mysteries. Took two off your Encircle Publications shelf. Didn't even know Maine had a quality publisher like that."

"You must've run into Star." Chabal snickered. "Crusty old fellow is putting it mildly."

Baylee was a good six inches taller than Chabal with legs that reached forever, and dark features with straight black hair. "Maybe we should introduce him to Crystal," she said. "We got a right-crusty lady as our administrative assistant."

The waiter brought over cocktails for Clay and Baylee. He then took their food order. Langdon went with a fried clam plate, Chabal the salmon, Clay simply a burger, and Baylee ordered the grilled seafood platter.

"What's that say on your coaster?" Langdon asked Baylee.

"Ooh, a clue," Chabal said.

Baylee picked up the coaster. "The weapon of choice shares a title with Lily Robinson." She looked up at the others and shrugged. "What's that supposed to mean?"

"Lily Robinson is the protagonist in the *Queen of All Poisons*, the first mystery in the series by BJ Magnani," Chabal said.

"Sounds like the weapon of choice will be poison," Clay said.

"Aconitine, to be exact," Baylee said, reading from her phone. "Which is considered the Queen of All Poisons. Also sometimes called Monkshood."

"I don't know about the rest of you," Langdon said. "But I'm not sure about my dinner order."

The four of them looked at each other for a long moment and then laughed.

"Would you call poison a weapon?" Baylee asked.

"Sure," Chabal said. "Professor Plum did it in the library with a vial of poison."

"Speaking of royalty," Langdon said. "Is that the queen of our festivities this evening?"

Down the center of the deck was a rectangular table with three people on either side and two on the ends. The woman in question had short-dark hair carefully constructed in organized disarray. She had a wide smile on her face that lit up her blue eyes like Christmas lights.

"That would indeed be Alyssa Maxwell," Baylee said. "And if there's a queen of Port Essex, I suppose it'd be her, and that'd be her court. Her husband, Jeffrey, is across from her with his back to us. He's an artist. To her right in order is the actor Vaughn Keller, then the wife of the town manager, Kelsie Hall, and on the end, Scott Martinson, who is the husband of the Major. Don't know what he does?" She looked at Clay.

"Think he has a lawn care in the summer and plowing in the winter business," he said.

"That sounds right," Baylee said. "Down the left from Alyssa is Major Wyetta Harlow, town manager Cameron Hall, and the artist Kiara Okaro."

"And you two weren't invited to sit with that particular coterie?" Chabal asked with a straight face.

"Only when they have need of the royal jesters," Clay said.

"Ha," Langdon said. "Looks like Vaughn is seated in the favored position, just to the right of the Queen."

"I think they were both in the same foster home when they were teenagers," Clay said. He, himself, had been orphaned at age eight, but at least he'd had his Grandpops to raise him and didn't get flushed into the system.

"What brings you two up from Brunswick?" Baylee asked.

"We got an invitation from the Queen's husband," Langdon said. "He came into the bookshop with a personal invite. Said he thought it'd be fun to have PIs at this soiree."

"Ah, that would explain our invite," Clay said drily. "Here I thought we were moving up in the world but I'm betting everybody here is from out to the Point."

Baylee pointed out over the harbor to an extension of land. "That's the Point. My house could fit in most of their living rooms."

"I can't breathe!" The high-pitched voice pierced shrilly through the open air in ragged gasps. Alyssa Maxwell stood at the head of the table of honor with her hands around her own neck, as if choking herself. "I can't feel my tongue." And indeed, the words came tumbling out thick and slurred. She was gasping for air, a fish out of water, and everybody froze, watching her.

"It's quite possible that this is part of the show," Clay said quietly. "AM is known for her outgoing personality and theatrics."

Major Harlow was the first to stand and take the woman's elbow.

Vomit spewed forth from Alyssa's mouth and dribbled down her chin, and then again—gagging noises interspersed with gasps of air as she tried to breathe and throw up at the same time.

Langdon noticed Vaughn Keller lounging lazily in his chair, making no effort to help. He was an actor, and maybe he was in on it, or could tell when somebody else was feigning reality.

"Help me. Please. Help me."

Kelsie Hall was the second to reach Alyssa, and her and the Major tried to guide the woman back into her chair, but her legs buckled, and she slid from their grasp to the wooden deck.

"I don't think she's acting," Baylee said.

"This is not part of the show," a man with a Jason mask shouted, pulling it free from his face.

"Call an ambulance," somebody yelled, and a hundred hands reached for cell phones.

"Let me through, I'm a doctor." A portly man with a bushy white mustache fought his way forward.

Half an hour later, Langdon, Chabal, Clay, and Baylee were again sitting together, but now they were on the second floor, one down from the top. They were in a room used for banquets and other functions. The paramedics had arrived and called in LifeFlight. Poison was suspected, whether by mistake or intent, it was not yet known. Clay had spoken in private with one of the first responders and told the man of the clue they'd received in regard to the poison.

The police were treating this like attempted murder. The staties were on their way from Augusta and they meant to interview everybody who'd been present. It had the making of a long night.

"What do you all say to us doing a little bit of investigating?" Clay asked. "As that is what we do. Can't hurt to ask some questions while we wait for the state police to show up."

"Absolutely," Langdon said. "I'm in."

"Ditto," Baylee said.

"Sounds better than sitting here on our asses trying not to think about eating," Chabal said. "Where should we start?"

"Let's break up," Baylee said. "Me and Clay, and you two. We'll cover more distance that way."

"Perfect," Langdon said. "How about we speak with Jeffrey Maxwell, Vaughn Keller, and that artist, Kiara?"

"Kiara Okaro," Baylee said.

"And you two can check in with the married couples as they seem to be sticking together," Langdon finished.

They all looked across the crowded room where Cameron Hall sat huddled with his wife Kelsie, and Scott Martinson stood in a corner with his wife Major Wyetta Harlow. Jeffrey Maxwell sat in a chair, alone, people giving him space like he was a leper. Vaughn Keller and Kiara Okaro were huddled together whispering. They were like islands in a storm as approximately one hundred people swirled around them.

* * *

Langdon and Chabal thought it best to start with the man himself, Jeffrey Maxwell. He was about forty, had mournful eyes, and shoulder-length brown hair tied into a ponytail by a leather hair tie.

"Hello, Mr. Maxwell. Is there anything we can do for you?" Chabal asked, sitting down next to him while Langdon sat across. People trusted Chabal. Langdon could be intimidating until people got to know him. It was their usual MO to let her break the ice.

"Who are you?"

"We're the PIs you invited from down Brunswick. I doubt that you thought you'd actually need our services, but here we are."

"Of course. You are Chabal and the tall chap with you is Langdon, as he so kindly informed me when I stopped by your shop. Just Langdon. Sort of like Cher, I suppose." He shook his head tiredly. "Please, call me Jeffrey. Just Jeffrey." He smiled wanly.

"I'm surprised you didn't go with your wife on... the helicopter," Chabal said.

"They actually had a passenger on board already and swooped in and picked up Al on the way to the hospital. No room left for me."

Langdon noted his pet nickname for his wife. "Portland?" he asked.

"Yes. The Chief asked me to stay and answer the questions from the state police and then he'd have a patrolman drive me down."

"Did anybody say what was wrong with your wife?" Chabal asked.

"One of the chaps, I suppose he was a paramedic, said something about Monkshood, some sort of poison. Thought maybe it was in the tea. I think Al might've had three cups of the stuff. Gave up drinking alcohol and has been swilling tea like there was no tomorrow." Jeffrey's ghostly face colored as he seemingly realized that there might not be a tomorrow for his wife.

"Can you think of anybody who had ill will for your wife, Jeffrey?" Langdon said gently. "Enough so to poison her?"

"No, of course not." Jeffrey rubbed his eyes tiredly. "I mean, Cameron has always been jealous of Al, him being the town manager, and everybody knowing it was really Al who held the reins of power. But poison her? No, I can't imagine."

"Let us know if we can do anything," Chabal said. "And if you think of anything else, please let us know. We're here to help. You invited us, after all."

* * *

Baylee and Clay decided to start with Major Wyetta Harlow and her husband, Scott.

"Hi, Wyetta," Clay said. They'd been in the same class in school, and while not quite friends, had shared many of the same classes.

"Hello, Clay." She stood with the ramrod posture of a soldier. Last year, for some unknown reason, a few years short of her twenty-year pension, she'd retired and returned to Port Essex. "I've been meaning to stop by and say hi."

"This is my partner, Baylee Baker."

"I know you," Scott said. "You're that lady who shot her husband." He was a lean and savage looking man with intense eyes.

"Scott," Wyetta said sharply.

Baylee stared at the man. He wasn't the first, nor would he be the last person, who blurted this out. "And you're the yard boy for people out on the Point," Baylee said.

"What brought you back to Port Essex?" Clay asked before things escalated.

"Alyssa asked me to head up her charity," Wyetta said. "It seemed like a good opportunity at the time."

But something had gone sour, Clay thought, reading between the lines. Her voice had a thinness to it that bespoke conflict. "She's certainly a busy woman," he said. "How would you describe her relationship with Jeffrey?"

"I'd say not good," Wyetta said coldly. "But Jeffrey seems a nice enough sort, even if a bit misguided. I think he might have something going on with that artist, Kiara Okaro. Wouldn't blame him a bit."

"What makes you think that?" Baylee asked.

Wyetta looked around the room and leaned forward. "I overheard Alyssa on the phone with her lawyer. She was telling him to cut her cheating husband out of the goddamn will. Mentioned Kiara by name."

"Who do you suppose would benefit if that happened?" Clay asked.

"I don't know," Wyetta said. "I don't think Alyssa has any family. She may just be the spawn of Satan, for all I know."

Spawn of Satan, Clay thought? That was pretty harsh. "How'd you first meet Alyssa?"

"Alyssa is attracted to success. My promotion to major a few years back cemented our friendship," Wyetta said. "But it could've been she was just interested in my husband."

"She has several properties in town, and I take care of the landscaping," Scott said hurriedly.

"Yes, you do," Wyetta said and walked off.

Scott went to follow her, then shrugged his shoulders resignedly, and turned back to Clay and Baylee. "Sorry about that," he said.

"Are we to take it that there is, uh, some sort of relationship between you and Alyssa," Baylee asked bluntly.

"It's not what you think," Scott said.

"You're not having sex with your employer?" Baylee asked. "And cheating on your wife?"

Scott took a deep breath. "She forced me."

Baylee gave him a 'don't fuck with me' stare.

"I'm screwing her for Wyetta, okay?" Scott said.

Baylee, again, gave him a 'don't fuck with me' stare.

"Look, this isn't for public consumption, but Wyetta was forced out of the military. No need to go into why, but she was offered the choice of retiring or being court-martialed." Scott sighed and looked across the room to where his wife was standing by the door as if trying to escape. "Alyssa must've found out about her…indiscretion. One day, when I was trimming her bushes, she invited me into the house for a glass of cold water. Then she tried to seduce me. I turned her down and she threatened to reveal Wyetta's secret."

"So, you had sex with her," Clay said. "To retain your wife's reputation."

"Every Wednesday."

"And Wyetta found out about it?"

"I told her," Scott said defiantly. "She doesn't like it, but she also doesn't want the world to find out what she did."

"Well, you already know what I'd do to you," Baylee said and walked off.

* * *

"Do you mind if we sit here?" Chabal asked, indicating the two chairs across the table from Vaughn Keller and Kiara Okaro.

Vaughn flicked his hand as if to say, 'go ahead'.

"That would be terrific," Kiara said. "Isn't it just the most horrible thing that has happened. I mean, one moment Alyssa was just fine and the next she's clutching her throat and laboring to breathe. And people are saying it might be poison? Who could do such a thing? I'm sorry, my name is Kiara, and this is Vaughn."

"I imagine they know who I am, my dear Kiara," Vaughn said.

Vaughn was a stunningly handsome man with a chiseled chin and smoky eyes that had made plenty of female hearts flutter in their time, but still, what an ass, Chabal thought. Kiara was a striking Black woman, dressed in a conservative gray pantsuit. Chabal had recently seen an exhibit of her art at a local gallery. It was entitled simply 'Lovers'. The entire collection had been abstract nudes of people having sex.

"My name is Langdon, and this is my wife, Chabal."

The introduction jolted Chabal back to the now. "They said it might've been something in her tea," she said.

"Oh, my." Kiara put her hand over her mouth. "That must be it. She was the only one drinking tea. Everybody else had some sort of alcoholic beverage, I believe."

"That seems to suggest that whoever made the tea poisoned her," Vaughn said.

"Or the wait staff could easily have mixed it in," Langdon said.

"That's indeed possible." Vaughn got a wicked glint to his smoky eyes. "I did see Jeffrey get her a cup of the stuff. The pot was on a hot plate atop the bar. Set up special for her, the Queen of Port Essex."

"Jeffy would never do such a thing, you know that," Kiara said. "He's too sweet and gentle of a man."

"For the proper motivation, men will do almost anything, my dear Kiara." Vaughn put his hand on her cheek. "Perhaps Jeffrey *really* is in love with you."

"Oh, we've just been having a bit of fun, nothing more." Kiara seemed unapologetic at sharing her affair with two complete strangers.

"You've been sleeping with Jeffrey Maxwell?" Chabal asked.

"Don't be so shocked, my dear, it's just sex. Just a spot of fun."

"I suppose anybody could've poisoned the tea if it was just sitting out on the bar," Langdon said.

"Come to think of it, you went up to the bar several times, didn't you?" Kiara said to Vaughn. "And you certainly have reason to dislike Alyssa."

"That waiter was abysmally slow in delivering drinks," Vaughn said. "Almost like he was doing it on purpose."

"What reasons do you have to dislike Alyssa?" Chabal asked.

"Nothing, really," Vaughn said.

"Nonsense, Vaughn," Kiara said. "She knows your big secret and threatened to out you if you didn't serve on her charity board and do promotional events for her."

Chabal thought that Kiara might be quite drunk. Her words didn't slur, but nonetheless, she seemed to have had a few too many. "To out you?" she asked.

Vaughn glared at Kiara. "My good friend knows not what she speaks of."

"Pish-posh, Vaughn. They're not the media. You're not the media, are you?" Kiara asked.

"Please stop talking, Kiara."

"Oh, so you can point out that me and Jeffrey have been doing the naughty, but I can't say that Alyssa was blackmailing you to keep the secret that you're gay?"

Vaughn stood up and walked off.

* * *

"It must be wonderful to have Alyssa in your corner," Baylee said to Cameron Hall. The man was frail and wore thin-wire spectacles. He had on a white-pressed shirt and a red bow tie.

"Ah, yes, very much so," Cameron said.

Kelsie Hall snorted. "She's a royal bitch and if she dies, ain't nobody gonna miss her."

"Don't say such things, honey," Cameron said. "Nobody deserves that said about them."

"Who would care?" Kelsie was as wide as her husband was thin, and where his cheeks were pale, hers were florid. "Jeffrey would leave her in a heartbeat if she didn't control the purse strings."

"Does Jeffrey have no money of his own?" Clay asked.

Kelsie snorted again. "Not one red cent."

"And why do you think he'd leave his wife?" Chabal asked.

"A, because she's a bitch. B, probably to run off with that Black florist lady he's always following around like a lost puppy dog, and C, because she's a bitch."

A lot of dog references, Baylee thought, hiding her smile. "You mean Kiara Okaro? Isn't she an artist, not a florist?"

"She's both, I guess," Kelsie said. "She creates artistic floral displays as well as painting those offensive perversions of hers. The arrangements tonight were done by her."

"Mind me asking why you dislike Alyssa so much?" Baylee said. "I've lived in town a long time and always thought she was, well, revered."

"She's all about power. She uses sex and fear to create power for herself, and the hell with everybody else. She pushes and pushes until something bends a bit, and then she pushes harder."

"Do you have a personal history with that?" Clay asked.

"She's been twisting Cam up and around her finger ever since he got into office. Convinced him to do a few things early on that were unethical and perhaps bordered on illegal, and she threatened to expose him if he didn't do her bidding. Good riddance to bad rubbish, I say."

"What sort of…improprieties are we speaking of?" Baylee asked.

Kelsie suddenly grew still. "You two are those private investigators from just next door, aren't you? Wolfe & Baker. I thought I recognized you. I got nothing to say about any of that."

* * *

Baylee and Clay rejoined Chabal and Langdon at an empty corner table just as the state police arrived and pulled the first witness to interrogate, the waiter who'd been servicing Alyssa Maxwell's table of honor.

"What'd you find out?" Langdon asked.

"Sounds like Alyssa may well have been the most hated person in town," Baylee said.

"Never would've guessed. She had her nose in everything and always had an entourage wherever she went," Clay said. "She seemed immensely popular, at least from afar."

"That's pretty much what we got," Chabal said. "Kiara admitted to sleeping with Jeffrey and it turns out Vaughn is actually gay and being bullied by Alyssa to do promotions for her or she'll out him."

"Vaughn Keller is gay?" Baylee said. "I know at least three women in town who claim to have slept with him."

"Maybe bi," Langdon said.

"Well, Kelsie Hall hates Alyssa with a passion because she's been pressuring her husband to bend the rules for her or she'll turn him in for illegal activities she convinced him to do," Clay said.

"Basically, blackmailing him," Baylee said. "What's more, Alyssa is forcing Scott Martinson to have sex with her, or she'll reveal something that Wyetta did that forced her out of the military. Wouldn't say what that was."

"The woman is a monster," Chabal said.

"But she's not the only monster here tonight," Clay said. "And I think I have an inkling who that other ogre is."

"You want to share?" Baylee asked.

"Give me a few minutes," Clay said. He was pecking text messages to his Grandpops, Cloutier, his newspaper editor friend, and Murphy, the old Irish barfly.

"No." The shriek pierced the somber room right to the core. Jeffrey stood facing two police officers. "No. No. No. NO."

"That's the Chief of police," Clay said. "C'mon."

The four of them walked their way over closer where they could hear. "She can't be dead," Jeffrey was yelling. "It was just supposed to make her vomit. She had me add it to her tea and make sure nobody else touched it. It was all for the show. Figured if she puked everywhere, people would believe she'd actually been poisoned. It wasn't real. She can't be dead. Why are you saying this?"

* * *

Langdon, Chabal, Clay, and Baylee now sat down on the first floor of the building, which was the main restaurant of the Pelican, along with the seven guests of honor who'd been at the head table with Alyssa Maxwell for her last supper. Clay had managed to gather the ear of

Chief Roberts, who was currently at the table, along with Jackson Brooks, the head of the Major Crime Unit of the state police.

"I don't know what happened." Jeffrey sat with his forehead resting on the table as he spoke. "It wasn't supposed to kill her. It was just Ipecac."

"Can I ask you a question?" Clay said. "Not to be indelicate, but this isn't a time to follow polite protocol. "Did Alyssa cut you out of her will recently? Leaving you nothing?"

Jeffrey picked his head up. "Yes."

"Why?" Clay asked.

"She found out I was having an affair with Kiara," Jeffrey said. "But I didn't care. We were going to run away together and be happy. Make art and love and not worry about money."

"Did this make you angry enough to kill your wife?" Chief Roberts asked.

"No. God no. I told you, I was happy to be out of her clutches. The woman is a dragon," Jeffrey said.

Clay looked at the text from his Grandpops, former lawyer, who'd proven he still had few strings to pull. Vaughn Keller. Why? "Do you know who the recipient of Alyssa's sizeable estate will be?" Clay asked.

Jeffrey shook his head. "No. No idea. And I don't care."

"Did you know that Alyssa and Vaughn were in the same foster home some twenty-five years ago?" Clay asked. "Foster siblings, if you will."

"Sure, I guess I knew that," Jeffrey said.

"What's that have to do with anything?" Vaughn asked.

"I'm betting that you're the person who'll benefit most from Alyssa's updated will," Clay said.

"So what if I am? What does that prove?" Vaughn said angrily.

Clay looked at the text message from Cloutier. Not in a movie for three years. Rumors of gambling debt. Not queer as far as I know. "How's your money situation?" he asked Vaughn.

"None of your damn business," Vaughn said.

"I have it on good authority that you gambled it all away and haven't worked in years," Clay said.

"That's not true," Vaughn said weakly.

Clay looked at the text message from Murphy, barfly, and lead town gossip. Vaughn K. and Kiara O. often together. Very cozy. "Are you and Kiara a couple?" he asked.

"No, she's…" Vaughn looked around the room wildly. "She's sleeping with Jeffrey." He pointed at the despondent Mr. Maxwell.

"But the two of you are actually in cahoots, aren't you Vaughn?" Clay asked. "She seduced the lonely man with the horrible wife, you slipped that information to Alyssa, she reacted as you knew she would, and wrote Jeffrey out of the will, leaving you as the sole beneficiary."

"That's preposterous," Vaughn said weakly.

"I first became suspicious when I noticed that you seemed the only one not surprised at the table when Alyssa started choking, gagging, and vomiting. That would've been a time to put some of your acting skills to work," Clay said.

"I thought it was part of the show." Vaughn's eyes were darting around the room like a trapped animal.

"And then I got to wondering why Jeffrey invited two sets of PIs if he really intended on killing his wife." Clay stood up and began a slow walk around the tables. "The two of you appeared pretty cozy earlier. I was momentarily thrown off by Kiara claiming that you were being blackmailed for being gay. But then Baylee commented on your well-known womanizing in town, and I realized that it was just a diversion to throw us off the scent. That you and Kiara are actually lovers and devised this plan together."

"That's a lie," Kiara said.

"Perhaps you should've kept a lower profile around town," Clay said.

"What the hell is going on?" Jeffrey asked.

"Kiara used you, Jeffrey," Clay said. "She found out that the only person in Alyssa's will other than you was Vaughn. So, she started an affair with you, the word was leaked to your wife, and presto, you were erased from the document and Vaughn became the sole beneficiary.

And once Kiara switched the Monkshood with your Ipecac, *voila*, you were not only out of the money, but you were also the prime suspect in her murder."

"You can't prove anything," Vaughn said.

"I believe the autopsy report will show that Alyssa Maxwell was poisoned with aconitine, known as Monkshood." Clay stopped behind Kiara so that he was looking at Chief Roberts. "And I'm fairly certain that the police will find this perennial growing in the greenhouse of the part-time florist, Kiara Okaro."

* * *

"Not bad, Mr. Wolfe," Chabal said as they walked from the police station some hours later.

Vaughn and Kiara had broken down and confessed to the entire plot. She had seduced Jeffrey to get him written out of the will, and then they plotted the murder, and when the opportunity of the mystery dinner theater escape room came up, it'd been too easy to pass up.

"You two staying around another day?" Baylee asked.

"Chief Roberts wants to talk to us tomorrow, so yeah, I guess so," Langdon said.

"How about we do dinner tomorrow night?" Clay asked.

"Food and good brown liquor to keep the poison at bay," Langdon said. "Sure."

Scott Lipanovich

Moonlight

The elevator door rattled open. State senator Allan Watkins stepped into the underground parking garage of the California capitol. He squinted against sudden darkness. His briefcase seemed to pull him downward as he lurched forward. Seventy years old, stout, Watkins had been on his feet twelve hours, cajoling, flattering, at times ambiguously threatening colleagues in both parties. The summer session was finally over. The last few days were always a scramble.

Parked at the curb nearest the elevator, Marci Watkins waited in their already-packed maroon Buick Regal. She had napped in the afternoon in preparation for the drive that night.

Watkins opened the passenger door, slid in. He turned, set his beige leather briefcase on the back seat, slipped off his blue tie and tossed it on top. "Sorry you had to wait so damn long. Once the cameras arrive, you can't get some of these guys to shut their traps."

Marci noted an absence of liquor on his breath. That told her the senate had met straight through without breaking for dinner; it was almost eight o'clock. She said, "You must be starving. Want to swing by somewhere for takeout?"

"What I want, is to get the hell out of this town."

There was no use in arguing. She exited the garage, made a few turns, and merged onto the freeway.

Watkins fidgeted. "We had the annual water subsidy fight." He gestured as though speaking to a crowd. "I asked Jerry Maher, right on the floor, how many of his brother's competitors in the almond business would go under if my amendment didn't pass. I requested an estimate." Watkins chortled. "You should have seen his face. I thought he was going to have a coronary."

Marci knew the only way to get him to settle down was to change the subject. She said, "It's nice driving at night when the moon's out. Even with a half moon, you see so much."

Watkins rambled on about legislative battles, pledges of support for November, a score he wanted to settle with a new member from Riverside. Marci grew tired of nodding. She reached down next to her seat for a Thermos of gin and tonic, and handed it to her husband.

"I forgot all about this. It should still be cold."

Watkins patted Marci's leg. He'd received the message: no more shop talk. He sipped gin. He began to feel rosy, then drowsy. By the time they passed Clearlake and headed through a short valley, into forest and toward the coast, he had finished the Thermos and was sleeping.

Their destination was a cabin five miles north of Sunset, a small town on the cool north coast. For two decades, the senator and Marci had made the cabin their retreat during holiday breaks. He was asleep when Marci parked the car, clicked off the headlights.

"Wake up. We're here."

Marci put their clothes away. Watkins went out the back door to a woodpile. Twice he filled his arms and brought split Douglas fir inside. Marci, tired from the drive, had gone to bed when Watkins finally sat across from a popping fire and cracked the seal on a pint of Korbel brandy. He couldn't sit still. He paced the living room. His mind, refreshed after three hours' sleep, kicked into high gear. Watkins went to his briefcase. He wanted to review the frenetic voting on more than three hundred bills from the previous twenty-four hours.

He decided to go to a restaurant/bar called The Cove. He'd work the old-fashioned way, pen on paper. He left a note on the kitchen table; Watkins had done this several times over the years. At The Cove he settled into a spot with a wall lamp beside it. He nursed two gin and tonics, keeping his mind on work. A few minutes prior to closing time, Senator Watkins left a twenty-dollar tip and walked into the purple night.

Driving, he took peeks at the half moon that showered the ocean with milky light. The way that light combined with flashes of pure white when waves hit the beach was hypnotic. He grabbed the brandy from the passenger seat, uncapped it, and sipped whenever the road straightened. For the first time in weeks, his stomach let go.

A figure walked along the shoulder of the road with a thumb out. The Buick's headlights splashed over a woman walking at a fast pace. She was wearing only a cocktail dress. As the headlights came nearer, she spun around and, walking backwards, stuck out her right thumb. Her hair was long and copper-colored. She wore tennis shoes.

Watkins pulled over, hit the button to lower the passenger window. The woman, who he gauged to be in her latter twenties, leaned into the opening. Her arms were bare. A sparkly purse, dangling on string, hung from her left shoulder.

Watkins said, "Are you okay? Where you headed?"

She grabbed a mop of long hair and flung it over a shoulder. "I'm going to see a man about a horse."

Watkins' head snapped back—he burst into laughter. "I haven't heard that one in years. Come in. It's cold out there."

The young woman shut the door behind her. Even while shivering, she offered a brilliant smile. Watkins got the window closed, turned up the heater.

"You sure you're all right?"

"I got a flat down by Schooner Gulch. No spare and no cell reception. It's closer to walk to where I'm going than to go back to town."

"You're headed for?"

"Garston Ranch Road. It's about a mile."

Watkins said, "I've passed it a hundred times," and pulled onto the highway. He offered the young woman the bottle. "This might help you warm up."

She surprised him by accepting and taking a full-throated slug.

She handed the bottle back. Watkins took a slug.

He said, "None of my business, but you're not exactly dressed for the coast at two in the morning."

She raked a hand through her hair. Her smile really was tremendous, as were her lithe arms, and legs encased in black stockings under the light-colored cocktail dress.

"I got a band. We had a gig down in Bodega Bay. I sure wasn't expecting to get stuck."

Watkins nodded, handed her the uncapped bottle. She took a smaller hit this round, and extended it back. Before taking the bottle, Watkins brushed a hand across a dark stocking.

She said, "Easy, mister."

His face crunched closed. Watkins felt his age in the wrinkles drawing together on his forehead. He said, "I've been wound up for a month. I'm not thinking straight."

The road curved outward, toward the moon and sea. Watkins looked at both. The road curved back. He took another peek at the young woman's legs.

She screamed, "Stop! God stop!"

Watkins saw a man hunched over, stumbling in the middle of his lane. He hit the brakes. Tires skidded over asphalt. Then: *thup*.

Impact hurled the body a dozen feet.

Watkins slammed the Buick into park. "Jesus H. Christ," he bellowed. Watkins climbed out. He saw the pint of brandy in his hand, crossed the highway and threw it toward the ocean as hard as he could. He looked for the young woman but didn't see her. He turned back to the body. He walked toward it. His legs felt like they were being filled with wet cement. He oozed onto the pavement.

Where was she? The senator heard crying sounds moving up the hillside on the inland side of the highway. He looked in that direction, but didn't see anything. Still on the ground, Watkins pulled out his phone and tapped 9-1-1.

No reception, as the young woman had said. The man's body didn't move. It had a disturbing twist at its middle. Everything in front of Watkins held the waxy half-light of a dream. Watkins made it back to the car. He left the engine running, flicked on the emergency flashers. From the trunk he took two flares and fired them up about fifty feet before the car, fifty feet beyond the body. He sat in the car for a few minutes, trying, and failing, to think straight. Over and over he saw the man stumble, then saw him fly. Watkins threw open the door, went to the back bumper and vomited onto asphalt.

Headlights shot around the curve behind him. They lighted the inside of the senator's Buick and the roadway; the body was hidden from view by his car. At reaching the flare, a pickup truck slowed. It swerved around the flare. Watkins waved down the driver. He'd ask for help in contacting the police. The young man driving kept his gaze straight ahead. He hit the gas and the pickup groaned.

Watkins blew on his hands and rubbed them together. Much calmer than before, it hit Watkins that he was not of sound mind. A function of shock, calmness did not bring clarity to his thoughts. Everything seemed mushed together. Waves carried hushing sounds over boulders and up a hundred feet to the highway. Watkins tried his cell again. Another set of headlights, this time coming toward him, spread over the road. As the vehicle reached the blue glow of the flare, a bank of red lights came alive. The police car pulled into Watkins' lane. It stopped twenty feet before reaching the body. A cannon of light burst from near the driver's side door and hit the senator like a blow.

The door opened. Out stepped a deputy. Watkins only saw an outline of him because of the blasting light.

"Officer," he said, "I'm glad you're here." His voice sounded dry, raspy.

The deputy unsnapped his holster. Right hand hovering above it, he said, "Don't you move a muscle."

"Officer, this is all a big mistake. I can explain."

The deputy walked forward. His voice grew louder. "Show me your hands."

Watkins flashed his palms. "There's no need for this, son. I'm Senator Allan Watkins, from Cottonwood."

The deputy said, "Anybody else involved?"

"No. But there…" How could he explain picking her up? He sure as hell couldn't volunteer that he'd shared a bottle with her while driving. And she'd run away. Where? Why? He paced back and forth in front of his car. The deputy knelt beside the body. He felt for a pulse. Watkins continued to pace.

The deputy said, "Listen, buddy, since you can't follow directions, I'm locking you in the back seat."

Watkins said, "This isn't what it looks like."

Rather than respond, the deputy took Senator Watkins by the elbow and marched him to the patrol car. "Give me your wallet." Watkins did so. "How much have you had to drink?"

Watkins said, "I'm sure I'll pass a blood test."

The deputy got a little rough, pushing the senator's head down when guiding him onto the back seat. He contacted the dispatcher and gave his location. He said there was a fatality, and told the dispatcher to send the county ambulance and to call the sheriff. Then he read Senator Watkins his rights. Looking through a grid of steel mesh, Watkins said *yes* a few times.

The deputy took a couple of deep breaths. His head dropped into his hands. "You son of a bitch. You killed Joe Garston. We grew up together."

"Son, the man was stumbling across the road."

"Tell your story to the sheriff."

"Son, if you'll just—"

"Shut up! Just sit there, and shut up, until the sheriff arrives."

"I'm telling you, I came around the corner, he was right *there*. Like it was a set up or something."

The deputy said, "Fuck you," and got out of the police car. He slipped his flashlight from his belt and began searching the vicinity of the Buick.

Watkins wondered how far he'd thrown the brandy bottle. He made a mental list of who to call. What in the hell was he going to tell Marci? The young woman could corroborate that the guy was in the road. But all she'd have to do is mention his hand on her leg shortly before hitting the man, and his career was over. Better to take the chance she just disappears. She had to be running away from something. Watkins closed his eyes and massaged both cheeks.

"Jesus Christ," he said aloud. "I killed a man."

The deputy returned. He opened a door to the back of the cruiser. He brandished a shiny purse. "Do you happen to know who this belongs to?"

Watkins said, "I have to talk to my lawyer."

Saralyn Richard

Mother's Day

The first day Sally Pearce returned to school after burying her mother, the faculty surprised her with a pancake breakfast in the cafeteria. Sally's administrative assistant, Pat, whispered in her ear. "The whole staff pitched in on this. Everyone at Lincoln High loves you."

Tears welled in Sally's eyes and spilled onto her cheeks. Even kindness caused her wounds to sting. It had been ten days, but grief over her mother's sudden death still dominated Sally's life. She'd insisted on coming back to school, despite Dr. Blank's encouraging her to wait a little longer. *There's no substitute for a good principal.*

Remaining at the doorway to the cafeteria, where she inhaled the aromas of coffee, maple syrup, and bacon, she watched the bustling scene—over two hundred faculty and staff members filling their trays with food and sitting down to eat—Sally crumbled inside. Such a normal event, people eating and chattering, and her heart and brain and belly felt anything but normal. She hoped no one would mention the word, "Mother."

Lincoln High School had thrived during this school year, Sally's first whole year as principal. The new student-centered programs that teams of eager professionals had implemented had gone a long way toward burying the unrest of the previous year. *Burying. Why can't I free my mind from death?*

Melody Singer, the new assistant principal for scheduling came up from behind and hooked her arm through Sally's. "Come on, Captain. It's a party, and you'll hurt a lot of feelings if you don't participate.

You'd better hurry, too. The students will be in the building in forty-five minutes."

Sally forced a smile and took a deep breath. "Okay, let's go." Still attached to Melody, she strolled into the seating area where someone had decorated tables with paper flowers and placemats in pastel colors. A microphone was set up at the front of the tables. Sally would be expected to speak, and what could she say that wouldn't cause her to drown in tears?

Baby steps. All you have to do is thank everyone. Say how good it is to be back. End with something inspiring, like, "Go, Warriors."

Sally patted Melody's hand and disengaged from her elbow. "Let's meet later. We have a lot to catch up on. I don't see Eric. I wonder where he is."

"I think he's taking care of a discipline referral. He told me to tell you he'd stop by if he finishes before homeroom. You know, he always puts AP duties before eating."

"I'm glad to have two dedicated and hard-working assistant principals, but sometimes we all need to come out of our offices and get to know our staff better. The school is only as congenial as its least congenial leader. I learned that from R.J. Stoker."

Sally worked her way around the tables, shaking hands with teachers, support personnel, administrative assistants, and maintenance workers. Whenever anyone mentioned the words "sympathy" or "condolences," she nodded and inched away. Before long, she found her way to the serving line and filled a plate with pancakes, sausage, and fresh fruit. She took a second plate for Eric and covered it with napkins. She'd stop by his office on her way back.

After scarfing down her food and giving a brief speech of gratitude, Sally was ready to get on with the day. There were people who needed her attention and assistance, and they would be the best distraction of all. The homeroom bell pealed through the intercom, triggering an automatic response. She strode out of the cafeteria and across the hall into Eric's office.

As she entered, a hard-faced woman and an obviously-pregnant girl were leaving. "We aren't going to take this lying down," the woman shouted over her shoulder at Eric. "We're going to the principal's office."

Sally paused to search the face of the disgruntled woman. "I'm the principal," she said, extending her hand.

The woman peered into Sally's eyes, as if she couldn't believe this fortyish woman could be in charge of all of Lincoln High School. She shook Sally's hand and poked her daughter. "This here's your principal? Shake her hand, Latrice."

Sally smiled at Latrice, imagining what predicament she must have gotten herself into, pregnancy and otherwise. "Why don't the two of you go to the main office and tell my assistant, Pat, that I told you to wait there? I'll be with you as soon as I meet with Mr. Simpson."

As she watched the two women lumber past the assistant's desk and into the hallway, Sally reflected on how different they were from her. She was motherless and childless. No matter how troubled Latrice was, she had a mother to champion for her, and Latrice's mother had a daughter to care for.

Sally's husband, Ron, and her puppy, Archie, gave her plenty of affection and companionship, but when she observed families at school or among her friends, she realized the enormity of what she was missing. She'd talked to Ron about it late one night, after her mother died, and he'd proposed adoption, as he had many times before, but there were compelling reasons not to, the demands of her job being one. She was doing what she loved, what she was good at—looking out for other people's children.

"What's going on with Latrice?"

Eric tapped the paperwork on his desk. "Five-day suspension for fighting."

"In her condition?"

"Yeah. The other party is the baby-daddy's other girlfriend."

"Who started it?"

"Witnesses say Latrice, but I really wish we could do something about these guys. We've got more than our share of students who take no responsibility for birth control or for the hearts they're breaking, the lives they're ruining. I don't need to tell you."

Sally swallowed. *Why did babies come so easily to people who hadn't yearned for them, weren't prepared for them?* "I'll support the suspension, but we need to come up with a way to teach our kids better ways."

"Agree. By the way, what's that in your hands?"

"Oh, I almost forgot. I brought you breakfast. Probably already cold, but still edible." She set the plate and utensils on the desk and turned to leave.

"Thanks, Captain," Eric said behind her. "And I'm so sorry about your mother."

Sally waved, but kept walking, not wanting anyone to notice the tears.

Normally, the hallway between Eric's office and hers was brightly lit this time of the morning, courtesy of the east-facing windows. Today the hallway was dim, reflective of Sally's mood. Arriving at the main office, Sally winked at Pat and motioned for Latrice and her mother to enter her personal inner office. They seated themselves in the two conference chairs, and Sally circled around to take her place behind the desk. Latrice's eyes were red and swollen. *Her eyes look the way mine feel. Perhaps her mother's been taking her to task.*

"I understand you've been involved in a fight, Latrice." Sally made eye contact with Latrice and then her mother. "And we have to take fights seriously at Lincoln High School."

Mother and daughter sat, glaring, with their arms crossed over their midriffs.

"Tell me your side of the story, and then we'll see where to go from there." Sally leaned forward, attentive and patient. *Sometimes all a person needs is to be listened to.*

As Latrice told how Sharonda had taunted her in the girls' bathroom in front of a group of onlookers, Latrice's mom uttered expletives under her breath. "So, I had to swing at her," Latrice finished. "I couldn't let her tear me down and get away with it."

Sally nodded. "I understand how frustrated and angry you must have felt, Latrice. Nobody likes being disrespected. But there are much better ways to express your anger without fighting. Especially as we get older, and especially as we take on adult roles." Sally's eyes passed over the bulge in Latrice's lap. "In adult society, fighting is called, 'battery.' That's a crime, and you could be arrested for it. Fighting can cause serious bodily harm, sometimes permanent. Just think how bad you'd feel if Sharonda punched your belly and caused damage to your baby."

"How'm I s'posed to get her to stop if I don't hit her?"

Latrice's mom uttered a monosyllabic grunt. Perhaps she didn't appreciate having another adult lecturing her daughter, or perhaps she wanted to know the answer to the question, herself.

"There are many ways," Sally said, leaning forward and lowering her voice, as if she were about to impart one of life's secrets. "One is to ignore her. You act as if nothing Sharonda says has the slightest bit of importance, as if Sharonda isn't worth listening to." Sally sat back. "If Sharonda sees she can't upset you, she'll stop picking on you and try taunting someone else."

Sally stood and leaned over her desk, making eye contact with Latrice. "The school is dedicated to teaching students better ways to express their emotions. You know fighting carries a consequence of suspension, and I have to uphold that. But there's something even more significant that I want you to learn."

Latrice opened her arms and sat forward, mimicking Sally's posture. "What?"

"You're about to become a mother, and your education is going to be more important than ever. What do you know about our Infant Care Center?"

Latrice shrugged, but her mother leaned forward this time.

Sally explained that the Infant Care Center was a state-licensed childcare facility on campus, established to help teen parents complete their educations and to educate them in the best practices for caring for and raising their children. "In addition to a certified director and full-time employees, the center is staffed by students who have taken required electives in childcare and child development."

"You mean the babies come to school with their mothers and have day care here at the school?" The woman's nametag said LaTonya Martin.

"Yes, Mrs. Martin. If she signs up for this program, Latrice won't have to miss out on her education. And the baby will be cared for by competent people in a clean, stimulating environment."

"How much does this daycare cost?"

"It's free of charge to Latrice, provided that she takes the classes and works in the center for an hour a day." Sally bent to gaze out her office window at the gathering clouds. "Looks like a rainstorm's headed our way, but I'll tell you what. Let's go visit the Infant Care Center. I want you to see how it works. And when you've served your suspension, I hope you'll talk to your counselor about enrolling in the classes for next fall."

As Sally had hoped, Latrice and her mother showed interest in the childcare program. Perhaps it soothed the sting of the suspension, while leaving the lesson of not fighting. As the trio walked across campus to the Infant Care Center, black clouds hovered, and large, splashy raindrops fell about them. The air was thick with humidity, but the temperature was not unpleasant. "I hope this squall blows over while we're visiting the center. I don't remember any rain mentioned in today's forecast."

Sally had called ahead, so the director buzzed her and the two guests in. "Ooh, looks like a storm out there. Come on in and make yourselves at home. I'm Dana Wells, the center director, and I'll take you on a tour. Please feel free to ask questions as we go along."

There was something about the ambience of the center that warmed Sally's heart, and today, that warmth served as an ointment for her grief. Dana began the tour with the infant room. Ten tidy cribs were lined up around the perimeter. Three student workers and a paraprofessional busied themselves, taking care of little ones. One was being diapered. One was being fed a bottle. One was being jiggled on a lap in a rocking chair. Three babies lay on their backs in their cribs, awaiting their turns. A sign over the door read:

>   **Everything Depends on Upbringing.**
>   —Leo Tolstoy, *War and Peace*

As Dana led them into the toddler room, Sally's radio buzzed. A call from 02. That was Eric. "What's your location?" he asked.

"Infant Care Center. What's up?" Sally moved toward the window to get better reception, and she noticed how black the sky had become.

"National Weather Service just issued a tornado warning for our area. I'm about to initiate a drill. You'd better stay over there."

Sally's breakfast transformed into a boulder in her belly, but she had rehearsed tornado drills throughout her career. The important thing was to move everyone into a window-free zone, to sit on the floor, head between knees. She'd never been in one of the outbuildings during a drill before, but the same principles would apply. Mainly, she needed to exert calm, confident leadership.

"Excuse me a moment," she said to the Martins, as she pulled Dana Wells aside to whisper in her ear.

Dana's response to the news was smooth as sea glass. She pointed to the long center hallway that connected the various rooms. "That's our shelter-in-place spot. I'll meet you there." She glided toward the student workers, touching them lightly on the shoulder and mouthing the single word, "Tornado." Within seconds the tornado alarm blasted over the public address system, three long beeps, two short ones.

Some of the babies and toddlers started to shriek, unused to the blaring sounds. Sally glanced at the quote above the door in this room:

>   **Mother is a Verb.**
>   **It's Something You Do. Not Just Who You Are.**
>   —Cheryl Lacey Donovan, *The Ministry of Motherhood*

She knew she couldn't stand by and watch the handful of student workers and adults protecting three or four times the number of children. She had to help.

She enlisted Latrice and her mother to help roll cribs from the infant room into the hallway, patting the babies calmly as they moved into the safe zone. After the babies were secured, she went back to where the toddlers had been gathered into a line. They marched like ducklings on parade, some on unsteady feet, and some carried in the arms of adults.

A third room held older children, three- or four-year-olds, also being shepherded into the hallway. A crack of lightning and a blaring rumble of thunder fairly shook the center's foundation, and a moppet of a girl with brown frizzy hair screamed, "Mommy." The word reverberated in Sally's heart. She too wanted to scream, "Mommy." But Sally's mommy was even more beyond reach than this one.

Sally lowered herself on one knee and stretched her arms out to the frightened little girl. "I'm here for you, sweetheart. I'm here." The warm little bundle against Sally's chest, rubbing a wet face into Sally's blazer, grew quieter, even as the distinctive whistle of the tornado approached, growing louder and louder.

Everyone was in the hallway, crouched on the floor in practiced postures, as the tornado rolled across the Lincoln High School campus, taking its electrifying centripetal force along with it. Sally sat on the floor, cradling the little girl in her arms, rocking her gently to and fro as she waited for the "all clear" signal. To her surprise, despite the tension of the moment, the child had fallen asleep in her arms, her little head turned to face Sally.

Sally thought of a time when her mother had held her and comforted her like this, how nothing could replace the warmth of a mother's embrace, the beating of a mother's heart. In this moment, her mother's quiet strength and love were with her. She was passing it on to this other person, someone who, in the moment, needed it.

After the tornado passed, everyone returned to normal. Sally gently woke her charge, who was sucking on two fingers. "Let's go back to the classroom, little one," Sally said. "You had a nice little nap."

As Sally deposited the child in the care of a student worker, she glanced at the sign over the door in that room.

**BEING A MOTHER IS AN ATTITUDE,
NOT A BIOLOGICAL RELATION.
—Robert Heinlein**

The workers in the center had a lot on their hands, calming everyone down. Now that the tornado had passed, the babies' mothers would be clamoring to be sure no harm had come to their children, and soon it would be time for lunch and naps. Sally couldn't linger. She had 2700 other students and lots of staff to worry about.

She tracked down Latrice and Mrs. Martin. "Thank you for helping us during the emergency. I have to return to the main building now, but Ms. Wells has indicated that she'd appreciate it if you stayed to help with the children a little longer. If you're willing, I'll shave two days of suspension off as time served."

Latrice grinned. "Really? I'd love to do that." She turned to her mother. "What d'ya think, Mama? Totally worth it."

Mrs. Martin nodded. "Funny how things happen. Latrice and I are sold on the Infant Care Center, too. Thanks so much for bringing us here."

Sally knew she was leaving the center in capable hands. She needed to check on the other buildings, other people. It was good to be needed, good to have the opportunity to open her arms and her heart to others. In two days, it would be Mother's Day, the first one without her mother. Now, Sally thought, she'd be able to bear it.

Jay Ruud

Nuns Fret Not

Madame Veronica, the prioress of Wallingwells, had given Tuck this small room off the priory's cloister to conduct interviews with the various nuns in the convent. She had not been enthusiastic about the plan, but at the urging of her chaplain Father Bernard, she had finally relented. She was not happy about having her sisters' daily routines disturbed, and not at all sanguine about their being alone in a room with a man, even if that man was a member of the clergy. But Friar Tuck assured her that the door to the room would remain open at all times, and Father Bernard that it would be good for the priory to have this matter—the bloody head of the gruesomely dismembered tinker Willie turning up at mass—cleared up and put to rest. So Prioress Veronica gave in and told Tuck he could have fifteen minutes with each of the sisters. Any more than that, she reasoned, might be an inducement to sin. Tuck himself considered that truly imaginative sinners could probably manage to sin in less than five, but made no argument.

It became quite clear to Tuck that the murder victim, Willie, was little known among the nuns. Several claimed to have no knowledge of him at all and, cloistered as they were, Tuck was not really surprised, since Willie had no official relationship with the nunnery. The cellarer, Sister Anne, did admit to a passing knowledge of the fellow, since he had repaired two of the priory's large kitchen vessels perhaps a year hence. When asked if she'd seen any conversation between Willie and any of her sisters, Anne scowled at Tuck with her dark eyes and said she had not, though she had left him for a time in the kitchen with the cook, and she did not know whether he'd spoken with anyone there. The infirmarian, the young and lovely Sister Mary Barbara, admitted to running into the tinker on the street some few months past, when she had been out paying a visit to the Widow Day during one of her frequent illnesses, and, batting her long lashes at the friar, confessed that Willie had made a suggestive comment to her at the time.

"Suggestive?" Tuck had questioned, raising his eyebrows.

"'You shouldn't hide that beauty in a nun's habit,' he said, or words to that effect." Sister Mary Barbara pursed her lush lips and pouted. Tuck shrugged. He remembered the Widow Day's wild charge that Willie had been the lover of some of the priory's nuns. Perhaps what Mary Barbara had told him was the kernel of truth behind that outrageous gossip.

Now Tuck began to question the rank-and-file sisters he had watched that morning in the chapel choir. The beak-nosed nun he had noticed among the singers was called Sister Lucy. She was a local woman who had become a nun at seventeen and had never left the immediate environs of the priory since, except to go into the village of Wallingwells on occasion. She could not recall ever having seen Willie the tinker on any of those visits, but she did volunteer that on the Sunday evening following the violation of the chapel by the bloody head, she'd heard violent weeping coming from one of the nearby cells. It might have had nothing to do with the murder, but she had thought she would mention it. The sisters closest to her own cell she named as Sister Anne, Sister Rebecca, and Sister Mary Eusebia.

Sister Anne turned out to be the older woman Friar Tuck had noticed in the chapel choir, the one with the prominent wrinkles about her mouth. On closer observation, Tuck realized that the woman's face was not at all as old as he had at first thought it was. She was perhaps in her mid-thirties, with deep hazel eyes that studied him intelligently and, he thought, coldly. But her face seemed careworn, weathered by what Tuck felt sure had been a hard and bitter life.

"Sister Anne," Tuck began cautiously, holding her eyes in his for as long as he could. "One of your sisters whose cell is close to yours mentioned that she heard loud weeping coming from one of the cells in your wing of the convent on the night after Willie the tinker's head was found aloft in the chapel. As Mother Veronica may have told you, my purpose here is to look into Willie's death, the better to find his killer if we can, and so prevent any others perhaps from being slain." This last excuse had only recently occurred to Tuck—in his conversation with the Widow Day—and it sounded more convincing, he thought, than his less tangible motive of "seeking justice." In any case, it seemed to work better with the nuns.

Not, as it turned out, a motive that worked so well on Sister Anne, who simply laughed ironically. "Seriously, silly friar? You think whoever killed this Willie person—whom I have never met, let me add—is likely to kill anyone else? Don't you think the manner of his death argues something very, very personal, so personal as to come from a very private and passionate hatred of this particular person? It's hard for me to imagine that anyone could hate more than one person so much."

Tuck blinked and turned his eyes away from Sister Anne's steady stare. "Perhaps you're right," he muttered, sounding more conciliatory than convinced. In any case, he wouldn't pursue that line of inquiry with *this* nun, he decided. "Well, what about this crying? Can you tell me anything about that?"

"Well it certainly wasn't *me*," Sister Anne asserted, and, looking at her sober, emotionless face, Tuck could well believe it. "As I said, I didn't know the victim, and I doubt if I'd have felt any sorrow at his demise in any case. Nor did *I* hear any weeping, whatever your other witness says. I have heard fairly loud cries from time to time coming from one of the cells in my neighborhood, though it sounded little like weeping to me. That night may have been one of the times. I must say I've learned to ignore such noises if they don't concern me."

Tuck decided to drop that line of inquiry as well, and was about to dismiss Sister Anne when it occurred to him to ask, "Tell me, sister. How long have you been here at the Benedictine Priory at

Wallingwells? I ask only because it seems most of the sisters I've talked to seem younger than yourself."

"Some of those youngsters have been here longer than I have," the woman answered. "It's only five years since I've taken the veil, and I did so here at this convent, under the current prioress."

"You weren't a teenaged postulant here, then, like some of the others? You'd had a life in the world before coming here, had you?"

"And what has that to do with the murder of this tinker of yours?" Sister Anne said, fixing her stony eyes upon him.

"Well, all right. I won't detain you further, then, Sister Anne. It doesn't seem you have any information that will help us." The woman rose to leave, until Tuck suddenly decided he couldn't let her go without asking what he still thought was the most important question. "Oh, one more thing, sister," he began, as if it had just occurred to him. "One of the other women we've talked to suggested that it's possible at least one of your sisters may have had a… a gentleman friend, perhaps even this Willie. Have you observed any of your sisters behaving in a strange way that might suggest such a thing? Wandering where they shouldn't, perhaps, or keeping strange hours contrary to the Rule?"

Sister Anne gave another ironic laugh, as if such a suggestion was absurd. Then, recalling herself, she put on her serious face again, and glared at Tuck, saying, "Young Sister Rebecca is a flighty little thing. I've seen her carrying flowers on occasion, holding on to them as if they'd come from some lover, perhaps. Now I come to think of it, I think I've heard those loud cries from the direction of *her* cell. Worth looking into for you, I suppose, Master Friar." With that, and a fleeting smirk, Sister Anne left the room. Decisively, as if to say she was done with him.

Sister Rebecca, for her part, also had a distinctive laugh, but hers was more like the tinkle of broken glass. And she used it not when she was being derisive, but rather when she was unsure or nervous, which was nearly all the time. She was the nun Tuck had noticed with the splash of freckles across her nose, and she had green almond-shaped eyes that squinted at him whenever he asked her anything. He was sure she must have a swirl of bright ginger hair under that wimple.

But she vigorously denied ever having known anyone by the name of Willie, and never, *never* would she ever consider breaking her vow of chastity with some horrid man. Sister Rebecca, it seemed, had taken the veil here at the priory at the age of fourteen, and had done so specifically to avoid having to marry a man chosen for her by her father, a local brewer. The man had been more than twice her age, and had breath that smelt of garlic to boot. The sister was still a girl at eighteen or younger, and when Tuck asked her about the flowers Sister Anne had observed, Rebecca gave her tinkling laugh and said she liked flowers, and sometimes one of her sisters might give her a small bouquet just for the sake of friendship.

"Before you go, Sister Rebecca, let me ask you one last question," Tuck closed off his conversation with the young nun. "A couple of your sisters mentioned hearing loud cries, perhaps of weeping, coming from the vicinity of your cell on Sunday night, after the victim's head was found in the chapel. Is there anything you can tell me about that?"

Sister Rebecca's face glowed a fiery crimson as her nervous laugh tinkled from her abashed lips. "I'm sure I…heard no weeping that night. Certainly not. Loud cries? I've no idea what they were talking about, I'm sure." She failed to meet his eyes as she rose from her seat and made her way to the door. "Probably somebody praying, that's what it was." And with that she left.

"Well," said the friar to himself. "*That* was certainly convincing."

* * *

Sister Mary Eusebia was the last of the nuns Friar Tuck had determined to interview today, and she stepped boldly into the small room off the cloister, as if she were entering some sporting event or university debate. She was a hearty young woman, in her early twenties the friar guessed, and had dark eyes as deep as caverns, over which loomed a dark pair of eyebrows meeting above her nose. Tuck, sensing she saw him as an adversary, took care to frame his questions gently, in a nonconfrontational manner.

"Mary Eusebia," Tuck began, good-humoredly. "Is that a name you chose for yourself when you took the veil, then?"

"Indeed it was." She looked at him as if expecting more, but he simply waited, assuming she would explain. "The name is Greek, and it refers to an inner piety or spiritual maturity. A kind of godliness."

"And you chose the name as a quality you wished to aspire to, did you?"

"Oh no. It's what other people called me." Tuck raised his eyebrows in surprise but again said nothing, waiting for the young nun to elaborate. "I have been associated with this priory since I was twelve years old, Master Friar. My father was a cloth merchant in Lincoln, and he knew the prioress then, old Sister Catherine. He bundled me off here to keep me away from unwelcome suitors and to have me educated. Wanted me to be of some use in his trade, so I could read and write and figure."

"A kind father, then, concerned with your welfare and your future?"

Sister Mary Eusebia blew the air from her nostrils in a little fit of pique. "He was a brute," she declared. And under Tuck's questioning eyes, she elaborated, "Just wanted to keep me for himself and figured I might as well be useful to him as long as he was going to keep me. But he'd already had his way with me before I ever had my monthly cycles."

Tuck turned pale as he felt his heart sink. And his mind flashed back to his own brutish father. "Oh my dear girl. Your own father?"

Her deep eyes looked back at him unmoved. Sister Mary Eusebia had long since transcended that shame and horror. "I was safe here." She waited. "He couldn't get at me here. My mother died my first year here, from shame and regret, I expect. My father waited hungrily for me to come home, but I wouldn't. Not even for mother's funeral. And when I declared my desire to become a postulant here, there was nothing he could do. I had him checkmated. I never saw him again. And I hope he died screaming. In any case, he did die, the day I turned eighteen. And that was five years ago. And that's when I became a nun. So to answer the questions you're here to ask me: No, I did not know this Willie the tinker whose head decorated our chapel on Sunday. No, he was no lover of mine. No, I haven't had any men paying me court here in the priory. And to answer one last question that you had no intention of asking me, no, I have never nor would I ever desire such a thing."

Tuck stared for a few moments into those deep brown eyes and then took a new tack: "Sister, it's clearly not a part of my investigation, but I am interested to know: you say it was others who gave you the name 'Eusebia.' Would you humor me by explaining why they gave you that name?"

She let a hint of a smile twist her mouth up at one corner. "It was because I learned so quickly. I could read Latin like a scholar by the age of thirteen. From that time I began to study the scriptures diligently. Every book, every line of the holy texts, and after that every commentary I could get my hands on from the library here, and some borrowed from other houses too. Jerome. Augustine. The Venerable Bede especially. The sisters took to calling me 'the Little Scholar' or 'Mistress Piety.' When I took my vows at eighteen, I chose 'Eusebia' to capture that idea of piety, of godliness."

Tuck thought about this for a moment and commented, "Your godliness seems of a singularly cerebral variety."

Sister Mary Eusebia gave Tuck a brief businesslike smile and then rose. "If you have no more questions, Master Friar, I want to get back to my cell. I have some reading set aside to finish this evening before compline."

As the young woman made her way toward the door, Tuck stopped her with another question: "Oh before you go, sister, I did have one more point I wanted to raise with you." At that the nun turned for a moment, her heavy right eyebrow raised quizzically. "A few of your sisters have mentioned that on the evening after Willie's head was found, loud cries or weeping were heard from one of the cells in the neighborhood of yours and Sister Anne's and the others in that part of the convent. Did you happen to hear such crying? Can you help us in clarifying where it was coming from?"

Sister Mary Eusebia stood still for a few moments, now with both brows raised in surprise. Or was it alarm? Tuck could not tell. But what she did next confused him even more. She turned toward the door again, and just as Tuck thought she was going to leave the room, she took hold of the door and swung it shut, turning the key in the lock. Befuddled, Tuck looked at the nun with blank eyes. She turned to him and said, "Brother Tuck, I want you to hear my confession."

* * *

Tuck's jaw dropped open, and in his startled state he babbled his first thoughts. "B-but I, I'm not prepared, er, this is not part of my responsibility here...shouldn't you be confessing to your own priest, Father... Father Bernard?"

"You're a friar. You're licensed to hear confessions. Friars regularly hear confessions of those who for one reason or another do not wish to confess to their parish priests. Your sacred duty is to hear my confession and I am requiring you to do so."

Tuck sighed. He was not prepared to argue with a scholar of Mary Eusebia's learning. "Very well," he conceded as she sat back down across from him with a look of triumph on her face. "How long has it been since your last confession, then?"

"Skip over the preliminaries, Master Friar. I'm familiar with the penitentials of Bede and of Theodore of Tarsus. There is one sin I want to confess to you that I have not felt at all comfortable confessing to anyone here. Let me just say that it concerns the loud cryings that have been heard of late coming from my cell."

"So it is *your* cell from which the cries are coming? It's you who are weeping?"

"Not me, Friar Tuck, and not weeping. Those are sounds coming from my special friend, Sister Rebecca."

"The little girl with the freckles?" Tuck said with surprise. "What is the meaning of these cries?"

Mary Eusebia lowered her head, raised her eyebrows, and looked at Tuck in disbelief. But it was clear she would need to spell things out with this friar. "Sister Rebecca and I. We sometimes lie together. We each need comforting and stroking sometimes. We stroke one another."

A slow look of realization dawned on Tuck's face. He searched his memory to those penitentials Sister Mary Eusebia had mentioned. A variety of sexual sins were listed, he recalled, but almost all he could think of involved sins by the male—varieties of adultery, of sodomy, in all of which women, if they were involved at all, were the passive participants, although of course they might have enticed the man into the sin. These were certainly sins a woman might confess. But it was difficult for him to even imagine sexual sins that might occur without a male present. But he did seem to recall a comment in Bede that specified "a woman fornicating with a woman," for which Bede prescribed three years of penance, or seven years if an "instrument" of some kind was used.

"So," Tuck cleared his throat. "You're confessing to fornication with another woman, then?"

"Am I?" The nun asked. Tuck was fairly certain she had thought about this a good deal. "Is simple stroking actually fornication? Had I been with a man would you call it fornication if he had only been stroking me?"

Tuck didn't know. "I…think not," was his only response.

"Doesn't fornication presuppose penetration? Isn't that why Bede suggests more serious penance for the use of instruments?"

"All right," Tuck agreed. "But then, in some way your relationship with your friend is at least an example of the sin of lust. Is it not forbidden in scripture? Might it be, shall we say, a version of the sin of Onan?"

"Not a word about it in scripture. I find nothing in Deuteronomy, or Exodus. Or Leviticus. But then, Moses was a man, wasn't he? As for the sin of Onan—but is it, though?" Mary Eusebia continued. "As I read the story in Genesis, Onan's act is sinful specifically because of the spilling of the seed. There's clearly no spilling of seed in my caressing and tickling my special friend."

"Perhaps not, but surely you are lusting in your heart," Tuck decided, feeling he was on surer ground here.

"Lusting? For what am I lusting, do you imagine?"

"For…for true fornication. I expect that as you fondle one another, you are thinking about true fornication, and that is what creates the excitement that leads to those cries you describe." Tuck really wasn't sure where he was going with this. How did he know what was in the minds of women? And how serious was this as a sin? Tuck regularly turned a blind eye toward Little John's relationship with Will Stutely, because he saw no harm in it—though the penitentials prescribed ten years of penance for that particular sin, and only three for this one. Didn't that make this more of a venial sin, if sin it was?

"Fornication? So you suggest that I am imagining being penetrated by a man while being stroked by my friend?" The young woman demanded.

"Indeed," Tuck nodded. "Of what else would you be thinking?"

Sister Mary Eusebia bowed her head to hide her smirk. "I assure you, brother friar. Before God I swear to you: lying with a man is the furthest thing from my mind at such moments."

Tuck sighed again in frustration. "My dear," he said to the young nun. "Just what is it you want to confess to, then?"

"I want to confess to breaking the rule of silence during the prescribed periods in our cells. Obviously, our cries have disturbed our sisters, and in breaking that rule we have broken our vow of obedience."

Tuck's mouth hung open for several seconds as he digested that. He had more than an inkling that this young woman was not approaching this confession with the proper high seriousness. What he was more than a little sure of was that she was telling him these things under the seal of the confessional so that he could never betray her secret to Mother Veronica, or Father Bernard, or anyone else. He, however, for his *own* part, would not debase the dignity of his office with regard to the confession. While it was clear to him he was not about to convince this young nun that her relationship with

Sister Rebecca was a sin, he would at least take seriously the sin she *had* confessed.

"You must take your vows seriously," Friar Tuck told the penitent sister, who now sat with head bowed and determined to do penance. "To fail in obedience is a manifestation of the sin of pride, the chief of the Seven Deadly Sins." Of that much he was quite sure with this young woman. "In your cell this evening consider your sins, and say a hundred Our Fathers. Now go," he told the nun as she rose, adding "and sin no more."

Sister Mary Eusebia turned and gave him a half-smile before she turned the key and exited the room. Friar Tuck sighed for the third time in this encounter, and wondered whether there was anyone on God's earth who could understand women.

CB Shanahan

Old Friends and Zip Drives

An overweight couple waddled past Biggs toward the casino. The husband, wearing a panama hat, jean shorts, and a Cracker Barrel T-shirt, boasted that he was up five hundred dollars in a voice set to the only volume he knew—loud. His wife's perfume steeped into everything as they passed.

Your winnings won't last, Biggs thought. *Gambling is a tax on idiots.*

The maple gelato trickled down his throat, endorphins coursing through his veins. His tongue was frozen, but he had built up a tolerance for ice cream headaches. There was a price to pay for every joy. He latched his mouth around another plastic spoonful and chewed to expedite the softening. The pain extended from his teeth to the base of his brain.

Biggs had been skin and bones since he was a toddler. An entire lifetime addicted to sugar hadn't budged his waistline. Even in his early forties, he couldn't grow a real beard, just splotches, so he stayed clean-shaven. His Brillo-pad brown hair was cropped tight to his head.

"It's like frozen waffles," he mumbled, his mouth muscles too cold to form the words as he stabbed into the creamy sweetness for another hit. He plodded down the hallway of the Bellagio Hotel, the clear plastic cup bearing his full attention.

"There he is," said Linh Pham, skimming off the top of her own cup of raspberry.

Biggs paused his intake, flanked by his two closest hacking friends. A large yellow banner stared him straight in the face, advertising the keynote speaker of the entire event, Chuck Zimmermann, founder of

Kawment—with his trademark ratty hair—in the Monet Ballroom at eight p.m. Biggs shuffled past the sign without a word.

He was attending DEF CON, the world's largest hacker convention, for the fifteenth year in a row. There were some big names here, Serina Castellano, who brought OPEC to its knees for nearly eight hours in 2015; Preecha Xu, the author of *To Catch a Multinational*, and Tommy Martell, the lead engineer for MindDump.

"You should tell him you're here," Mickey Watts added, a supersized latte heating her palms through the cardboard insulator.

A short sleeve, button-up shirt dangled off Biggs' shoulders like a scarecrow's, hanging over a set of khaki cargo shorts and albino-like toothpick legs. He didn't reply.

"Why?" asked Linh. "What, does he know him or something?"

"Yeah," Mickey replied. "They went to school together. Chuck used to cheat off him in class, didn't he?" She elbowed Biggs' arm.

He shrugged.

Mickey was only in her early twenties, younger than Linh. Unlike Biggs, she struggled with her weight. But at DEF CON, it didn't matter and that's the way she liked it.

Linh was a healthy version of Biggs' bony physique. She'd been born in Vietnam, but spent her entire life since then in California. "I never knew that," she said. "How come you never told me that?"

Biggs took his attention off of the gelato long enough to roll his eyes at her. She might as well have been attending Comic-Con, her stick legs wound with thick-striped tights and a skirt barely down to her thighs. She wore combat boots, suspenders, and a Ramones T-shirt, her black hair in pigtails, and a thin layer of white foundation, making her skin extra pale. Her lips were painted glossy black, and she had sparkles around her eyes. She smelled of bubblegum.

"What?" she said. "You don't know him then."

"He totally does," Mickey said. "Tell her."

"I'm not interested in Chuck Zimmermann," he replied, stuffing the spoon into the cup and grabbing hold of the back of his head, grimacing.

"You're full of shit," said Linh. "The guy's worth seventy billion dollars and he used to cheat off you. Mickey, he's lying."

"No he's not. He went to Goodwin Knight High and so did Zimmermann and they both graduated in ninety-eight."

"Who told you Biggs graduated Goodwin Knight in ninety-eight?"

"He did, but that's when Zimmermann did too."

Linh shook her head. "He just told you that. Have you seen a yearbook or something?"

"No, but why would he make it up?"

"You're going to have to ask him. If he introduces me to Zimmermann, I'll believe it. Until then, he's full of shit."

"Aww, man." Biggs stopped in his tracks. There was a table set up outside the Monet Ballroom with two DEF CON goons manning it.

"What?" Linh asked.

"Jeff Achterberg and Walter Dubois," he replied. "Those guys are always in the wrong place."

Linh was not impressed. "*That's* Jeff and Walter?"

"Yeah," said Mickey. "Total wankers."

"They look like wimps."

"Jeff's a good hacker," Mickey replied. "Not as good as my man here, but he can make trouble."

"Well, come on. We have tickets. What, are they not going to give them to us?"

"I'm not going," said Biggs.

"Because of these two idiots?" Linh's voice was getting higher.

"No, I didn't reserve one. I don't idolize Chuck Zimmermann."

"You're not going?" Mickey seemed offended.

"No, there's a ton of other better stuff than watching Chuck."

"Well, we still have to get our tickets," Linh said, pulling at Biggs' upper arm. They stepped up to the table and were greeted by a pair of smirks. The man seated on the left kept shoulder length, stringy blonde hair tucked underneath an Australian-type hat; black-rimmed glasses made his eyes pop out. He wore a T-shirt that read, "The internet is full. Go away."

On the right sat a heavyset man in a short sleeve, apricot orange button-up shirt, with cropped brown hair and a replica Predator computer system strapped onto his left forearm.

"What can we do for you ladies?" the man on the left asked.

Biggs greeted the man matter-of-factly. "Jeff."

"Oh, hello Gabriel. I didn't notice you next to two women."

"It's Biggs."

"You wish. I knew you before you became the Chuck Cunningham of Star Wars."

"What's that supposed to mean?" Mickey asked, a fight brewing in her eyes.

"I got it," Biggs said, turning his attention back to Jeff. "I believe these two ladies have reservations."

"Gabriel, don't tell me you weren't ready when these tickets became available. You're losing your touch."

"Which wasn't much to begin with," the second man said.

"Shut up, Walter. No one's talking to you," said Biggs. "I have better things to do tonight than watch a Kawment infomercial."

"Besides," said Mickey, "he knows Chuck Zimmermann anyway."

Jeff forced a laugh, followed by Walter. "Is that right?" Jeff asked. "So let me get this straight, you didn't fail to get a ticket when they disappeared in the first minute; you opted out of DEF CON's biggest talk because you're old pals with one of the richest guys in the world." He shot an eye toward his companion, who chuckled.

"Can we just get our tickets?" Linh asked, her face rolling up to the ceiling.

"No skin off my back," said Jeff.

Walter was eyeing Biggs' cup of gelato. "What flavor is that?"

"Maple," said Biggs, stuffing another spoonful in his cakehole.

"Is it any good?"

"Wouldn't *you* like to know."

Biggs stared at the Eiffel Tower, just on the other side of the palm trees that split Las Vegas Boulevard down the middle. Then he spun around to face Caesar's Palace and the Bellagio. Though the inferno in the sky had crested past the horizon, leaving just a faint yellow glow, his sneakers were still in danger of melting to the sidewalk. The earth below him was returning the heat baked into it by the daylight, like a giant oven door left open. The scent of softened blacktop wafted over him in a roasting wave from under the never-ending traffic.

The temperature aside, Las Vegas was magical at night. Every inch of space was abuzz with activity, from honking horns to the constant flow of fountain water crashing back into giant pools. Flashing neon, massive LCD screens, pedestrian overpasses, streetlights, and billboards for personal injury lawyers all vied for attention.

He leaned on the stone railing that fronted the Bellagio's fountains as a Frank Sinatra song blared over loudspeakers, the water display keeping time to the music. It was mesmerizing, but his elbows were starting to cook, so he straightened himself up.

The Chuck Zimmermann event was in full swing inside the hotel. Outside was as good a place to be as any.

Biggs wasn't lying. He was friends with Chuck in High School, but he doubted the man would want to rehash the old days. Decades ago, Biggs had to correct lines of code for Chuck, but today that same C student would be as likely to be meeting with a president or a movie star.

Was Biggs jealous? Maybe a little. He hated to admit it to himself, but Chuck was a computer newbie in high school. Biggs practically passed computer science for him. How could he not resent that same kid sitting on more money than several small states combined?

"That's fucking awesome, isn't it?" A kid of about twenty had his arms crossed in front of his chest and was staring at the water show, as a mist from the display breezed over them.

"Yeah, I guess." Biggs never felt at ease with strangers, especially in a city like Vegas, where scammers were always on the lookout for patsies, but he recognized the T-shirt, yellow with Chuck's face, today's date and DEF CON scrawled across the bottom. "Are you a goon?"

"Yeah, just checking out the town, you know. Never been here."

"You're not watching Zimmermann?"

"Nah. Kawment is for tools. I'll head back before it ends. I might hit the slots or something."

"Say goodbye to your money," said Biggs. "The house always wins."

"I know. It's fun though. You're not a betting man?"

"Never have been."

"You can't win if you don't play."

"I'll remember that."

"Do they got any good burgers within walking distance, do you know?"

"They got some in the hotel."

"Yeah, I'm just getting out of there, you know what I mean?"

"I get it. There's a Wahlburgers right over there," Biggs said, pointing toward Flamingo Road. "They're pretty good."

The man spun in that direction. "Oh, I see it. All right, dude, thanks."

"Hey, hang on."

He turned back toward Biggs, who was reaching into a lower pocket on his cargo shorts. Biggs retrieved a small notebook and pen and wrote on a slip of paper, ripping it out of the book and offering it to him. "If you happen to run into Chuck, I went to school with him. Can you tell him Gabriel from Goodwin Knight is here?"

The goon accepted the paper. "Are you serious? The chances I run into him are somewhere in the neighborhood of zero."

"Well, if you do."

"Did you really go to school with him?"

"Yeah, we used to be friends."

The kid examined the slip of paper and shoved it in his back pocket. "I'll give it my best shot."

Biggs had taken up residence at a sofa in the center of the Bellagio lobby. He was sizing up two men, probably in their early thirties, drinking bottles of non-alcoholic beer on a Saturday night. He typed into his phone. "Two, corner of Petrosian."

"Def," came the immediate response.

He was engaged in a game of "spot the feds," and the men he had fingered looked too awkward. They had the right clothes, but they couldn't stop themselves from scanning the room. DEF CON was infiltrated by NSA and CIA undercover ops. They took pictures of every attendee for their databases, so they'd have somewhere to start whenever something big was hacked. Biggs didn't blame them. He understood the need to protect the country, but that didn't mean they were trustworthy.

His phone buzzed. It was a blocked call. His heart jumped. His mouth felt dry. The smell of the shampooed rug was hitting him and irritating his nasal passage. There was no way the government would target him because he was playing a stupid game. Was he right about the two men? Was the National Security Agency trying to scare him?

He clicked a button on the side of the phone, sending the call to voicemail. Then he scanned the lobby, his jittery eyes darting between the men and any other possible agents. One of the ladies behind check-in. She was on the phone. He tried to avoid looking directly at the hotel cameras all around. It was likely that the hotel had allowed access to the video system for the feds. That was probably how they got a lot of their recon. The cameras were already set up and ubiquitous.

His phone buzzed. There was a message. He held the phone to his ear.

"Gabriel, holy shit! I can't believe you're here!" There was no mistaking the voice. It was Chuck Zimmermann. "You gotta come by. I'll have someone let you in at the pool door by the stage. Come on back, you old dog!"

Biggs leaned his elbows on his knees studying the phone for a moment. This was unexpected. His note getting to Chuck must have been a million to one shot. Maybe a thousand to one. He shrugged and raised himself up from his perch. There were doors leading from the lobby to the pool area. He made his way to them and stiff-armed one open.

The pool was still busy as the heat from the day had yet to cool to overnight desert standards. Most of the people looked like DEF CON goers, but he didn't recognize anyone. The scent of chlorine hung in the air. There was a glass door past the Pool Café that led to the Monet Ballroom. Biggs pulled it open and reentered the air conditioning. He preferred the heat to the fake atmosphere inside.

The room was large and garish, hundreds of brown plastic chairs facing the front, where the stage was set. Over the speakers, a rap song thumped out a beat, loud enough to make conversations difficult. Dozens of people in small groups were shouting over it anyway.

"How you doing? Who are you?" There was a Middle Eastern woman wearing a black polo shirt and a jumble of passes around her neck. He hadn't noticed her when he had entered. He was startled off balance.

"Biggs," he shouted. "Um… Gabriel."

"Great," she replied. "I'm Alicia. Do you want to come with me?"

She led him past a burly man in a black shirt and a no-nonsense face, up a set of rollable steps to the side of the stage and onto it. A single microphone was illuminated by a spotlight in its center. They walked around the red curtain into the backstage area, which was dark and utilitarian compared to the plush front of the house. A set of stairs plunged them into the depths underneath the main floor to concrete halls and eventually to a red door adorned with a paper star. On it was Chuck's name, written in Sharpie. She passed that room and several catering tables—from which Biggs stole a slice of cucumber, dipping it in ranch dressing and chomping it down before his guide could catch him.

The next door was already ajar and revealed a much grander space, with sofas and glass coffee tables. It smelled musty for the middle of a desert. Framed posters lined the walls from previous Bellagio shows, many of them autographed. A metallic sounding speaker played the same music from the Monet Room, but at a much more preferable volume.

He almost didn't notice Chuck, who was seated on the corner of a couch, a bottle of Stella Artois in his clutch. There were no paparazzi, just one man seated next to him. The two were talking. Chuck jumped up when he spied Biggs.

"Gabriel! Oh my god, I can't believe it!" He lurched at Biggs, wrapping his arms around the stick of a man. "Hi Chuck," Gabriel replied, his face stuffed into the corner of Chuck's shoulder. Biggs hadn't really gained weight since high school, but Chuck seemed bigger. Not much fatter, just bigger.

Chuck released his hold. "Look at you, man! You look exactly the same."

Biggs didn't know how to respond. "I'm kind of going by Biggs now."

"Biggs? That's awesome. What, like Luke Skywalker's buddy?"

"That's the one."

"I love it. Hey, you know what I still got? Wait, do you need a drink? Alicia, can you get my buddy a drink? What are you having, Biggs?"

"I'll have a Coke."

"Still on the Coke? Man, how do you stay skinny?"

Biggs was beginning to remember why he liked Chuck. He was just an all-around good guy. They stuck together in high school partly since no one else wanted to hang out with them, but they had similar tastes.

"Anyway," Chuck continued, "I bet you can't guess what I still have after all these years."

"Herpes?" Biggs always liked to deliver take-downs with a straight face.

Chuck doubled over with laughter, which forced a smile from Biggs as well. Alicia handed a plastic cup of soda to Biggs. "Thanks."

"Other than that," Chuck said. "Remember when I came over your house to borrow your ZIP Drive? What did those things hold, like two hundred and fifty meg or something?"

"The later model. The original was a hundred."

"A hundred meg. Yeah. That's the one I have. I still have it, dude. I kept thinking I was going to give it back to you, but I never did."

"You can have it," Biggs replied. "I have the two-fifty now."

Chuck laughed again. "Oh man, I miss hanging with you."

"I'm kind of surprised you got my message. I mean I just gave it to a goon outside and he said there was no way he was going to run into you."

"He wouldn't have. Alicia…" he waved at the woman. "She heard him telling one of the guys on my team and he would have just tossed it, but she knew you 'cause I've told her stories about us back in the day. She's the only reason I got it."

"You're still telling stories about us in high school?"

"Sure, I mean it's not like you get rich and forget the stuff that happened when you were young. Who ever gets over their high school years? We were bros, weren't we?"

"Definitely."

Alicia tugged on Chuck's arm. "We gotta go," she said. "Gabriel, it was great to finally put a face to the stories." She held out her hand and Biggs accepted it, feeling embarrassed by his sweaty palm.

"Do you remember when I asked if you wanted to help start this company?" Chuck asked.

Biggs didn't have to think it over. He'd regretted the decision every time he checked his bank account. In high school though, Biggs had no confidence in Chuck's vision. "Yeah, the conversation has played in my mind once or twice."

"This is the guy," Chuck said to Alicia. "He was the best programmer there was. It would have been the two of us running Kawment."

"Yeah, but you got Stickie Evans. He was awesome."

Chuck nodded. "I lucked out with Stickie. Listen man, what are you doing now? I can get you a position if you're looking. We pay pretty good."

"Geez. I'd have to think about that."

"Let me give you my number."

Biggs' eyes bulged out.

"Do me a favor and don't give this to anyone. There are a lot of crazy people out there and I've had to change my number a bunch of times. It's a major pain in the ass."

As the door inched shut behind him, Biggs stared into a hallway devoid of DEF CON attendees. The check-in table beside him was empty, but the sound of Las Vegas still called for suckers beyond the confines of the immediate area. It hit him that he hadn't secured any proof that he'd met up with Chuck. He should have grabbed a photo for the naysayers. It would have been great to stick in Jeff Achterberg's face.

"Where r u?" came a text from Mickey. "Zimmermanns bn ovr a haf hr."

"Where are you?" he replied.

"Me and l at lilys. Getn drnk."

"K." Biggs lowered his phone and set off for the lobby. He passed by the closed gates of Café Gelato, where he'd picked up the maple goodness earlier in the day. The racket from the casino clamored from around the corner.

Lily's bar was a mix of plum and gold, with stone tabletops and leather sofas, a dim room filled with DEF CON attendees and goons. Mickey and Linh had snagged the stools at the far corner of the bar, half glasses of red wine at their fingertips. Gentle piano music played from hidden speakers.

"Where have you been?" Mickey asked. "Zimmermann was pretty lame. You were right. It was like a Kawment commercial."

"I took a walk around, checked out the city. It's plastic, you know, but cool."

"Hello ladies." The voice came from behind. Biggs spun around to disappointment. It was Jeff and Walter. They were smirking. "You two should think about ditching Gabriel. He lost his hacking mojo like two decades ago," said Jeff.

"He never had it," Walter added.

"He's better than either of you," Mickey replied.

Jeff snorted a laugh as Walter eyed him and threw out a smug smile, nodding along. "In his dreams," said Jeff. "So tell me, Gabriel, how's Chuck doing? He must have been dying to catch up."

"That's for me to know and you to find out."

"We don't need to find out because we already know."

"No you don't."

"*Pfft*. Come on Walter. These guys are too much fun for me." The pair turned and headed for an empty table.

"Did you try to see Chuck?" Mickey asked.

A vein bulged out of Linh's temple, her face flushing. "God, if only you could have gotten backstage. That would have made Jeff's head explode."

"Who said I didn't get backstage?"

"Oh please. Nobody's going to believe you really went to school with Chuck Zimmermann."

Mickey motioned for the bartender. "What are you having Biggs, Coke?"

"Yeah, Coke is good." He eyed the wall of liquor and did a quick scan of the room. "You know what? I'll be back in a minute."

"Where are you going?" Mickey asked.

"It's Las Vegas," he said, a grin taking over the lower half of his face. "I gotta make a call. You have to gamble once in your life."

Sue Baumgardner

Patsy of Harlan County

Patsy, 1938

Freckle Face and Ole Cow Eyes were two of Patsy-June's nicknames that had followed her right up into high school, and Danny Booker had given her both names twelve years ago. She had been standing by the steps at recess, in her new grain-bag red calico dress, waiting to hear the bell ring and to go back inside. It was her first day of school and she didn't know anyone except her older brother Bill. He played cowboys and Indians with his stick-gun-toting pals and ignored Patsy. Too shy to make friends, Patsy stood alone and scanned the playground, listening to the laughter, watching the play, and wondered if she would ever join in the fun. Would she ever have friends?

Danny who was two years older—same age as her brother Bill—sauntered up to her with his hands in his overall pockets, and looked out from under a thick, wiry shock of chestnut hair. Looking down at Patsy-June's little upturned face, he grinned and said, "Hey Freckle Face, would you like to see my pet frog?"

Noticing his fist in his right pocket, attempting to pull something out, she answered quickly, "No, thank ye."

Seeing Danny's hand still pulling something from his pocket, Patsy took a step back and upwards—up that first step into the school house.

"How about my new tiger eye?" Danny pulled out a fistful of agates.

The two became friends. While they each understood that they were special friends, no one else realized it. Danny and Patsy didn't play together. Patsy did eventually make friends with many other girls after she summoned up some courage and stepped out of her initial shy demeanor. She and her friends played on the girls' side of the playground. Jumping rope, the girls giggled when Danny strolled by them as he retrieved the boys' basketball, which had rolled over near the rope jumpers. They whispered; someone said "He likes the girls. That's really why he comes over on our side." But Patsy knew, and Danny knew; she could tell.

On a dusty October day, Patsy ran for the steps as the bell rang. Remembering her sweater, she turned back to the swing set to retrieve it. Grabbing it hurriedly, she turned back in mid-stride. With everyone else inside, the playground was vacated. One of her Brogans had come untied; she stepped on the lacing in her rush. Almost to the steps, she skidded across the hard-packed dirt and fell to the ground. Still in a hurry, thinking she was alone, Patsy rose as she wiped at the flowing tears. Danny Booker stood over her. "C'mon, Ole Cow Eyes, let's go get you cleaned up."

He reached for her hand. She slid hers into his, even though hers was bloody and smarting. He led her into the school and down the hall to the deep white sink at the end, where a big gray mop rested upside down in the corner. Tearing a sheet from the roll of brown paper towel, he washed her knees first and then each of her hands. Finished, he passed her a clean, damp piece of towel and said, "You might should take this to class with you, Freckle Face. Hold it in one hand for a few minutes and then t'other for a few. It'll take the sting away."

Patsy, 1949

By her senior year in high school, Patsy's freckles had mostly dissolved. But those cow eyes? They were bigger than ever, and now she curled her long, dark lashes with a little tool few boys even knew of. That blazing Kentucky sun, with a little help from a bottle of hydrogen peroxide, had bleached her dishwater-blonde hair, through the summer, to a soft, golden wheat color. She was pleased with her blossoming maturity.

Patsy held Dan's letter in her hand, remembering the summer when she was sixteen; he had plowed up her mother's garden, same as always. Smiling, she cast her mind back further—eight years ago—the first time he had plowed up Momma's garden. 1941. Danny was but an eleven-year-old boy then and she was nine. He stood there barefoot in his overalls with galluses, and a front bib pocket, stained and bulging with a cut of chewing tobacco. He had removed his dirty boots before he stepped into their kitchen. Patsy appreciated that. No one else bothered. And she was the one who did the housework around there. Momma played with the younger kids, sewed, cooked, gardened, sang ditties and played the banjo. Patsy did the housework—partly to please Daddy and keep his nasty temper in line, but mostly because it just came natural to her, as natural as laughter and music came to Momma.

Patsy had not seen Danny since he last plowed their garden, nearly two years ago now. Someone said he had gone and joined the Army.

Not a word from him in two years, and now this letter. Sergeant Booker. Humph! Patsy swung open the porch screen door, stepped into the kitchen, and found her mother and Dickie-Ray, her twelve-year-old brother, feasting on a bowl of cornbread and cold milk.

"Momma, you won't believe what that Dan Booker has written me. Listen to this." And she read Dan's entire letter. Near the end of the last page was where Patsy fell into peals of laughter while clutching her abdomen. Danny's letter dangled in her right hand; she wiped the tears from her face with the back of her left hand, then continued to read through Dan's proposal, if you could call it that.

It was more like he told her. "I will be coming home in a couple of months. You are a big girl now, Patsy-June, and it's time we start thinking about getting married."

"That foolish thing," Patsy grinned, her laughter abating.

Biting her lip, Patsy thought of Hugh-Noble Owens. The one and only boy she had ever dated, he was a bright and sensitive young man who adored Patsy. Hugh-Noble was not your typical suitor back in that coal mining town in Harlan County of 1948. Well-suited, Hughie and Patsy were both good-humored, poetic, and shy.

Danny, 1949

Danny Booker arrived in Crummies during the Christmas break. He took Patsy out to a movie in the shiny new Chrysler he had bought for his parents, who had never owned a car before. Swaying like Cinderella, Patsy-June stepped boldly into the red lacquered pumpkin-coach, as Danny held the long sleek door for her and smiled appreciatively. What was he more pleased with, Patsy or the car? It was debatable.

As curvaceous and sensual as that pin-up calendar girl by the cash register down at the Gulf Station, this automobile had seduced Danny from the moment he first stepped onto the lot down at Rideout's. Line after line of chrome streaked full across the front; first the bumper then three more horizontals of lesser value with a mesh of chrome shining in the background space. Like a woman standing in her panties, with ribs rippled under sweet, sweaty flesh, those two headlights sat high and protruded round and bold on either side of a cleavage. Ah, and the cleavage; it exposed its own visual. That smooth and shiny V-shape, thrusting up and out, Danny found reminiscent of one pubic mound he had seen on a Korean-lady exotic dancer in a European bar. The boys had called her the 'White Tiger.'

The car had been a good deal. Just two years old, this 1947 Chrysler Town & Country had Danny's pulse racing. Old man Rideout had owned her himself and was now driving around in a brand-spanking-new one. Paint, chrome and leather—its very essence bolstered Danny's brash nature, and kindled a sense of adventure in Patsy as well. He hadn't missed her bold sashay.

Checking her reflection in the rearview mirror, Patsy smoothed on a touch of red lipstick. She added a dash of the red to each of her cheeks and rubbed it into a faint blush, before dropping the gold encased tube back into her purse.

Danny pushed the clutch in, slipped her into first gear, glancing across at Patsy. They smiled at each other like two children, co-

conspirators with their hands deep in the candy-jar. The wood strips, so highly polished, that streaked both sides of the car, flashed in his mind's eye and somewhere in the back of Danny's brain, he connected it with the old-timey stage coaches. Yes, and Patsy was riding shotgun. He sucked air between his two front teeth, lifted his right arm, pantomimed a whipping motion, and yelped, "Ye-haw!"

After leaving Patsy that first evening, Danny felt torn; he wanted to rush home with the new car and surprise his folks, but he needed expert advice on winning Patsy-June's hand in marriage. Grandpa Led was easy to talk with. And ever-one knew that while Granny Led sure knew her Bible, Grandpa was the expert on good whiskey, fine horseflesh, and wily women. Grandpa Led might be Patsy's kin, but he was Grandpa Led to a whole community of Harlan County young folk. Danny drove up to the Ledford's and found Grandpa smoking his pipe on the front steps. Grandpa shared his best moonshine with Danny and listened with great interest to his tales about Army life while Granny Led went to bed with the Good Book.

Next morning, after a fine breakfast of white country gravy with sausage on biscuits big as tea cups, and a heaping pile of scrambled goose eggs, Granny shooed them off, asking Grandpa to take some ground cornmeal down to Laurie. Grandpa took the long-way-round, after dropping the cornmeal off at his daughter's house. He drove Danny down through Slack Holler, and up through Crummies to Saw Mill Holler. They even went up on Grave Yard Hill and surveyed the gravestones of the grand-daddies who were responsible for their families living on this piece of God's creation purely encircled by, and hidden in, the foothills of the Appalachian Mountains. They rattled along in that old company truck so fragrant with apple peels strewn behind the crackled leather bench seat. Grandpa was a wise man. He had that truck smelling of apples, Danny was sure, to mask the smell of moonshine whiskey from Granny's sensitivities. And Grandpa's advice? Well, it had been just the encouragement Danny Booker had needed. "Hellfire boy, you don't want a fine gal like Patsy-June pissing her life away with that mealy-mouthed little sissy!"

Patsy, 1949

The following evening Hugh stepped up on the front porch at Patsy's and found her sitting on the porch swing with Dan. Patsy's family could be seen through the window at the far end of the porch, all seated around the console radio and phonograph. The Grand Ole Opry was just getting into full swing; they were teasing a fellow about his height. A man was introduced as Wesley Tuttle from Colorado, and began entertaining the audience with his newest release.

"Good evening, Patsy," Hugh drawled, blushing. Attempting a smile, he darted a glance at Dan, "Sergeant Booker." Hugh's smiling gaze fell away under Dan Booker's steely-eyed inspection.

Dan tapped his fingers on the swing seat between himself and Patsy. Patsy, and Hugh too— she was sure—both mentally counted the ten finger rolls. Sergeant Booker placed his palms above each knee cap and pushed himself to a standing position. He stood a good six inches taller than Hugh. He glared from above Hugh's downcast face. Patsy looked up at Dan's hard-set jaw and then into Hugh's gentle, stricken face. She noticed Hugh stared at the smoldering cigarette in her hand; her hands began to shake. Dan spoke softly, slowly enunciating each word, "Owens, don't you come round here no more. You stay away from my girl, you hear?" Neither Patsy nor Hugh, by all appearances, thought to question this.

Wesley Tuttle sang, "*Go on and cry yourself to sleep, the way I've done a million times…*"

Hugh raised his head until he looked Patsy in the eye, "Well, goodnight then."

"Hugh? Good night," Patsy called after him as he descended the steps and evaporated into the darkness.

Danny, 1949

That night, Danny left Patsy's porch feeling like king of the mountain. Time to surprise his parents with their shiny new automobile, he took his leave from Patsy. Danny inched down the holler. He didn't want to stir up the dust on the road and dull the sheen. Events of the past two days ran in review through Danny's mind. Everything had gone perfectly since he had stepped off the bus yesterday and walked over to Rideout's Auto Sales, with his wallet bulging. *Well, it ain't a-bulging now, but the look on their faces is going to be worth ever dime.*

He was glad he had gone over to Grandpa Led's last night. Danny smiled, recalling how his knees had shook, as he assumed that voice of authority and dismissed Hugh-Noble. Tempted to feel sorry for Hugh now, he reminded himself of what Grandpa had said, "Hellfire boy, you don't want a fine gal like Patsy-June, pissing her life away with that mealy-mouthed little sissy!"

Danny killed the lights as he approached the curve in Ten Spot, and there, bathed in the moonlight, sat the old homestead. All the company houses were just the same, four-sided with four rooms and a front porch. Yet, each was different. As the company electrician, Bradley Booker made better money than most, though that was still a mere pittance. It did, however, allow for an occasional luxury which was rare in that coal mining town. The two silver maples out front were respectable in size now, and the latticework around the bottom of the house was the only lattice in Crummies.

Danny stepped up on the back steps and knocked. Light spilled into the kitchen from the front room. That was the parlor now that three of the kids had left home. A real parlor with a radio and upholstered rocking chair. Danny thought of his fourteen-year-old kid brother; Ronnie-Rob sure had things good, and now he would be riding around with his parents in a big, shiny, new car. *Damn, I shoulda had it so good. Maybe I wouldna had to join the Army before I dared ask Patsy-June out.*

Danny watched through the glass as his father walked slowly across the kitchen to the back door. *Pa's gotten old. He never used to be bent over like that. Hell, he looks like he's spent his life shoveling coal with the rest of 'em.*

Bradley Booker snapped on the porch light above Danny's head before he looked up and peered through the glass. A mixture of emotions flickered across the old man's face, and he squinted his eyes as he opened the door. "Son," he breathed. They held each other in a prolonged bear hug, for the first time in their lives.

"Go get Ma," Danny whispered. "Don't tell her it's me. I want to surprise her, too."

"She's not here, son, but come on in and sit'cher bones down with yer ole Dad, and tell me what kind of deviltry my boy's been up to."

Bradley led the way to the living room, and with a sweep of his hand, offered his recliner to Danny. Another first. Danny was honored and knew better than to refuse his father's offering.

"Where's Ma? What time will she be home, Pa? I'd really like to surprise her."

"She won't be coming home, son."

It was to the smell of hot biscuits, gravy, and sausage, that Danny woke up in his old bed the next morning. He thought he would rather face Satan himself than go out into that kitchen and face his father. His Pa always was a good cook, but Danny wondered—*how does he do it, even now?* Danny had heard the words from his father's own lips, "Your mother has left me. She wants a di-vorce. She wants to marry Everett Owens. Says he treats her like a real lady."

Danny had poured his father a large glass of moonshine and then drank the rest himself, right out of the mason jar. He vaguely remembered backing down the yard, but the rest was just one big blank.

"C'mon son. Breakfast is on the table."

"Be right there Pa."

Headache or not, his father needed him.

"Dad, do you know what time I came in last night?"

"Yes, Dan." His father paused long enough to pour Dan's coffee. "Bobby-Lee brought you in this morning, about ten o'clock. It's four in the afternoon now, son. You were vera drunk." A minute of silence stretched long and naked between them before Bradley continued, "You went into the commissary and unzipped right in the middle of the place. You pissed all over the radiator. The piss hit that hot thang, the steam began to rise, and the ladies all a-screaming and a-running ever-where. Bobby-Lee said Fat Fannie Reardan was bending round the corner, trying to get a look at-cher and fell right atop a stack of twenty-four dozen boxed eggs, and just barely missed Bobby-Lee's old hound, Earl, a-lying thar. Ye gave them ol' ladies something to talk about, now that's fer sure. Don't misunderstand me, boy. I'm mighty proud of ye. I think ever-thing you do is fine as frog hair. But it's ye I'm a thinking of. Don't get all het-up about this thang with your mother and me. Got along without her once and I'm a guessing I will again, the good Lord willing and the creek don't rise..."

Patsy, 1950

It was a warm spring evening with the scent of dogwood and honeysuckle heavy in the air. As Danny held Patsy close on the swing at the end of her parents' front porch, she turned and faced her intended in the moonlight. He placed one hand on the small of her back, then slid the other onto the nape of her neck and pulled her face to his. Danny held his mouth tantalizingly close to hers. She felt the warm vapor of his breath and smelled the mint even before he licked her lips lightly, moistening them. Patsy's innocent lips quivered, then parted slightly, willingly. He kissed her possessively, while out of the darkness a sweet mantra trilled and floated lonesome on the air, *whip-poor-will... whip-poor-will...*

Patsy lay across the double bed she had shared with her younger sister, Mary Lee. This was to be her last night here in the only home she'd ever known. This room had grown-up with her—with them, really—her sister Mary Lee and herself. A dusty light bulb hung from the ceiling, casting its yellow glow around the room, reflecting light in the window across from the bed, beside the highboy dresser she and her sister shared. That one cracked pane of glass had been cracked for how many years now?

It was the year she turned eleven and Mary Lee had been eight.

Seven years ago! Christmas night had found them sitting on this same bed, goodness—on this very same quilt! They sat Indian-style in their new nightdresses Momma had sewn for them, with their combined Christmas stash strewn on the quilt between them. Mary Lee had grabbed the one orange and started to peel it. Patsy snatched it away from her, saying, "Hey, you little thief, that's mine!"

"No it's not; it's mine," Mary Lee had whined. She always was a whiner, getting out of doing the dishes with a 'headache,' and never had to empty Grandpa Green's slop jar because her stomach was just too sensitive.

"Look, you little baby, maybe you ate yours already, or Dickie-Ray ate it. I really don't care, but this one is mine, and I'm not giving it up to either of you spoilt brats." Patsy had dropped the orange into the lap of her new pink flannel nightdress, only to have Mary Lee's scrawny little paw snatch it right back. With her tiny little hands, Mary Lee's grasp was tentative at best. Patsy caught her hand in mid-air and easily reclaimed the orange.

"Momma!" Mary Lee wailed as she turned on the bed.

"Girls." Momma had been standing in the doorway; the startled girls turned as they dropped their heads in shame.

Momma's hand held an orange high for them to see. "I found this orange beside the kitchen sink and was going to ask if it belongs to one of you. But from what I hear, it couldn't possibly be either one of yours, so it must be Dickie-Ray's. Well, I best go fetch him from the tub so's he can have his orange a'fore bed."

"Momma," Patsy-June said in a low, contrite voice, "that's my orange. I remember now. I left it beside the sink. I was heating water for Little Dickie's bath and carrying it over, one dipper at a time. By the time I finished, I plum forgot about my orange."

"I knew that," Mary Lee asserted. "But you wouldn't give me a chance to tell you. You're a big bully." And with that, she grabbed at the orange in Patsy's hand. Patsy knew she should let it loose. It was her sister's, but Mary Lee was being such a little snot. Patsy's fingers dug in. Mary Lee's little fingers let loose and her hand fell, only to rise back up and quicker than a copper-head, she struck at the orange. Somehow the orange had become airborne and fell to the floor only after it hit and cracked that window over there.

Momma shook her head smiling and both girls thought they just might get out of this easily, seeing how it was Christmas.

"What the hell?"

Lord-a-mercy, they had woken Daddy up. He was mad as a hornet, darting back and forth behind his pointing finger, but no one got whupped; it was Christmas, after all. But Daddy did seize both the oranges. He said he should give them away to some poor and more grateful children. "I'm going to have to sleep on this," he said wearily as he turned and headed back to bed with an orange in each hand.

Patsy-June and Mary Lee carefully picked up their treasures from the bed and stored them in the bottom dresser drawer. Momma pulled the string, shutting out their light. The two girls crawled beneath the cover and waited, as Momma eased in and settled on their bed. They expected her to lead them in prayer, which she did do eventually. First though, she reached into her apron pocket, pulled out her own orange, and peeled it as the two sisters sat up. Momma placed the peels in her pocket and broke the orange in half, tearing off a wedge and biting into it, sucking noisily. Then she giggled and tossed the rest of the orange into Patsy's free hand. "Do you know what to do with this, child?"

"Yes Momma." With that, Patsy handed the orange over to her sister and said, "I am really sorry, Mary Lee; I was mean to you. You deserve this orange. I don't."

Patsy had felt better before she even finished that last sentence. It wasn't in her nature to be mean like that. But then Mary Lee and Momma had both thrown themselves on her and hugged her fiercely. It was when they drew their faces back from hers that she felt the wetness on both her cheeks, and it wasn't hers. Mary Lee and Momma both were crying. Well, Patsy commenced to cry, too. They laughed, hugged again, then split the orange three ways. Whispering so as not to wake Daddy again, each told their favorite part of the day…

* *

Patsy looked around her bedroom. One broken pane of glass had taken her on quite a trip down memory lane!

Mary Lee came bouncing in, "Well, what are you doing still up? Tomorrow is your big day. Don't you think you need your beauty rest?"

"Yes. I was just thinking that tonight is my last night sleeping here in our bedroom, with you. And I was thinking how you and I have done a lot of growing up in here. And in a way, the room has grown up with us."

"Huh? Patsy you speak in riddles. Could you just say straight out what you mean?"

"Well, you know… like remember how we used to take a cardboard box and cut out doors and windows for a doll-house?"

"And make stick-people to go in it with Momma's clothes pins?" Mary Lee chimed in.

"Yes. And remember how we took Dickie-Ray's baby clothes and dressed the cat? What was that cat's name?"

"Her name was Lily and she was *my* cat. But you guys never called her Lily; I think just because I named her, y'all called her Kitty-Cat just to spite me."

Patsy laughed, "You and I lugged that cat ever-where, remember? And we were *not* trying to spite you, and that cat was *not* yours. It was a stray that came to us. And Lily was a boy cat—that's why we refused to call him Lily. But no one wanted to explain that to a five-year-old."

"You're kidding!"

"Naw," Patsy drawled. "But Mary Lee, there is something that's been bothering me."

"What Patsy? You sound so serious."

"Well, you know planning a new life with Danny is all very exciting."

"But?"

"But," Patsy took a deep, shaky breath. "I worry that I'll miss sleeping with you, and fighting with Daddy, and Momma's laughter. How do people live without laughter, Mary Lee?"

"Oh, there you go again, Miss Poetic."

"And that's something else. I've missed Hugh coming over here. I long for more discussions on literature and poetry, religion and philosophy. Now I'm afraid to face the fact that I will never have that again. He was a true friend, Mary Lee. I've lost a true friend. Why does life have to be like that?"

"I guess no one gets everything, Patsy. But the real loser here, as I see it, is Hugh. I've always felt bad for him. Ever-one knew he adored you, and you just dropped him like a hot potato just off the coals when Danny came home for Christmas. That's not like you Patsy. How could you do that?"

Patsy sighed. "I never wanted to hurt Hugh. I loved—I *do* love him dearly. But Hugh never held me like Danny does, Mary Lee, and Lord knows, he never kissed me."

"Did you want him to?"

Silence fell upon them, but within moments, Mary Lee's bubbling laughter erupted. Patsy raised one quizzical eyebrow before she joined her sister in the merriment. They laughed until their faces were tear-streaked. They said their prayers together one last time, then cried themselves to sleep in each other's arms.

Bill, Patsy's older brother, was in the Navy now, out in California. What would he say when he found out his old friend Danny had married his little sister? Patsy had the house all to herself. *Thank ye, Mary Lee… Thank you, God*, she whispered. Just then she heard music—a mouth harp playing "You Are My Sunshine." She flew to the porch door and there stood Hugh-Noble. "Oh, Hughie!" Patsy embraced him fully and the past five months of silence dissipated like morning fog lifting from the holler.

"Patsy, sweet Patsy. You truly do look like the sunshine today. What a beautiful dress. This is to be your wedding dress, then?"

"Yes Hugh." Patsy hung her head. "Dan bought the dress for me yesterday. We're getting married today, but you knew that. How?" Patsy looked up into the kindest eyes she had ever known.

"I just kind of figured it out. But I wasn't sure until I saw you."

"The new dress, huh?"

"No, not the new dress. It's that radiant smile on your face, girl."

"Sweet Hugh-Noble, that smile was from my joy at seeing my best friend in all the world at my door."

"Yes, I know that, too, but I also know that you would not look so radiant if it were not for the fact that you are marrying Dan Booker today. I couldn't be happier for you, Patsy. You are my best friend, too. I always knew that we would never marry, that someone else would come along and carry ye away. I always knew we were best friends, not lovers."

Patsy said nothing; only nodded.

Hugh pulled back from her and affected a stern voice. "Now, my friend, your dress is definitely something new. And I see you are wearing Mary Lee's white pumps from the prom; they will take care of something borrowed. That leaves what? Something old and something blue. Do you have something old, Patsy?"

Patsy blushed. "Plenty."

"Okay then." Hugh-Noble slid his hand out of his trouser pocket and held up a heart-shaped blue cameo pendant which hung from a string of yellow velvet.

"Oh Hughie!" Patsy reached out and caressed the dangling cameo with her finger tips before taking it from him and inspecting it more closely. The intricate carving depicted a young couple sitting and facing each other on what could easily be a porch swing, and behind them was a full white moon in a cameo blue sky. "Oh Hughie, this is too much!"

"I thought… Well, it's supposed to be you and Dan sitting there."

"I know, I know… But how did you know to get yellow for the cord?"

"I must confess that when I went into Butlers in Harlan, I heard Miss Fannie telling Mrs. Franch about your new dress."

"Oh Hughie, how am I going to live without my best friend?" She clutched his two hands in hers, with the yellow velvet cord dangling from her right thumb and the cameo tugging at her heart.

"Same way that you will live without your Momma and Daddy, and your brothers and sister, Patsy-June. It will be bearable because you will be sharing your days and nights with the love of your life."

Once again, Patsy only nodded. Hugh pulled a clean folded hankie from his pocket and wiped her tears. Using a single thumb, she wiped one lonesome droplet from under his right eye, even as a car roared up in a cloud of dust, with the horn blowing profusely.

Hugh-Noble bent and kissed Patsy, their first kiss. It was slow… soft… and sweet.

Alison L. McLennan

Sisters of Grace and Mud

On May 8, 1869 people all over the world waited for the word *done* to come over the telegraph wires. A big ceremony was supposed to take place in Promontory, Utah where Thomas Durant, the president of the Union Pacific railroad, would drive the final spike made of gold, which would connect the land from the Atlantic to the Pacific Ocean with rail track. People would soon be able to board Pullman train cars and travel from the east coast to the west coast of the United States without ever smelling a horse. Impatient hands held uncorked champagne bottles. But Instead of the word *done*, the word *delayed* came. The ceremony was held up for two days while Thomas Durant wired for money so that he could pay the angry mob of unpaid workers who had derailed his train and held him hostage until they were paid. Despite the delay, people celebrated. Bubbly flowed down bottlenecks and the brass bands played.

The saloon dwellers on Fifth Street in Ogden didn't care much for pomp and circumstance anyway. Nor did they need a reason to drink. By late afternoon, Pearl Kelly had drunk enough champagne to dissolve her aloof exterior. A flame of fiery red hair by the bakehouse caught her attention. She fluttered down the boardwalk like a moth drawn toward light. Mesmerized and determined, she jostled past clusters of people blocking her way, and even stepped into the muddy thoroughfare, because she was certain that the red-haired girl she saw in the distance was her sister.

"Annie, Annie," she called.

The red-haired girl sat slumped against the windowless bakery wall on an old split rail bench. She did not turn toward Pearl, nor even look up as Pearl stood over her. She clenched a worn crumpled bonnet and seemed to be searching the faded pattern for an answer to her troubles. Pearl's hands were clasped in hope and the vestiges of failed prayers. The girl finally noticed the shadow Pearl cast over her and looked up in confusion. Her dusty tear-streaked face was weathered beyond her years.

"My sweet sister, we're reunited at last." Pearl knelt, hugged the girl, and wept.

Behind Pearl, Johnny Dobbs stood slightly inebriated yet stern. "That's not your sister Pearl. Annie is dead. Let her go." He cast an irritated glance at them and returned his gaze to the street. With countless enemies in town for the big day, his nerves twitched, and his hand never strayed too far from his pistol.

Pearl hardly heard Johnny as the image of her dead sister's body appeared in her mind like a profane exhibitionist. The men delivering the body had claimed that Annie was murdered by road agents. But her bruised face and the gaping knife wound across her neck alerted Pearl there was more to the story than highway robbery. She shouldn't have looked. Annie's gruesome face always haunted her. Riddled with guilt and regret because she put her younger sister on a stagecoach unaccompanied, Pearl was paralyzed by the memory. She froze. Her lower lip trembled.

Johnny's voice softened, "Now Pearl, you know this girl ain't your sister unless it's her ghost." Johnny was trying in his way to throw her a lifeline, so he could pull her from the pit she so often fell into when her thoughts turned to Annie.

Pearl turned to the girl, held her chin with one hand, inspected her face, and searched her eyes. "But Johnny, she looks so much like Annie: the red hair, the blue eyes, and those little freckles on her nose. Poor Annie, God rest her soul." Pearl wept again. She couldn't help it, all the champagne, and then the girl.

Johnny Dobbs pulled a handkerchief from his pocket and handed it to her. "Pearl, this here's a celebration. Don't ruin it by mourning and mooning over the dead." He shook his head in exasperation. A man passing by stopped and stared. Pearl dabbed her eyes.

"Women. They cry like dogs piss." Johnny explained. The man nodded in commiseration and kept walking.

Pearl glared at Johnny for his callous remark. His insult riled her enough to pull her from her paralyzing grief. She was about to retort, but he spoke first.

His words came out like a bugle call. "Pearl! This is a big day. There's money to be made. Let's get back and see to business."

Seeing his impatience growing, Pearl dropped her rebuke. For the first time, she addressed the girl. "What's your name? You look so much like my dearly departed sister, Annie."

The girl hesitated. Her gaze drifted from the ground to her burlap sack. "My name is—Ruby. Ruby Dollhouse," she said. "It's very nice to meet you. I'm sorry I brought you grief by reminding you of your sister."

Pearl stood, threw her head back, and roared with laughter at the girl's obvious fib. "Ruby Dollhouse? What a name! You are Ruby Dollhouse and I'm Jane Eyre! I like your imagination, Sis. Where are all your people? How did you come to be such a wretch?"

At the mention of family, tears welled in the girl's eyes. Pearl smiled, dismissed her question, and tried to cheer her. "Never mind about that. Come, follow us. I'll get you a bath, some new clothes, and a hot supper. Would you like that Sis?"

"Pearl!" Johnny Dobbs exploded. "No one's going to want that lousy girl. She's a flying mess, as poor as Job's turkey."

Johnny was a bear, but he was Pearl's bear, and she knew how to make him dance. She left the girl's side, went to him, slipped her arms around his waist, gazed up into his eyes, and whispered, "I want to keep her. We can kill the lice and fatten her up. We've done it before. Look at that hair color—lot of men pay extra for that. I'll bet you five dollars I can turn this ugly duck into a swan!"

He melted as fast as a candlestick thrown into a forge. His eyes softened and he smiled at her. But he turned a doubtful, scrutinizing look toward the girl.

"I'll work real hard, sir," she said.

Johnny and Pearl looked at each other. They smiled, and their eyes filled with amusement.

"Come on then," he said and strode away.

Pearl grabbed Ruby's hand and pulled her from the bench. The girl gathered her sack and walked. Pearl noticed she was trying to hide a limp. Lucky, Johnny Dobbs hadn't seen it. He strode ahead and rudely bumped people out of his way. Composed and sober now, Pearl held her head high. It was going to be a busy night, so it was a good thing that she'd cried out most of the champagne.

When they reached the back door of the saloon, Johnny held the door open for Pearl and Ruby. Before entering, Pearl looked up and admired the three-story brick building. Not long ago, she, Johnny, and seven soiled doves had been living and working in canvas tents. With all they had saved following the railroad, they managed to buy one of the only brick buildings on Fifth Street. It was next to a bathhouse and close to the railway station. If she had hedged her bets right and Ogden became the official Junction City, they would make a fortune. The saloon sported a brass rail and a long mirror, which gave the illusion of space. Soon they'd replace the makeshift partitions upstairs with real walls. The soiled doves had risen the ranks of whoredom to become upstairs girls. And yet some of them still had the gall to complain.

As soon as they entered, Pearl smelled smoke coming from the kitchen. She scolded two girls for loafing, and then directed them to gather all the girls on the back stairs for a meeting. She ordered another girl to pump and heat water for baths. They had their own tub, but no running water yet.

When all seven sallies finally had their fannies seated on the back steps leading up to the cribs, Pearl gave them a lecture on how to conduct themselves. She warned them it would be a busy night and reminded them which token meant what, exasperated by how easily they forgot. The girls stared at Ruby. Finally, Pearl introduced her. "This is Ruby, she's my second sister. Tonight, she's just going to be a barmaid. And she's going to have the first bath." The girls glared at Ruby with menacing expressions. Pearl pointed at the girls. "Anyone who mistreats her will suffer my wrath."

She dismissed them and climbed the stairs to her room on the top floor. She took off her shoes and rested on her bed with her eyes closed. From her open window, she heard voices, horses neighing, and wagons rattling down the rutted road. Restaurant proprietors lured travelers by shouting the evening specials. It was going to be a busy night. She'd have to hurry, gussie up Ruby, and then get downstairs. Johnny Dobbs could handle the saloon, but when he tried to manage the girls and johns things always went south.

The girl appeared at her door looking like a newly sheared lamb, shivering and raw. An old rag was all that covered her. Of course the whores had given her a rag instead of a decent towel. She should have looked after Ruby herself. But she was tired from the long day and the canceled ceremony.

She wrapped Ruby in a robe and used the rag to squeeze the water from her hair.

"That was my first, ma'am," Ruby said.

"Your first? Your first what?"

"My first hot bath."

Pearl sighed in relief. "You had me worried for a minute. Did you enjoy it?"

"Oh yes, once I got used to it; it was heaven."

Pearl frowned at the girl's milky skin blotched with pink from the hot bath water and scrub brush. From her dressing table, she retrieved a bottle of her best skin oil. She put a few drops in Ruby's hand.

"Rub that all over. It'll keep your skin from getting dry and itchy."

Ruby sat at the vanity. Pearl pulled, combed, and pinned her hair. Finally, she dabbed rouge onto her lips, stepped back, and stared, both awed and ashamed of her creation. If Annie had lived, Pearl would have had to do this very same thing to her. There was no other way.

Ruby was so skinny it was difficult to find a corset that would tighten enough to give her an ample bosom. She instructed her how to pull on her first pair of stockings and attach them to the garter. A gust of wind slammed the bedroom door shut. The curtains billowed like ghosts, and the scent of rain filled the room. Pearl scurried over and shut the window. The rain pelted and tapped on the glass. Pearl placed her hand on it and watched the rain bleed translucent down the pane. Was there another way? Could she have spared her sister the brothel life? Could she save this girl from ruin? Pearl shook her head and sighed. Based on the condition she found her in, it was probably too late.

Pearl opened the door. Even from the third floor and with rain drumming on the roof, she could hear a commotion from the saloon downstairs as people packed in to escape the unexpected downpour. She finished dressing Ruby, gave her a new pair of high-heeled lace-up boots, and placed her worn holey boots out of sight under the bed.

The saloon was packed and noisy, yet the general din subsided as Pearl and Ruby made their entrance. Men stared. Johnny Dobbs stood behind the bar, arms wide, leaning on it as if it was his pulpit. Pearl led Ruby to him. He nodded and placed a fin in Pearl's outstretched hand.

"Thank you, Johnny." Pearl turned toward Ruby, tucked a piece of Ruby's hair behind her ear, and adjusted her dress. "Now, listen," she said to Johnny. "I'm going to get her some supper. She'll barmaid tonight. No whoring, unless I can find the right prospect. I need to get her trained and educated."

Johnny stopped wiping the bar and aimed an explosive look at Pearl. "Are you out of your goddamn mind? Look how busy this place is already. We're going to need all the girls we have on their backs upstairs. I've got plenty of men to help me down here."

Pearl put her hands on her hips, tilted her head, and spoke softly but firmly. "Johnny Dobbs, remember that you said the brothel is mine, to run how I see fit? I don't want to turn her out just yet. She needs training."

He leaned over the bar toward her and yelled into her face. "What training? You open your legs, lie back, and let the man do his business!"

Pearl shook her head and looked exasperated. "I didn't build what I've built, the reputation I have, on that kind of simple thinking."

"It's screwing, Pearl! Can't get much simpler than that!"

That night, Ruby held her own, carrying ale and whisky through the crowd to patrons who couldn't reach the bar. Unattended coach bags and instrument cases sat in corners tempting sticky fingers. Men played tense card games. They had more business than the upstairs girls could handle, so Pearl let the bats and owls in out of the rain, and told them that for a cut, that night only, they could ply their trade in the saloon. Every hour or so, she had Ruby bring the girls shandies, freshwater, and sweets.

Some brawls broke out, but overall the night was manageable until Pearl heard a piercing screech. She followed the sound until she saw Johnny Dobbs with his hands around Ruby's throat. Pearl pushed her way through the crowd and squeezed between them. She managed to free one of Johnny's hands from Ruby's neck by bending his thumb back. He hollered in pain and grabbed her. His thumbs dug into her arms as he tried to push her out of the way, so he could get back to strangling Ruby. Two of Johnny's men broke it up and shuffled them to the back. One man held Pearl and one held Johnny. It had happened before.

Pearl heaved and tried to catch her breath. "Don't you dare hurt her. She's just an innocent girl."

"Innocent!" Johnny yelled. "Do you know what that bitch did?"

"No, what could she possibly have done to deserve immediate strangulation?"

"She told every man in the whole damn saloon that she has syphilis."

Pearl looked at Johnny in shock and disbelief. "There's not a pox on her body." She turned to the girl. "Is it true? Do you have syphilis?"

Ruby averted her eyes and shook her head. Pearl tried to control her growing rage. If she struck the girl, Johnny would too, and that was more punishment than anyone deserved. Pearl had underestimated the girl, as she had always underestimated Annie: the fire in her eyes and the impish grin hidden by a charade of meek innocence. On countless occasions, Pearl had rescued Annie from the dire consequences of her own antics. Had her sister been murdered by random road agents, or had she incurred the wrath of a duped man?

"Pearl! What are you going to do? If you're not going to let me beat her, put her out right now," said Johnny.

Pearl looked through the opened back door at the steady rain and felt the chilly night air. Ruby met her eye with a pleading look. *Annie, oh Annie, what have you done?*

"She will undress to her undergarments. She will stand on the bar and confess her childish fib. And then she will stand by the piano, and let anyone who wishes inspect her for pox. At the break of day, she will gather her meager possessions and leave us. Does that satisfy you?" she asked Johnny.

Johnny scowled and glared at Ruby. He stormed back into the saloon. Ruby grimaced and looked at her hands.

"You should be grateful," Pearl said.

Ruby rose to the occasion. She stood on the bar, stripped to her undergarments, and with her chin up, and her voice loud and clear, she spoke. "I told y'all a fib tonight. I don't have the French Pox. I just said that so—I don't know why exactly. But it's not funny and it's not true. I'm going to stand there next to the piano and anyone who wants can come get a closer look. There's not a pox on my body." Catcalls and whistles, hoots and hollers erupted. The girl held up her hand for silence, and to Pearl's surprise, the saloon quieted. "And there's one other thing, I lied. My name's not Ruby; it's Ophelia."

She stepped off the bar and stood next to the piano, still as a statue with her eyes closed.

The ruckus continued. And from then on the girl was engulfed by men, so that Pearl could no longer see her. As night moved toward morning the fever pitch finally died down. Men were slumped over tables; drinks were abandoned half full. The piano player's fingers rested on the keys. With his eyes closed and his head bobbing, he managed an occasional broken tune. And yet there were still enough live ones stirring about that the saloon hadn't closed. The crowd of men around Ophelia was gone. She stood—skin sullied by sooty handprints; hair a wild mess; scratches and bruises all over.

A solitary fiddler appeared. He played *Amazing Grace*, first softly and then louder as he approached Ophelia. He hopped, still playing, from a chair to a tabletop, and onto the bar. The piano player awoke, found the tune, and accompanied him. The fiddler looked at Ophelia with large luminous eyes. She gazed up at him—entranced.

Pearl marveled. The girl had been mauled by men for five hours without a break. The music transformed her. Although her skin was bruised and battered, her eyes were at peace. She smiled at the fiddler and then sang alone with such clarity and soul-stirring beauty even the drunkest of men lifted their heads in wonder.

When the song was over she walked forward, stood in the middle of the saloon, removed her torn undergarments, and kicked the fancy high-heeled boots from her feet. Like a ragged, horseless Lady Godiva she walked naked and proud through the saloon toward the door. Her shoulder blades were so prominent they could have been attachments for wings. Silence filled the saloon. She walked out into the night. The wind blew the door shut behind her with a resounding thud. And then the din instantly returned. Patrons drank, cackled, and shouted. The piano player played a bawdy tune. Everything returned to normal. Only the fiddler put his instrument away and quietly wept into a glass of ale.

Pearl followed Ophelia out into the night. It was way past midnight but before the crack of dawn. The rain had stopped. Mist and steam rose from the muddy ground. Pearl spotted Ophelia walking east toward the settlement of Eden away from the railway's binding iron bands. Pearl tried to follow her, but as soon as she stepped off the boardwalk, she sank ankle-deep into the mud. The naked girl seemed to be walking on top of the mud without sinking. Mist swirled around her like an ethereal snake; her red hair rose from her head. Pearl blinked, and the girl was gone.

She tried to run after her, but she slipped and fell. "Wait! Annie! Ruby! Ophelia! Come back! Where will you go?" She stretched a muddy arm toward where the girl had vanished. "What will you do? How will you live?"

Bruna Gomes

The Terrace, Saint-Tropez

She smells of red onion. She should have picked them out of her sandwich. It's her third day on this job, she should know better. What are the tour guides going to think, or worse, the conservators? Should have asked the waiter to leave the red onion out when she ordered. A gardener walks past her with a spray-bottle of fertilizer and a pair of shears. She better introduce herself. Bends a stick of spearmint gum into her mouth. No, don't chew at work. Spit it out. The gardener kneels to the side of the footpath and plucks a yellow leaf from the stem of an orchid. She taps him on the shoulder. A bit unprofessional of her. Fixes her blazer. He turns around expectantly, as if ready to answer a tourist's question.

"Cille Beaufort," she announces herself, outstretching her hand. "The new director."

The gardener removes a glove and shakes her hand warmly.

"Welcome to The Gardner. I'm Marco, just part-time." He's got a slender face with hollow cheeks and large eyelids like French awnings. His hair, parted down the middle, swoops around his face. "You've got big shoes to fill," he laughs.

"I'm sure I do."

She looks around the courtyard. Some would consider this a dream job. Others would consider it a waiting room, a transition, a dream in progress. Elegant ferns curl through the air, green tendrils like ringlets. The ancient statues are smooth and staring. Tiny red blossoms adorn autumn-twisted branches like earrings, austere as a matriarch, and the air smells mossy and undiscovered, as if she was intruding.

She is no intruder.

She is the director.

She is almost stunned that she is the director of the Isabella Stewart Gardner Museum, but then again, of course she is the director. She is Cille. Blazer button fastened or unfastened? Fastened. The gingham looks good. Hanging nasturtiums fall like the skirts of a belly dancer around medieval arches, and ancient women of white marble gaze at her beneath helmets of stone ringlets. Persephone looks smug. She has always been Cille's favourite. In all Persephone's two thousand-ish years of living, she probably never smelt of red onion.

Marco was right, Cille *does* have big shoes to fill. The leather loafers of Anne Hawley are heavy with prestige and initiative. But she knows better than to wear someone's shoes to do their job. No, she will strut around in her own black stilettos and the renaissance halls will echo with the *clop-clop* of her impeccable direction. History will not repeat itself, there will be no robbery. There will be no shame. Years ago, she once befriended a thief and she knows what became of that. A red coffee machine and too many credit card bills for overseas flights. *Mon Dieu*, she is a good friend. Now she will be a good director.

She walks to the Yellow Room, where a conservator had said he should start working on the Matisse soon before the dust gets too thick. Matisse's soft, impressionist brushstrokes are blurred beneath the dust, making the scene yellow and hazy. The sunny landscape hangs above a cane lounge that looks dusty, too. In fact, the entire set of cane furniture in the Yellow Room looks dusty.

Cane always looks dusty; these people should know that.

Her grand-maman used to dust her cane twice a day.

She interrogates the rest of the paintings with a menacing squint, half to make an accurate judgment and half to look the part, before landing back on Matisse's *The Terrace, Saint-Tropez*. It is the one she always returns to, no matter what. The painting reminds her of her grandparents' house in the south of France that she used to visit as a child. Mornings of cherry jam and Persian orange cake. The stink of cheese from the cellar and the assortment of vials for Grand-maman's hypochondriac fantasies that rattled in her pocket like a bell on a cat's collar. The chamois heads that jutted out from the walls and the carpets of genet fur that Grand-maman walked around, never on. Horned walls and furry floors. Sometimes Cille thinks that Grand-maman wore a blue kimono on the balcony overlooking the sea, but she's not sure if she made that up because of the painting.

The painting comes first, and then her memories.

The painting is her memory.

Or maybe Grand-maman wore kimonos even before the Japanese wore kimonos.

Grand-maman is the woman in the painting.

That sounds right. That sounds like her ancestry: a legacy of pioneers. Her phone rings and two visitors turn quickly to stare down the unsolicited noise. She answers it.

"Yes?"

"Cille?"

"Speaking."

"We need you in the security room. We've got some updates."

"Good. I'm on my way."

* * *

When she gets home, she feels nostalgic for her mother's voice. She calls her and she picks up in the middle of the first ring.

"Maman! I have a new job. The Isabella Stewart Gardner Museum, you know the place."

"In Boston?" Her mother's accent is strong and alcoholic, so thick that the sound oozes like treacle.

"Yes."

"But I thought you got a job at The Met? In New York City."

She recites the excuse she had planned since the day they called to say she didn't get the job.

"I did, Maman, but I was told what I could and could not wear, and it was against my moral standards to work for such a sexist organization."

Her mother tuts through the speaker, tongue clicking against teeth.

"You are stubborn, you couldn't just wear a long skirt?" She had expected her mother to praise her. "What are you going to do in Boston?"

"The museum is a living museum, you would love it."

"They got burgled, Cille. Biggest art heist in history. What are you doing in a place like that?"

"Maman, do you remember Grand-maman's blue kimono?"

"Of course I do. She was the only woman in all of France to own such a fine kimono."

From the age of seven, Grand-maman treated Cille like an adult. She taught her how to moisturize her skin in upward strokes with her knuckles so she would never have to go to a dermatologist, because dermatologists always find something to burn off or cut away. She showed her how to crochet blankets and use them to decorate the living room. She fed her diluted glasses of wine at the dinner table and took her to the tennis club to gossip. She was a tall woman with a masculine face, liquorice eyebrows and a bulbous nose like a proboscis monkey. She wore her black hair in a small knot at the top of her head that made the rest of her hair balloon around her temples. It was always winter when Cille visited, in line with the Australian summer holidays, and she wishes she had been there on a hot day to see Grand-maman sit on her terrace with her face tilted to the sun, the silver hairs on her chin glowing and her eyes squinted shut. But she must have seen her sit in the sun like that, she can picture it so clearly. If she dusts off the memory even more, she can see all ten of Grand-maman's fingers strangled with thick gold rings and precious stones to make up for the wedding ring she no longer wore. She has asked Grand-maman about Grand-papa several times. She hardly ever answered. When she told Grand-maman about her Master's Degree of Art History she scoffed and said, "Cille, you do not need university for that. Study me. I am art history."

She pours herself another glass of red wine, not minding that it's a Wednesday night. She is an adult, art museum director, university graduate and almost-resident of New York City. She takes another sip of wine and it spills onto the couch. *Dieu*, she can't believe she *almost* lives in New York City. The red stain is going to annoy her now. She needs to scrub it with hot water before it dries. She could use the embroidered handkerchief her friend once gave her. It is an ugly handkerchief, but she likes that it's from Spain. She's getting groggy but she still has emails to reply to. She goes to the kitchen and turns on the espresso machine to let the water heat up. She pours coffee beans into the grinder and thinks how good the red machine looks in her apartment. She wonders if Marco the Gardener is single. She wonders if The Met has any new job openings. She knocks back her espresso and feels her teeth turn yellow so she goes to the bathroom and brushes her teeth. Minty fresh, minty fresh.

* * *

She tucks *The New York Times* under her armpit and rushes out the door, frustrated with herself for not waking up when the alarm went off. She knows better than to sleep in. No time to stop for breakfast, so her stomach will make whale sounds by mid-morning. She has a meeting with the head of the education department in twelve minutes and she is a seventeen-minute walk away from the office. To get there in time she is going to have to sweat, which will stain the pits of her houndstooth blazer, and if she ruins the blazer then she ruins the whole pantsuit set. Her feet disappear beneath the orange carpet of fallen leaves from the green ash trees, tickling her ankles. She stops every couple of minutes to bend down and itch them. She can feel her nose turning red and glacéd. The autumn is cold enough to preserve her suit.

Ainsley, the head of the education department, smells of tinned beetroot and Chanel No. 5. Cille can tell the perfume was an afterthought. Ainsley has a reddish bob that curls around her jaw and a smile of wide teeth that seems to go for infinity into her cheeks. The walls of her office are covered with posters about international art conferences and third-world art programs that happened so many years ago that the poster corners are too curled to lean against. She offers Cille coffee and she accepts it politely. She does not drink from it once throughout the entire meeting. Ainsley talks of proposals about a new high school program that works with the schools' syllabuses, smiling as she talks slowly.

"We need to build up our art community," she says, "we want the youth to be excited about the art community."

She repeats "art community" too many times.

"Do you know what pieces in our collection are already in the syllabus?" Cille asks.

"The Rembrandt, of course, Daddi's *Virgin and Child*. Mostly portraits. Schools like teaching portraits."

"What about a portrait of Isabella herself?"

"No, but they do Mancini's portrait of John Lowell Gardner Jr."

"Pa," Cille scoffs. "Boston has its own art history painted right in front of them and they choose her husband instead." Ainsley shakes her head in solemn agreement. "Alright, so tell them to swap out John with Zorn's portrait of Isabella. The light, the sensuality—perfect for a high school essay. Then I think we encourage more pieces from the Chinese Loggia, and please, get some landscapes in there. Start with *The Terrace, Saint-Tropez*. They cannot say no to Matisse. If they refuse, remind them of the kimono-d woman and call it a portrait. There, we have a program, yes?"

Ainsley frowns. Cille was quick. Cille was straight to the point. Ainsley can't find any faults in her suggestions. So, she smiles and says, "Fantastic. I'll get started." Before Cille leaves, Ainsley peers at her cup of cold coffee and asks, "So, does your love for art run in the family?"

Cille's eyebrows raise in surprise at her interest. "In a way, yes," she answers, halfway to the door. "My grand-maman crocheted her living room decorations and my grand-papa was a taxidermist. Turned the dead into the living."

"But he hunted the animals first?" Ainsley's teeth filled her face when she spoke. All chomp and no brain.

"The French! What can I say?"

"So you grew up there?"

Cille considers saying yes, but here, the truth is even more interesting.

"No, in Australia. Bondi. I went to France during the summer holidays."

"Lucky girl, your friends must have been jealous!"

Her hand is on the doorknob, ready to leave.

"I better return to the museum. I've got a job to do, make sure the past is still living, right? Maybe taxidermists aren't so bad."

She can hear Ainsley's confused laugh as she walks out and closes the door behind her.

* * *

From the courtyard, she spies Marco hanging nasturtiums from a third-floor balcony. She walks up despite the noises her stomach is making, quiet belches that echo at the back of her mouth. When she reaches him, he is delicately arranging the vines so they sit neatly over the ledge.

"How long do they last?" she asks from behind. He turns around to her. He's wearing a clean button-down tucked into brown chinos that are fastened with a belt. Neat and professional. His sleeves are rolled and buttoned. Casual and nimble.

"A little to the right!" a voice shouts from the other side of the floor. Cille peers across the balcony and sees a woman with a fluffy ponytail standing in the third-floor arch opposite her and Marco. Marco turns back around and does as he's told before answering,

"We swap them out every ten days or so. They grow in a greenhouse about a half hour away from here. We bring them in a van."

Cille knows all this but pretends she is intrigued.

"How long have you been a gardener?"

"Horticulturist."

"Horticulturist?"

"A few years, about six." Marco wipes his hands down the side of his pants and gives a thumbs-up to the woman at the opposite balcony. "Clem and I mainly look after the flowers in the courtyard, but every now and then we get to do some decorating. Makes the building look more alive, doesn't it? Less of a museum and more of a… history."

"Like my grandparents' house," Cille says. "Trees and vines bending this way and that, leaning into the house." She can remember the way the plants followed Grand-maman as if she were the sun, warping out of the shady corners and into the light.

"The plants here have to be resilient, because they are in the shade so much," Marco says, sort of ignoring her, sort of not really caring about her grandparents' house or the plants around it. It is strange of a horticulturist to not show much interest in such a monumental setting. What's the difference between a horticulturist and a gardener, anyway? "Well, I better leave you to your job. I'm sure you're much busier than me."

Cille smiles tightly to him and nods her goodbye, walking away with a tight chest, wondering what room she should check for dust next.

She enters the Tapestry Room like she is entering a medieval castle, making a b-line for the French chateaux fireplace. She already feels calmer. The lively Flemish tapestries hung around the wooden walls somehow remind her of Grand-maman's crocheted throws and blankets even though they look nothing alike. She supposes it's because they're woven, but these threads have woven scenes of heroism of historical episodes. She is sure that if she looked closely enough, Grand-maman's throws would depict something historical, too. Her phone rings, scaring her out of her stillness. It is her mother.

"Cille? Are you there?"

"Yes, Maman. What is it? I am working."

"I am going to France," she announces. "I need to check up on the property. I am due for a visit, we cannot let the house disintegrate into dust. Come with me. I will pay for your flight."

"But Maman," Cille says through a clenched jaw, "This is my fourth day as the director. I cannot just go to France, you know better than to ask that of me."

"Pa! You will miss out."

"Do you remember Grand-maman's crocheting?" She stares at the woven Persian scenes of Cyrus the Great.

"Of course. She began crocheting after she found out Grand-papa was having an affair."

Cille glares at the wool and silk hare that's concealing a letter.

Cyrus the Great does not look like Cyrus the Great.

He looks like a medieval European fake.

Not a Persian king.

"Are you sure, Maman?"

The historically inaccurate fashion is just a representation of political scheming.

It connected the past and the present.

She knows this, she studied this.

539 BC connected to 16th century.

"No," Maman's reply sounds woven and unsteady, "I think she was just distracting herself from her loneliness. Your grand-papa was always out hunting for his taxidermy."

"But she had you to keep her company in those days, right?"

"Of course!"

"Ok, Maman. Kiss Papa hello for me."

* * *

Cille wakes up at 5:00 in the morning and goes for a run around Back Bay Fens in the blue dark. She couldn't fall back asleep after she woke up before her alarm even though it is Saturday. She needs the exercise anyway. She wears a headband that covers her ears and she wears leg warmers even though she had to stuff them into her shoes. The park is empty and noiseless, wet with the smell of dew. She doesn't think she has ever seen France in the dark. She runs beneath a ghostly canopy of skeletal tree branches. She doesn't think she has seen a bare tree in France before. The sweat on her face turns cold and numbs her cheeks. She should check again if The Met has any new job openings. They have Van Gogh's *Wheat Field with Cypresses* and Cassatt's *Lydia Crocheting in the Garden at Marly*. Imagine what her mother would say if she got a job there, working in the swirling French fields beside the wonderful crocheting Lydia dressed in blue. She weaves her way around the Emerald Necklace as the sky turns pale, creating milky lines on the river.

Turning off the park and onto Queensbury Street, she runs back to her apartment, does her laundry, and drinks two espressos to thaw her cheeks. Light slowly warms the kitchen as the sun rises onto the crisp day, and she thinks she should look through her directory of employees to find Marco the Horticulturist's number. She doesn't yet have many friends in Boston. She finds his name under the heading Landscape and Gardens and she dials his number promptly. He picks up, confused as to why the director is calling him on a Saturday, so when she asks if he wants to come over, he says yes out of wary politeness. He asks what time and she says it doesn't matter.

After he hangs up she goes to Jamaica Plain Farmers Market and fills a canvas tote with produce. The fruit stands are bright and the tent of jarred honey perfumes the air, smelling of Spring. She returns home and prepares a Persian orange cake, not because she likes baking but because she is good at it, and she reads *The New York Times* while it bakes. She changes into a square-neck blouse and then changes again into a collared linen shirt. She spoons dollops of cherry jam onto thick slices of camembert and arranges them on a plate. She ties her hair into a bun but because she recently got it layered, pieces fly out and it looks messy. Before she can untie it the doorbell rings and she's letting Marco through the door.

He looks sallow and handsome, like a man ready to be fed. He's wearing the same outfit as the other day, but his chinos are beige and his shirt is untucked. He sits at her dinner table in front of the cheese plate while she stands in the kitchen slicing the cake. She unties her hair while he isn't watching. "I hope you weren't busy today?" she asks loudly.

"No, I like to leave my weekends free to relax."

She carries the cut cake to the table and puts it next to the cheese. "Help yourself."

He nods a thank you.

"You said you work part-time at The Gardner?"

He nods again, not bothering to look at her. "I do maintenance at the James P. Kelleher Rose Garden."

"I ran past there this morning."

Marco smiles with uninterested surprise. His hair looks freshly washed, its buoyant sweep falling above his eyebrows and over his ears. He's sitting uncomfortably with skewed shoulders and Cille wonders if she should move the conversation to the couch. His face shutters between confusion and boredom. He's waiting for her to make it clear as to why he was invited.

"My grand-maman used to make this cake for me when I visited her in the summer," she offers.

"It looks good," he says, still leaving her food uneaten.

"It is. Those are rose petals on top."

"I know."

"And pistachios."

Marco cracks his knuckles and yawns into his collar.

"How has your time been as a director so far?" He shimmies back in his seat and crosses his arms on the table.

"Good. It's what I set out to do."

"You've always been interested in art?"

She pours herself a glass of mineral water and takes a long sip. "Ever since I first visited France, yes. The view of the sea is enough to inspire anyone with an artistic passion."

"How old were you when you first visited?"

"About eight months old," she says. She sounds defensive. He smirks rudely. "My grandparents demanded that my mother show them their baby granddaughter before she became a toddler. I am an only child. It was important to them. Everything in France is important."

"I can tell."

"Of course, in Australia, the art culture isn't as rich, but I learnt so much in France that it did not matter."

"Naturally. And what of the Indigenous art?" His voice is squeaky with amusement.

"Indigenous Australian art is wonderful. Like maps. It just doesn't point me to my ancestry. My ancestry, my artistic history, lives in France. Like a living museum."

"Your artistic history."

He's mocking her now.

As if he has the right. As if he isn't her employee.

Cille puckers like a Totalitarian.

"Yes, well, if you're not hungry, don't let me hold you up. I am sure you have things to do."

Marco laughs in surprise at his sudden dismissal and scratches the back of his neck. "Did you need anything else?"

"I'll see you at the museum on Monday."

"I'm at the Rose Garden on Mondays." Marcos stands up and knocks on the table as a sort of farewell.

It echoes throughout the apartment.

His chinos are wrinkled behind his knees.

He sucks his cheeks into his mouth, making them look so hollow that he becomes a skeleton, and as she walks him to the door she can smell the soil beneath his fingernails, like decomposed sunlight. As she turns the doorknob her phone vibrates in the pocket of her jeans. It's her mother again. She smiles tightly to Marco and as if asking for his patience and answer the phone.

"Maman?" She takes her hand off the doorknob.

"Cille. You remember Grand-maman's blue kimono?"

"Of course I do. She wore it even before the Japanese."

"I cannot find it."

"What do you mean Maman?"

Marco is staring at his feet and Cille starts staring at them too, panicked. The rubber edge of his shoes is also dirty with soil, and she realizes he has probably trailed it all over the apartment.

"Just now, I went to check her closet to check that nothing had mothballs or silkworms, like I always do. I cannot find the kimono, Cille. It is not here."

Her face must look as contorted as her thoughts, because Marco puts his hand on her back and asks if everything is alright. She turns his hand away with a violent twist. Suddenly her hand is reverberating with an incoming call, and she hiccups. She holds the phone in front of her to see the call from the head of museum security.

"Maman," she rushes, "stay there. The museum is calling, stay there."

"That Boston museum?"

"Hold on Maman."

She switches calls and answers security. Marco is looming in front of her like a marble sculpture.

"Cille?" The voice says her name regretfully. "*The Terrace, Saint-Tropez* has been stolen."

Anne Britting Oleson

Ulnar Splint

Genevieve consciously smoothed her facial expression into impassivity, keeping her eyes wide and focused on the red-headed doctor as he indicated the x-ray. The widening eyes were meant to give him—or anyone else, such as the nurse laying out a tray in the corner—the impression of a doddering old woman; to minimize her height, she remained seated, too, squinting at the computer monitor: doddering old women were not taller than condescending upstarts of doctors half their age.

The fifth metacarpal of her right hand: the hairline fracture midway along the bone was visible as a tiny crooked pathway of light.

"If it were further up toward the fingers and the cap of the bone—" he tapped the screen with a fingernail—"we'd have called it a boxer's fracture." He turned toward her and chuckled. "You haven't been boxing, have you?"

Genevieve tittered, judging that to be an appropriate response. "Oh, no, Doctor. At my age?"

The nurse looked up sharply as she wheeled the tray closer. Genevieve smiled vaguely at her. Perhaps the tittering was too much?

The doctor turned his attention to the sterile packs on the tray the nurse had moved to his elbow. Genevieve watched his fingers sift among the implements. "We'll have to splint this, of course, to keep it immobile while it heals." He pulled a stool closer with a foot, then settled on it, taking up the packaged flexible splint, and some scissors. He looked up. "It could take a while—up to four weeks." He held out a hand, and after a moment Genevieve realized he wanted her right arm. Too late, she realized she should have trembled a bit as she gave him her own hand—old women trembled, didn't they? *Focus*, she admonished herself.

She winced as he fitted the splint along her pinky and down to her wrist. Using the scissors with the angled blades and blunted tip, he cut the material to fit.

"So… how *did* you break your hand?" he asked.

Genevieve kept her eyes wide, her posture less than straight, her expression vague. *You are an old woman.* "I fell," she said.

Too late she realized the trap.

She left a message on Lance's voicemail. He called back within the hour.

"Can you take some days off and travel up? I might need you."

She heard him suck in a breath. "Is it Paul? Is there something wrong?"

"It's not always about Paul, young man," she said briskly. But there was affection in her voice. "In any case, he'd ring you up before he would me."

Lance laughed. "I suppose."

"So do come. Take the earliest train. I'll repay you for the ticket when you arrive."

"I'll try." There was a pause, then, "What do you need?"

Genevieve's laugh was short. "A great-grandson."

Lance coughed slightly. "Mrs. Smithson—I'm Black."

"I'd noticed," she said dryly. "Doesn't matter. Three generations removed? There could be any manner of genetic permutations."

Now Lance sighed mightily. "I'll try," he repeated.

Genevieve had read people for so long that she knew she'd hooked Lance. She allowed herself a few moments of remorse for manipulating him, and then got on with business. Going through to the kitchen, she flicked on the kettle before realizing with annoyance that, with this blasted ulnar splint, she'd have to curtail the full tea-making process she'd always enjoyed. She should have learned to be ambidextrous. Her husband—she paused momentarily and allowed herself a brief smile at the thought of Honoré—had been ambidextrous; no broken bone in his dominant hand would have set him back. Of course, had she been twenty years younger, or forty, no bone in her dominant hand would have *broken*. Had she just kept in practice, pounding the side of her palm against the table as they'd had to do at Arisaig, she would not have found herself in this predicament. With a sigh of annoyance, she drew out a mug and a single tea bag. She wondered how Lance would fare, making tea.

He appeared shortly after five, knocking twice at the door, then waiting a beat before knocking twice more. Genevieve worked all the locks more slowly than she usually did, but opened the door at last, smiling. Lance's dark eyes creased at the corners.

"What took you so long?" he demanded, though in jest. He hefted his backpack and weekend bag, and brought them into the hall. Then his gaze fell on her splinted and wrapped arm. "What happened?"

Genevieve waved his concern away. "Long story."

"And if you told me, you'd have to kill me?"

"Very funny, young man." She lifted her chin toward the stairs. "Your usual room. Take yourself up, then join me in the kitchen."

She watched his retreating back, then checked the locks on the door before heading back down the hall to the rear of the house.

"I made a mistake," she said in the kitchen.

Lance nearly spit out his tea. "*You?*"

"Stop it. I'm an old woman. It happens."

He used the tongs to drop another sugar cube into his tea. Genevieve grimaced in distaste, just watching. He sipped from the mug before tipping his head to the side, a rather endearing mannerism.

"Mrs. Smithson, you only use that as an excuse when you're trying to deflect. You're the most capable person I've ever met. In fact, you're damned frightening."

"I'm not now," she said. "I *am* an old woman, and I *did* make a mistake. I told the doctor I broke my hand in a fall."

He sipped some more tea. She did too. Hers was black. So un-English.

"And?"

"My GP has been agitating for the past several years for me to leave my house and move to some sort of care facility." Genevieve grimaced again; this recurrent theme tasted worse in her mouth than did over-sugared tea.

"You've resisted."

"Of course I've resisted. I will only leave this home in a body bag." Like Honoré. But *that* body had not housed Honoré, she reminded herself; *that* body had not housed Honoré for years. "Still, I'm fully expecting a visit from Social Services tomorrow, or perhaps the next day. Because I fell."

"And you need me for moral support?"

Genevieve raised her bandaged hand in impatience. "Oh, do hush, Lance, and listen to me."

Lance held up both hands in surrender. "My mistake was telling the doctor I fell. I had to tell him something. But I'm fairly certain that as soon as I left that office, he was on the telephone to Social Services. You see? I played right into his hands."

"And you're not going to tell me what happened."

"If I did, Lance—"

"You'd have to kill me."

They both laughed.

The knock came the following afternoon. Genevieve let Lance answer the door, while she waited in the library, pretending to read. *A Year in the Life of Mobius,* by Aventurine Morrow. She set the book aside as Lance ushered the visitor through. "This is Patricia Folger, from the

Council," he said. He brushed a hand over his dark hair. "I'll get some tea, shall I, Great-grandmother?"

"Thank you, Lance, if you'd be so kind."

Genevieve stood and straightened her back: she thought she had about six inches over the visitor. She made no move to meet her halfway, but forced Patricia Folger to cross the length of the Aubusson carpet to her. She was gratified that the other woman had to lift her chin to meet her eyes. She waved her bandaged hand toward the settee. "Please. Have a seat. Forgive me for not shaking your hand, but as you can see, I've sustained an injury."

Patricia Folger was wearing a twinset, and a practical purse was tucked over one arm. She set this aside once she had brought out a small notebook. "Thank you, but I don't need anything. I'm making this call at the behest of your GP."

As if on cue, the cat wandered in from the front hall, wispy tail at attention. She headed toward the settee, noted the stranger, then changed course to leap into Genevieve's lap. There she curled up, while Genevieve stroked her fur with her left hand. "Ah, yes."

"About your injury." Patricia Folger flipped through several pages of notes, then squinted and read. "He is concerned about your fall." She looked about her at the furnishings, the mirror over the fireplace, the long curtains at the windows that pooled on the floor. "And your age."

Genevieve nodded again. "Ah, yes," she repeated, giving no help at all. She continued to stroke the cat.

There was a noise from the hall, and Lance appeared, carrying the silver service. Genevieve smiled at him, as devotedly as she knew how. She was surprised to realize that it wasn't difficult. She moved the Morrow book aside, and he lowered the tray onto the table beside her. "Thank you, darling," she said, then turned to their visitor. "Milk, Miss Folger? Sugar?"

"It's *Mrs.* Folger, actually, and thank you, none for me."

"Very well." Genevieve fixed a cup for Lance, with milk and two sugars, then poured out a cup, black for herself. He settled into the other armchair. "You were saying, Mrs. Folger?"

The woman was clutching her notebook as if for support. She looked from Genevieve to Lance and back again. Her jaw tightened. "I was sent to check on your well-being."

Genevieve turned to Lance. "Because of my fall, and my age," she said.

"Ah, yes," said Lance. He turned to Mrs. Folger, tilted his head. Genevieve tilted hers, too.

"I'm fine, as you can see, Mrs. Folger," Genevieve assured her. "Lance here is taking wonderful care of me."

"And how *did* you fall, Miss Smithson?"

Genevieve raised an eyebrow. "It's *Mrs.* Smithson, actually, and I fear the cat here tripped me in the kitchen while I was feeding her."

The cat, on cue, yawned, showing off her fangs. Genevieve scratched behind her ears.

The other woman wrote something in the notebook. "I'm sorry," she said, turning her gaze on Lance, "but I don't recall what you said your full name was?" *And who you are*, her narrowed eyes clearly added.

"Lance Miller," he said. He sipped his tea.

"He's my great-grandson," Genevieve lied cheerfully.

Mrs. Folger wrote, then stopped, looking up. "But—"

"I'm Black," Lance finished for her. "Everybody notices that."

She winced, put up a quick hand. "No, no—"

"It's three generations removed, Mrs. Folger," Lance said.

"And there could be any manner of genetic permutations," Genevieve added.

Lance showed a flustered Patricia Folger to the door, and returned with the post and the newspaper in his hand.

"They'll send someone else, probably tomorrow, trying to catch us up," Genevieve said, leaning back in her chair and drinking from her refilled teacup. "If you could stay through, that would be useful."

But Lance was only half-listening. He had set the post aside, and now shook the paper out. "Did you see this?" he asked, holding it up to show her the front page above the crease.

Body Found at Rose Theatre Identified

"Of course I hadn't. You just brought in the newspaper." Genevieve leaned forward slightly in her chair, the better to see what the paper had to say.

Lance cleared his throat. "'The body discovered in the ladies' toilets at the Rose Theater two nights ago has been identified as that of Natalya Vasilyevna Balakin, a Russian national. Unofficial reports suggest the cause of death was a crushed windpipe. Balakin was named as a person of interest in the death of British statesman David Corwin by poisoning last month, authorities say.'"

"Oh, dear," Genevieve sighed. She leaned back again, took another sip of tea.

"A Russian spy," Lance mused, peering at her with his dark eyes. "A Russian assassin."

Genevieve finished her tea and set the cup aside. She met his gaze steadily, cradling her injured right hand with her left. "Right here in York." She shook her head. "Imagine that."

Joe Kilgore

Waitin' for the 12:15

six o'clock

The way I see it, mornin's not really mornin' 'til that first cup of coffee's in your hand. When that hot black brew slides across your tongue, well, seems to me it fires your soul as well as your gullet. Assuming you have a soul. Reverend Ogilvy tells me everybody has one, but I have my doubts. Too long in the job I guess. Seen too many things I'd give a brood mare not to remember, but for whatever reason simply can't find a way to forget. Heard it said there are some people who actually don't drink coffee. Not sure I believe that. But if there are some of that persuasion, I don't think I'd trust 'em. Course, there are a lot of people I don't trust for one reason or another. Don't get me wrong, I'm not one of those—what do they call 'em—oh yeah, one of those misanthropes you hear about now and then. It's just that doubt and mistrust are load-bearing occupational hazards when it comes to being Sheriff of Concho County.

Once I've had one or two cups of coffee I'm generally ready to kick off the day. Though in my line of work, one day is pretty much like another. Hell, I've never been one to go out of my way to make tomorrow different from yesterday. There's a lot to be said for routine. Keeps a man centered, squared on what needs to be done and how he ought to go about doing it. So, for me, it's generally coffee first, saddle up and ride to the jail second, then just sit around and wait to hear from some fearful or disgruntled citizen that the general peace is being disturbed in one way or another and someone needs to do something about it. That someone would be me, of course. And what

I have to deal with, plus how I go about it, provides what passes for variety. Yep. Each day is pretty typical. I'd like to think this one will be too. But I know there's little chance of that. You see today, Galworthy Primrose is comin' in on the 12:15.

seven o'clock

Galworthy is a former citizen of Paint Rock, our little oasis that is pretty much smack dab in the middle of the sand and dust that is central Texas. I refer to Galworthy as a former citizen because for the last five years his official residence has been the state lockup. It's a mystery to me how he managed to survive life behind bars alongside the miscreants and malcontents that populate that place. Never one to go along to get along, Galworthy, or GW as he preferred to be called, never met a man he didn't insult or a woman he didn't offend. Maybe to endure the hell of his environment he got even meaner in prison than he was in Paint Rock, though I wouldn't have thought that possible. Oh well, for good or ill—and I damn sure know which it'll be—I'm going to be his welcoming committee.

There are some folks who've been around Paint Rock even longer than I have. Not as long as the Lipan Apache who likely drew the pictures on the cave walls that gave the town its name. If the Lipan had known GW, there's no doubt in my mind that he wouldn't have grown to manhood. He would have surely done something rank enough to warrant a young brave lifting his hair and hanging it on his lance. But white folk seem to be able to put up with a lot. And old-timers tell me that's exactly what they had to do with Galworthy.

Apparently GW started out bad and just kept getting worse. As a kid he often drowned cats, threw rocks at dogs, and chopped the heads off chickens whether they were meant for supper or not. His rampage through puberty was a bit like Sherman's march through Atlanta. Young females eagle-eyed enough to see him coming, would scatter like startled quail. Those who didn't spot him in time often were petted and pawed without permission. A hellacious slap in the face might pause his behavior temporarily, but history was apt to repeat itself regardless. Nor did he give a good goddamn for honoring his father or mother or respecting his elders. The more feeble the codger, the more likely GW was to trip him, pull his chair out from under him, or accidentally-on-purpose step on his spectacles. There are those who claim without reservation that Galworthy was actually born an asshole, and something resembling a human being merely grew up around him. Nature can produce some strange things, alright. And there's no doubt that GW is one of the strangest.

As he grew into what could be called young manhood, our paths crossed from time to time. But like most bullies, he kept his contemptible conduct under wraps when any real authority figures were around—preferring to have his way with those who he saw as weaker or more vulnerable. All things considered, while he was always a detestable human being, he wasn't a hard core criminal. At least, not yet. But then, fate stepped in. His old man died and GW inherited his paw's .44 Walker Colt. And wouldn't you know it, the kid took to that gun like buzzards take to carrion. He learned to shoot straight and draw fast. Faster than most of the young bucks in Concho County. And he wasn't scared to draw blood either. Fact is he goaded more than one testosterone-filled cowboy into gunfights that ended with their imminent demise. But GW always made sure they drew first—keeping him legally innocent. Though that word sours the stomach when it's used in connection with Galworthy Primrose.

8 o'clock

The event that sealed our undying animosity toward one another is remembered in Paint Rock by more than just GW and me. Hiram Ludlow owns the only mercantile in town. He was in the back taking inventory while his daughter, Mercy, was responsible for any customers that might wander in. GW did the wandering, stewed to the gills on Tangle Leg Rye and raging hormones. He grabbed Mercy by the arm and started dragging her toward the back of the store. Little Joey Wilson was by the candy counter at the time. He may not have been old enough to know exactly what GW had on his mind, but he was old enough to know that Mercy's screaming and crying was a direct result of Galworthy's obnoxious behavior. So he lit out to find me.

GW, with Mercy in tow, had to pass through the storage area on his way out the back door. Hiram heard the commotion, dropped his inventory notes immediately, and stepped forward to put a stop to what was about to happen. GW never broke stride. As he walked and yanked Mercy, he simultaneously pulled his colt from its holster and used it to backhand Hiram across the bridge of the nose. The force was such that the storekeeper careened over a box of canned beans, fell to the floor, and immediately passed out, bleeding profusely. Once outside, GW started reaching for Mercy's various lady parts while trying to plant a kiss in the middle of her mouth. But the outraged young woman was in no mood to give up without a fight. Hitting, punching, scratching and clawing, she was giving GW a hell of a lot more than he bargained for. So he quickly put an end to her protestations by delivering a right cross to the firebrand's jaw. She hit the dirt comatose, but her lack of responsiveness didn't seem to assuage GW's romantic ardor. He began to unbutton the fly of his trousers slowly, savoring what was about to come next.

Unfortunately for Galworthy, what came next was me. On my way through the store I picked up a tool and carried it with both hands to the back of the mercantile. GW heard my boots banging down the wooden steps and started turning to see if he was about to be further interrupted. He was. Just as his peripheral vision began to catch sight of me, I swung and caught him square in the forehead with the business end of a long-handled spade. He didn't wake up 'til he was behind bars and awaiting trial.

Both Mercy and Hiram Ludlow recovered from their injuries and testified against GW. You could tell the judge was moved by their retelling of the heinous events, yet unmoved by the defense attorney's plea of diminished capacity, or that abstract concept some easterners refer to as leniency. He brought the hammer down and sentenced the offender to five years hard time. Galworthy, seemingly oblivious to the victims' or the judge's role in determining his fate, saved his ire and his promise of revenge for me. Before they led him out of the courtroom, GW looked me in the eye and said, "We'll settle this the day I get out." That would be today.

nine o'clock

This being Saturday, Wayne Gardner should be at the jail by now. But his horse's not hitched out front. Wayne's my weekend deputy. I use him on Saturdays because folks tend to get a lot more liquored-up on this particular day, and I can use the help. Sundays are generally pretty quiet, so I have Wayne watch things while I take the day off— unless duty calls—and Wayne always knows how to get hold of me.

But here's the odd thing. Wayne's not at the jail. Not in the office. Not in the cells. Not in the outhouse either. That's odd because Wayne never misses his weekend stints. Likes both the job and the money. If you can say one thing about Wayne, it's that he's reliable as sweat in July. Hope he's not ailin'. Guess I should ride out to his place and make sure he's okay. It's not that far. Just north of town a bit. Things seem quiet anyway. I'll go check on him.

ten o'clock

Apparently, Wayne ain't home. Neither is his wife. I yelled for 'em out front. Even got off my horse, strode across the porch and knocked on the door. No response. Turned the knob, or tried to. Door was locked. Which is kinda odd. Don't see much of that in Paint Rock. Oh well, I'll head back to town. Maybe I'll learn later where Wayne and his better half has gotten off to.

Now I know what some of you are thinkin', but don't go jumping to any rash conclusions. Like I said, Wayne's a responsible man. Sure, he and just about everyone else in Paint Rock has heard that Galworthy's served his time and that today he'll be comin' in on the 12:15, but that's no reason to start casting aspersions on my deputy's character. Wayne Gardner is no coward. It's not out of the realm of possibility that his missus might have tried to talk him into stayin' out of harm's way, but Wayne's not one to crabwalk trouble. Wouldn't have made him my deputy if he shied away from confrontation. You get a boatload of that in our business. My guess is they both got called away for some emergency, you know? Like a family matter or something like that. Probably had to light out in hurry. No time to let me know. Probably planning on filling me in soon as he gets things under control…or soon as he gets back…whichever comes first. You know what I mean.

eleven o'clock

Been back in town for some time now, and things just keep getting stranger. Thought I'd walk over to Ludlow's Mercantile and let Hiram and Mercy know that they needn't have a concern about Galworthy Primrose being back in town. Wanted to assure both of 'em that I'd make sure he kept his distance. I figure even GW's not stupid enough to get back involved with the folks who stimulated his ultimate undoing. Though that may be giving him a lot more credit than he deserves. GW and stupid have been on intimate terms for as long as I can remember.

Was unable to give 'em any peace of mind though, cause they were nowhere to be seen. Store was locked up tighter than a spinster's knees. Which is particularly confounding. Saturday is one of Hiram's busiest days. Folks come in from out of town to replenish supplies or pick up fabric for the ladies, candy for the kids, or an extra jug or two for the coming week. Doesn't make sense that Ludlow's would be shuttered today. Course a lot of things have stopped making sense. Making my rounds, I found that Reverend Ogilvy had the door to the church closed and latched. He keeps the place open all the time. So sinners can repent day or night, he says. But that sure ain't the case at the moment. As you might expect, the saloon's doors swung open when I shoved, but the place was devoid of customers. Nobody sittin' at the poker tables. Nobody with a foot on the rail at the bar. The piano player wasn't there. Even the bartender was missing in action. And there's generally beaucoup action in that place on a Saturday. It's just weird. No horses at hitchin' posts or water troughs. No pedestrians strollin' the sidewalks. No cowhands ridin' in hard ready to raise hell. The whole dang place is kinda like a ghost town.

Even dropped in to see a lady I know. Well, lady is definitely bein' kind I guess, but she sees her way to not accepting any form of remuneration for the time we spend together. Which is the polar opposite of her regular modus operandi. Thought I might at least get a kind word or two from her, seeing as how it's gettin' mighty close to what's liable to be mine or you-know-who's last noon. Hell, even she wasn't in her room.

twelve o'clock

Time to face facts, I suppose. Everyone's assuming Galworthy and me are gonna go barrel to barrel. And no one wants to be in range when the lead starts to fly. I won't call 'em deserters. Yeah, there was a time when citizens respected the ones they paid to maintain law and order. Even backed 'em when it was needed. But times change, and I guess people do too. Guess the way they see it, they're not the one wearing the badge, and they're in no hurry to risk life and limb when they have someone like me gettin' paid to do just that. Plus, they ain't at all sure who'll be walking away when it's done. I ain't so sure either. Like I said before, GW was fast. Damned fast. And accurate too. It's possible that five years wearing a ball and chain instead of a sidearm might have slowed his hand or dulled his eye. But goin' mano a mano is a hell of way to find out.

I could walk down to the depot, to check with Harvey Beckwith, the station agent, to see if that iron horse is gonna be on time. But there's really no point in that. If all these other folks have hightailed it, you can bet Harvey's exited the premises some time ago. Guess I'll just walk out and wait in the middle of the street…after making sure I have a full load in my Colt Dragoon.

12:15

I'm sweatin'. I admit it. The closer it gets to showdown the wetter my shirt gets. Hope GW won't notice that. Might bolster his resolve. Maybe give him an advantage. Got a feeling he don't need one. I used that shovel on him five years ago so I wouldn't have to find out if he was faster than me. Gonna' find out today though, no getting' around that. Well…might as well man up. Cause here he comes now.

"That you Galworthy?"

"It's GW. And I ain't changed that much."

"I see you're packin'."

"Told you we were gonna settle this the day I got out."

"That you did."

"Well, I'm out."

"I can see that, Galworthy."

"It's GW, damn it."

"We do have a bit of a problem, though."

"Oh yeah, what's that?"

"You still committed to always letting the other man draw first?"

"Yep. That way, I don't get in trouble with the law for sendin' other yahoos to hell."

"But you see, I am the law. And being a lawman, I'm encumbered from drawin' first.

"You're en… what?

"I'm not allowed to draw first. So…we have a problem. What do you think we should do about it, GW?"

"Well, I don't rightly know."

One thing obviously hasn't changed. When it comes to usin' his brain instead of his gun, Galworthy is still a few ponies shy of a remuda.

"Tell you what. Why don't I count to three, then we'll both draw at the same time."

"You mean like one…two…three."

"That's what I mean."

"And when you say three…we both draw?"

"That's what I said."

"I'm good with that."

"You sure I can't talk you out of this, GW? I mean you just got out of prison. Seems a shame you ought to go right back in or take up permanent residence on Boot Hill."

"You ain't talkin' me outta nothin'. You took five years of my life. Now I'm gonna send your badge-totin' soul to hell you lily-livered, scum-suckin', chicken-shit lawman."

"Worked on your vocabulary in the pen, did you Galworthy?"

"It's GW, you wise-ass. Now start countin'. And say that three good and loud."

"Well, if there's no gettin' round it… then here goes. One!"

I never got to two. After that first number cleared my lips, there was a thunder of gunfire the likes of which hadn't been heard in Paint Rock since a war party of Lipan tried to put the whole town to the torch. Galworthy was sent into a spasmodic dance of death as bullets bore down on him from multiple directions. Unbeknownst to me, Deputy Wayne had concealed himself on the roof of the bank and used his Sharps Carbine to drill GW just about heart high. Hiram Ludlow, who was on one side of his store, had taken a brand new shotgun off the shelf in order to empty both barrels into Galworthy's gut. Mercy, on the mercantile's other side, aimed her Winchester somewhat lower and obliterated GW's manhood. Reverend Ogilvy, hidden in the hotel's doorway, squeezed off a round from a single action army revolver and delivered a message of salvation to the right side of Galworthy's skull. That lady I mentioned seeing from time to time, stood behind a barber pole and used her pocket derringer to indent GW's right kneecap. The boys from the saloon, who had taken up positions in the buildings' shadows all around main street, had apparently finished their drinkin' before I scoped out the bar earlier. They fired numerous rounds that found purchase in Galworthy's arms, neck, and feet. Believe it or not, even little Joey Wilson, crouched behind a water trough, used his air rifle to riddle GW's corpse with BBs.

There's no gettin' round it. I had initially entertained the notion—only for a moment, mind you—that the citizens of Paint Rock had deserted me in my hour of need. Nothin' obviously, could be further from the truth. They recognized evil when they saw it, and they weren't about to give it an opportunity to prevail. Course, I am the sheriff. I am responsible for maintaining what passes for law and order in this town. And while I'm certainly not a proponent of vigilante justice, I do understand that nobody wants to live in a place where they're constantly in fear of menace and bodily harm from an unrepentant sonofabitch immune to rehabilitation like Galworthy Primrose.

The circuit judge will be by next week. He may want an explanation as to exactly what happened to that ex-convict who had the gall to come back to the very place he terrorized for so long. Guess I'll just have to tell him the truth—that GW was unaware we were having our annual marksmanship competition—and the poor bastard walked headlong into the firing range. Judge probably won't think twice about it. He'll likely see it as Mother Nature culling the herd, and chalk it up to that Darwin fella's theory of natural selection. No doubt he'll then depart this little slice of heaven we call Paint Rock, on the 12:15.

Richard J. Cass

What's Your Name?

In the hard brown clay hills above and behind the Stop & Shop on Cummins Highway, Mickey Barksdale and Norman explored the warren of shallow caves and tunnels left by construction and the glaciers. Five years from now, in the parking lot, Mickey would have his first time, with Patty of the dangling earrings and the jellybean perfume, in the wide back seat of his father's Plymouth Fury.

But today, he was a prisoner. They both were.

Frank and Joe Goodman, twin brothers from Roslindale, were two years ahead of him at Washington Irving Junior High School.

"What do you want to be when you grow up?" Frank said.

He was the brother who looked and acted most like a thug, with a forceps-squashed face and rayon shirts, but it was Joe who'd pointed the sharp end of his stick at them and made them sit up on the rocks, like witnesses at their own trial.

Norman, as always, sucked up.

"A doctor. I want to help people get better."

"Good. That's good."

Joe, younger by a minute, which his brother lorded over him, poked Mickey in the ribs.

"What about you, Fatty?"

"A detective," Mickey said.

He'd been reading the Hardy Boys, Nero Wolfe. A dim light burnished Frank's stony eyes.

"Like a cop? You want to be a cop?"

Mickey felt a thrill of fear, all the way down into his balls.

"Yeah. Put people like you away."

Norman squeaked.

"Not cool," Frank said.

He looked off into the middle distance, where a cop car crawled up the entrance road to the grocery store, closed on Sundays.

"Joe."

Joe tapped Mickey on the ear with the stick, the lightness of the blow an insult itself.

"Keep an eye out, pudgy."

And the two of them disappeared down a tunnel Mickey thought came out on the far side of the hill.

* * *

Mickey's old man liked to call himself a ward-heeler. He was the state representative's guy in Hyde Park, responsible for getting out the vote and making sure it was for the right candidate.

"You want to make some money Saturday?" he asked Mickey one morning before school, Mickey spooning up Rice Krispies and milk, knowing that was all he'd get to eat 'til dinner. "I need someone to leaflet Fairmount."

Mickey liked to stay as far away from his father's temper as he could, by keeping his grades up to an acceptable (but not genius) level and never sassing his mother. He was trying to save enough money for a slot car set, and birthdays and Christmas, when Grandpa Frank slipped him a fin, only came once a year. He was still ten dollars shy, but also wary.

"Sure, Da." His father liked to pretend they were more Irish than they were. "How much?"

His father clucked at something on the front page of the Herald.

"You'll be taken care of. Full day, mind you."

"What do I need to do?"

His father glanced over the top of the paper like he wondered how he'd borne such an imbecile.

"Carry a bag. Stick a pamphlet in each door until they're gone. Think you can manage that?"

It sounded simple, though Mickey felt a sliver of worry saying yes.

Saturday morning was the third day of September, still hot and humid for New England fall. Mickey regretted missing the Saturday football game on Ross Field with Greg and Dominic, but the slot car set glimmered in his imagination like one of the stars in a Nativity scene. And he didn't want to wait for it until Christmas.

The bag was the size of the canvas ones the paperboys carried. The strap dug into his shoulder as he trudged from house to house, tucking the flyers in between doors. His father had told him not to use the mailboxes, which could get the campaign in trouble.

He sweated through his shirt in the first half hour, but the heat also put the dogs to sleep. None of them even barked at him, though if he'd been on his bike, on a cooler day, they would have chased him.

In the hottest part of late afternoon, he still had a hundred or so left and he thought about pushing them down the sewer and quitting, but he gutted it out. Pride surged as he stuck the last one in an aluminum storm door.

Back at the campaign office on River Street, he tossed the empty bag in a corner and stood before the rotating floor fan. His father stood in the next room with two tough-looking guys and the candidate, whose face Mickey had been looking at all day. All of them wore short-sleeved cotton shirts and suit pants.

"What?"

The receptionist returned, from the ladies' room, probably. She looked at him as if he wore short pants.

"Finished the leafletting. Can I get paid?"

She frowned, as if it were a calculus problem.

"Minute."

She walked into the other room and spoke to his father, who casually ran his hand over her sleek rear end as he listened. He laughed and raised his voice so Mickey could hear.

"He probably dumped them down a manhole and went to play ball."

Mickey felt a flush of shame, as if his thought had been the deed.

The candidate walked back out of the room with the receptionist, bent down to talk to him.

"I know you wouldn't do that," he said. "You're your father's son, aren't you?"

Mickey frowned. How would this faker have the slightest idea what he would or wouldn't do? But, the money. He was hoping for twenty, but he'd settle for ten. He nodded.

"I did what I was supposed to do."

"OK. OK."

The candidate straightened up and put his hand in his pants pocket. Mickey lightened up. He was going to get paid.

The man fished out a handful of change and stuffed it, jingling, into Mickey's hand.

"Here you go, champ. Good work."

He turned back into the other room and said something to Mickey's father that made him laugh.

Mickey counted the silver in his palm: four quarters, six dimes, and two nickels. No pennies, at least. A dollar fucking ninety-five.

"Fuck that," he said and flung the coins against the wall.

The men turned as one at the sound. Mickey ran out the door into the hot humid streets, laughter jangling in the air behind him.

* * *

Mickey, one year older, not a lot smarter. At least that's how high school made him feel. He'd be sixteen in another month and legal to quit, not that his mother would like it.

Until then, though—if he couldn't quit, at least he could skip. A warm May day and even if he wasn't the outdoor type, he could enjoy the sun.

He brought a Creamsicle from Topalian's store on the corner of Hyde Park Ave. and walked up the short hill to the Episcopal Church, empty and quiet on a Thursday, and sat on the low rock wall in front.

He was down to the stick and chewing on it, when an unfamiliar sight strolled around the corner.

Kid was maybe twelve or fourteen and dressed in Walmart jeans and a cranberry-colored Henley shirt. His skin was so dark Mickey thought he must have come from Africa. Not one of the city Negroes, African-Americans, whatever you called them.

"Hey."

He tossed the stick up into the Episcopal flower beds. This neighborhood was Irish and Italian, solid white. This kid belonged in Roxbury or Mattapan, high up on Blue Hill Ave.

"Yeah. You."

This kid wasn't even smart enough to look scared. Hyde Park High had been like a war zone this year, all the bussing shit Mickey didn't understand except as another example of people in power forcing things on people without. Fucking liberals, his father called them, the only time Mickey heard him swear.

Kid was skinny, too. He stopped on the sidewalk, well out of reach, and put a hand in his pocket.

"You want a piece of gum?"

Mickey almost broke out laughing. He grabbed the package of gum and tossed it up onto the church lawn.

'No. I don't want your stupid gum. What are you doing on my street?"

Kid looked stunned, turned his head. The church took up the whole block.

"Your street? You live here?"

Mickey pushed himself up off the wall and got in close. The kid smelled like cold ashes, a little spearmint.

"You getting wise with me?"

"No sir."

That was better. His eyes widened up, the whites stark against his skin.

"You have to pay the toll," Mickey said.

The kid stiffened up.

"Got no money."

Mickey could tell he was lying. The street was a shortcut from River Street to Topalian's. Boy's mama probably sent him out to buy her smokes.

"Give it." He balled his fist to show the penalty.

Shoulders slumped. Kid gave up easily. Mickey'd hoped for a little fight.

The skinny hand reached into his pocket and brought out a handful of change, nickels and dimes mostly, dropped it in Mickey's outstretched hand. Mickey felt a power so pure he wanted to feel like that always.

He stepped in and looped his arm around the boy's neck. Kid was shaking now.

"What's your name, pal? What do you want to be when you grow up?"

About the Authors

Sue Baumgardner is the author of *Where Sin Increased* and the forthcoming *Rocky and the Changer*. To learn more, visit https://encirclepub.com/baumgardner/.

Mike Befeler is the author of the Paul Jacobson Geezer-Lit Mysteries, as well as *Back Wing* and *Front Wing,* and many more. Watch for the forthcoming *Old Detectives Home*. To learn more, visit https://encirclepub.com/befeler/.

Richard J. Cass is the author of the Boston-based, Jazz-inspired Elder Darrow Mysteries, and a forthcoming new series in 2022. To learn more, visit https://encirclepub.com/richard-j-cass/.

Dane Cobain is the author of the Leipfold Mysteries *Driven* and *The Tower Hill Terror*, and *The Leipfold Files*, publishing in June, 2022. To learn more, visit https://encirclepub.com/cobain/.

Matt Cost is the author of the Goff Langdon Mainely Mysteries, the Clay Wolfe/Port Essex Mystery series, and the historical fiction novel, *Love in a Time of Hate*. Matt's new historical mystery series starts with *Brooklyn Eight Ballo*. To learn more, visit https://encirclepub.com/cost/.

Sharon L. Dean is the author of the Deborah Strong Mysteries *The Barn* and *The Wicked Bible*, with book three, *Calderwood Cove*, publishing soon. To learn more, visit https://encirclepub.com/dean/.

Catherine Dilts is the author of *Survive or Die* as well as the Rock Shop Mysteries. Catherine has a new cozy mystery series, the Rose Creek Mysteries, that begins with *Rose Creek: The Body in the Cattails*, publishing in May, 2023. To learn more, visit https://encirclepub.com/dilts/.

Bruna Gomes is the author of *How to Disappear*, her debut novel. She is also an award-winning poet. To learn more, visit https://encirclepub.com/gomes/.

Vaughn Hardacker is the author of the Dylan Thomas Thrillers including *The Exchange*, as well as many other critically-acclaimed novels. To learn more, visit https://encirclepub.com/hardacker/.

Joe Kilgore is the author of *Insomniac: Short Stories for Long Nights*, and the first Brig Ellis Tale, *Fool's Errand*, publishing April 1, 2022. To learn more, visit https://encirclepub.com/kilgore/.

J. K. Knauss is the author of the historical fiction novel, *Seven Noble Knights*, and the Medieval short story collection, *Our Lady's Troubadour and Other Miraculous Tales*. To learn more, visit https://encirclepub.com/knauss/.

Scott Lipanovich is the author of the Jeff Taylor Mysteries *The Lost Coast* and the forthcoming *The Golden Ceiling*, which publishes in July, 2022. To learn more, visit https://encirclepub.com/lipanovich/.

BJ Magnani is the author of the Dr. Lily Robinson Novels *The Queen of All Poisons*, *The Power of Poison*, and the forthcoming *A Message in Poison*, publishing in April, 2022. To learn more, visit https://encirclepub.com/bj-magnani/.

S. Lee Manning is the author of the Kolya Petrov Thrillers *Trojan Horse* and *Nerve Attack*. Book three in the series, *Bloody Soil*, is publishing in November, 2022. To learn more, visit https://encirclepub.com/manning/.

Alison L. McLennan is the author of *Ophelia's War* and *Ophelia's War: Dangerous Mercy,* as well as the literary fiction novel, *Falling for Johnny.* To learn more, visit https://encirclepub.com/mclennan/.

Anne Britting Oleson is the author of many novels including *Aventurine and the Reckoning*, the first Aventurine Morrow Thriller. Her next novel, *The Springs*, is publishing in March of 2023. To learn more, visit https://encirclepub.com/britting-oleson/.

Saralyn Richard is the author of *A Murder of Principal*, *Bad Blood Sisters* (publishing in March, 2022), and the Detective Oliver Parrott Mysteries. To learn more, visit https://encirclepub.com/richard/.

Jay Ruud is the author of the Merlin Mysteries, as well as a new series, the Robin Hood Mysteries, starting with *Sleuth of Sherwood*, publishing in June of 2022. To learn more, visit https://encirclepub.com/ruud/.

Lois Schmitt is the author of the Kristy Farrell Mystery series, including *Something Fishy* and the latest, *Playing Possum*. To learn more, visit https://encirclepub.com/schmitt/.

CB Shanahan is the author of *Hollis Whittaker*, his debut novel. Book two, *Hollis Whittaker and the Bolivian Incident*, will be published in July, 2022. To learn more, visit https://encirclepub.com/shanahan/.

Kevin St. Jarre is the author of *Aliens, Drywall, and a Unicycle*, *Celestine*, *The Twin*, as well as the forthcoming thriller, *Absence of Grace*, (April, 2022), and a new historical mystery, *The Book of Emmaus* (July, 2022). To learn more, visit https://encirclepub.com/st-jarre/.

Karen Hanson Stuyck is the author of many novels including *A Deadly Courtship*, the first Alexandra Sinclair Mystery. Book two in the series, *Death of an Unfortunate Woman*, publishes in May, 2022. To learn more, visit https://encirclepub.com/hanson-stuyck/.

A. J. Thibault is the author of *Deadly Serious*, and his new novel, *Identity*, will be published in October, 2022. To learn more, visit https://encirclepub.com/thibault/.

Lara Tupper is the author of multiple novels including the critically-acclaimed *Off Island*. To learn more, visit https://encirclepub.com/tupper/.

About the Editor

Cynthia Brackett-Vincent is Lead Editor at Encircle Publications, and is a Pushcart Prize nominated and award-winning poet. Her co-edited anthology, *Women on Poetry: Writing, Revising, Publishing and Teaching* (McFarland, 2012) was named "One of 100 Best Books for Writers" by *Poets & Writers* magazine. To learn more, visit https://encirclepub.com/about-us/.

If you enjoyed reading this book,
please consider writing your honest review
and sharing it with other readers.

Many of our Authors are happy to participate in
Book Club and Reader Group discussions.
For more information, contact us at info@encirclepub.com.

Thank you,
Encircle Publications

For news about more exciting new fiction, join us at:

Facebook: www.facebook.com/encirclepub

Instagram: www.instagram.com/encirclepublications

Twitter: twitter.com/encirclepub

Sign up for Encircle Publications newsletter and specials:

eepurl.com/cs8taP